advance praise for *rules for the perpetual diet*

"In Burns' (*The Amazing Adventures of Working Girl*, 2009) novel, a perpetual dieter decides, after her best friend dies, to follow through on "The Plan" they had made to go to Paris.

Recommendations for writing a can't-put-down book: Make your protagonist funny, introspective or complicated—better yet, all three—as well as someone whom readers will immediately recognize and feel compassion for. That compassion has to hold up no matter how dubious the protagonist's choices. For 29-year-old Amy Brodie, the decision to go to Paris is hardly questionable, but how she goes about it is. While her engineer husband is away on business, she sneaks away from their Phoenix home and boards a plane, intending to use cash she has stored away and to lie to her husband during daily phone calls. "Kat's death, William's wanting to start a family, the siren song of food—I traveled ten thousand miles…to get away from those things," she says. Food, or the avoidance of it, controls every aspect of Amy's life. She lives by a set of dieting rules. Rule No.11: "abstention is easier than moderation"; rule No.25: "feast your eyes first." Of course, Paris isn't exactly the best place to avoid carbs; neither is it a great place to avoid self-awareness. The Plan doesn't go quite according to itself, and before long, Amy is trekking through Paris' underground with a ragtag team of Frenchmen and sampling buttery croissants. Although Burns excels at the "rules" of good writing, her well-crafted novel is too moving to be formulaic. Amy's struggle through her grief is touching, as is her feeling of being trapped. "Being demoted from independent working woman to dependent unemployed spouse can freak out a person" she says. "I want to get away from this life that has somehow become my life." Her attempt to escape never stops being an absorbing adventure—not until the gratifying final moments, when we find out whether she succeeds.

A lovely ode to Paris, friendship, spontaneity and forks—both on the plate and in the road."

— *Kirkus Reviews*

praise for *the amazing adventures of working girl*
(also by K. S. R. Burns)

"Working girls (and boys) will likely find something to relate to in Burns' part memoir, part self-help tome for career professionals, filled with no-nonsense advice, job survival tips and humorous anecdotes."

— The Seattle Times

"Burns is encouraging and funny, but also a hard-nosed pragmatist who isn't about to do the work for you—but neither is she going to waste your time with pages of condescending instruction. Instead, her snappy chapters provide perspective and action points for a cascade of work conditions."

— Publishers Weekly

"With equal amounts of insight and entertainment, *The Amazing Adventures of Working Girl* is an ideal tome for any gal, whether she loves, hates or needs a job."

— Marie Claire Magazine

"*The Amazing Adventures of Working Girl* is a book that promotes spunk, common sense, courtesy, curiosity, and ethical behavior."

— The Bookmonger

rules for the
perpetual diet

k. s. r. burns

Booktrope Editions
Seattle, WA 2014

Cover Design by Tatiana Vila
Edited by Laurel Busch

This is a work of fiction. Names, characters, places, brands, media, and incidents are either the product of the author's imagination or are used fictitiously. Any resemblance to similarly named places or to persons living or deceased is unintentional.

PRINT ISBN 978-1-62015-626-1

EPUB ISBN 978-1-62015-637-7

Library of Congress Control Number: 2014921293

everything I write is for Steve

one

SEVEN P.M. A Wednesday. Two weeks to the day after the funeral.
Kat is dead. I am not.

What I am is hungry.

And majorly pissed off at William.

And did I mention hungry? Which isn't strictly William's fault,
but when he wanders into the kitchen as I'm putting away leftover
schweinhaxen and sauerkraut—Wednesday night is German food
night—I do not acknowledge his existence.

"Amy," he says. He must be pissed off at me too, because normally
he calls me "Ames." "Almost forgot. Next week? Prototype testing
in Teterboro."

I dump cucumber salad and braised red cabbage into plastic
storage containers. At least those are less-caloric-type foods I can eat.
But you know what? They don't satisfy.

"Okay," I say, still not looking at him because on the drive home
from the funeral he said, "Well, I guess that's that," and I flipped out
and screamed, "You're *glad*? You *bastard*," and since then I've hardly
spoken to him, not even to mention that my period is two days late.

"Leaving Sunday," he says now. "Back Friday. Five days."

Five days. In my brain, Kat's voice bellows, "The Plan! The Plan!"
as loud and real and strong as if she were right there in the kitchen with
us, as if she were still alive, in this world. But she isn't, and the last
thing I want to think about is The Plan.

Anyway, five days isn't long enough for The Plan.

William returns to the family room and the television, where the
Diamondbacks are now down two to nothing. I grit my teeth and slide
the rest of his apple strudel into the fridge without stealing even a

single crisp golden flake of its crisp golden pastry. Seven p.m. is my hardest time of day. The evening meal is cooked, consumed, and cleaned up after, and my stupid body knows nothing more is coming down for hours, not till tomorrow, not till breakfast, and it starts to whine. It wants food. Fatty, salty, crispy, sugary, creamy, crunchy, meaty, tangy, anything-that-fills-your-belly-and-brings-you-peace food.

Shut up, stupid body.

Because I can't give in now. This time it's only twenty pounds, and then I'll be back to where I need to be, want to be. I gather up my hair into a grapefruit-sized knot and fix it with a pencil to the top of my head. So far I've lost eight of that twenty, in spite of German night, Italian night, Mexican night, Thai night.

William used to cook these crazy-lavish meals for me. Then we did it together. Since my layoff, however, I've been doing it alone. I enjoyed it at first. I enjoyed it for quite a long time.

"No way! He was safe by a mile!" William shouts at the television. He is trying to be normal.

I join him in the family room. "Your trip to New Jersey. Is it that T-30 project again?" I ask, because I want normal, too. In fact, normal is all I've ever wanted. The red cabbage, or maybe it's the cucumber, urps up into my throat.

He nods and twiddles a solid blue jigsaw puzzle piece between his middle and ring fingers. When Kat found out about William's jigsaw addiction she cracked up laughing. "Seriously? How old is this guy?" she asked. I said, "Actually he's only six years older than us. But he was raised by his grandfather, so he does jigsaws, and wears a wristwatch, and balances his checkbook, in addition to being a gourmet chef. He really has a ton of talents." Kat guffawed so hard she fell off the bed.

A burger flashes onto the TV screen. A high-definition, super-sized burger, thirty-four inches wide and twelve inches tall, oozing ketchup and mustard and lettuce and cheese and pickles and bacon. I jump to my feet and flee to the kitchen. It's spotless, but I rerinse the dishcloth, Swiffer the hardwood floor, and buff the fingerprints off the stainless steel refrigerator. Rule number one of the perpetual diet: Fidget as much as possible. Fidgeting burns calories. Fidgeting gives your hands something to do other than to stuff fat piggy food into your fat piggy face. Fidgeters are slender.

When we go to bed we make love for the first time since the night Kat died. In college Kat used to tell me that sex with a man could be pretty damn good, great even. I didn't believe her then, but she turned out to be right. Tonight of course there is no conversation, just sex. Still, it is ardent. Sex works between William and me when nothing else does. Plus he is always ardent before leaving on a business trip, as if paying ahead on the mortgage.

He falls asleep thirty seconds later and I lie next to him, watching his chest rise and fall. I will wait two more days and then I will take the home pregnancy test I have stashed behind the towels in the linen closet. Meanwhile I won't bother William until I know more, because he would be sure to get all excited and I don't think I could stand that. Not now. Not yet. Besides, my period is often late. Sometimes it doesn't show up at all.

Lord, a handful of potato chips would be amazing right now. Or a spoonful of chunky peanut butter. Or a Snickers. Or a bowl, a big bowl, of chocolate chip cookie dough ice cream with fudge chunks. Or even just a few bites of the apple strudel that I prepared and served without tasting. Which means I am not a real cook because William's grandfather—who like William is a master chef—says a real cook tastes everything. Which makes me a fake cook I guess.

I roll over onto my back, bunch up my pillow, prop up my head, and survey my tortilla-flat body. Of course you always look your thinnest while supine but I smile anyway. I run my hands over the speed bumps of my ribs and let them come to rest on the sharp peaks of my hips. Rule number two of the perpetual diet: Nothing tastes as good as feeling skinny feels.

Rules. They are imperative. Because while any moron can lose weight, it takes a talented and dedicated and—let's face it—fanatical self-brainwasher to keep the weight off. Which I am. Not that this is anything to be proud of. But better to think about food, or the lack of food, than about Kat and the lack of Kat. Damn. Too late. Tears slip from my eyes, slide past my ears, and soak into my hair. I jump up to get a box of tissues from the bathroom. I don't worry about waking William because he's a dead sound sleeper—not even the thunder and lightning of an Arizona monsoon storm stir him. Certainly not the telltale aluminum odor of tears.

At six a.m. the alarm tweedles and I scramble out of bed.

"Wassup?" William mumbles, sitting up and rubbing his eyes. He's normally the one to get up first and I am normally the one to whine and burrow under the covers, but this was a night I never fell asleep at all. Seriously. Not for an hour, not for five minutes. And I am tired. So tired.

"Gotta pee." I sprint to the bathroom, scrub my face, glug down three glasses of water (rule number three of the perpetual diet: Drink a ton of water), and thump down the stairs. I start the coffee—God, I need coffee—and, twenty minutes later, just as if it were a normal day, William cruises into the kitchen dressed in a clean white shirt and smelling like vanilla. He sips his orange juice while scanning the headlines on his phone. He doesn't comment on my hollow eyes, my pasty face. Kat would've. She commented on everything.

But Kat is not around to comment on everything. Kat will never be around again.

At 7:32, the garage door still lowering after William's Jeep, I microwave a bowl of oat bran. In April in Phoenix it's too hot to eat cooked cereal for breakfast, but I love, love, love my oat bran. I make it with no salt and no sugar, adding only fat-free milk and cumin.

"Cumin. Interesting choice," William remarked one morning not long after our shotgun wedding, four years and one month ago. "Cumin is my favorite spice," I explained. When I told Kat about this later she shrieked, "Yikes! You told him you had a favorite spice?" and I said, "Yes. Yes, I did. He thinks it's quirky. He thinks it's delightful."

Yeah, William uses words like "delightful." Another of his many fine-slash-irritating qualities.

I rinse the cereal bowl and grab my keys. I want to do something, to go somewhere. I want to get away from this life that has somehow become my life.

Fortunately it's Thursday, grocery day. After the layoff I launched myself big time into homemaking. I collect recipes and pore over household tip books. I follow urban homesteading blogs and The Food Network stars. They all advise having a system. It was systems that put a man on the moon, as William likes to say. Ergo—as I like to say—systems can create a perfectly happy, orderly home right down here on good old Planet Earth. A normal home.

Kat never tired of harassing me about my housekeeping-by-the-book binge. Even William's grandfather, who comes down to Arizona to visit us for two weeks every Christmas, finds it a little puzzling. But who can argue with shining floors and organized closets and home-cooked meals? No one, that's who.

I head north on the 101. "The Plan!" Kat's voice yells in my head.

Stop it. Shut up. Even if five days were enough time, which it isn't, without Kat The Plan is toast. Because the fact is, I don't have the cojones. At one time in my life I did, but now, at the alarming age of twenty-nine, I do not. I wonder what happened to my cojones.

Whatever, it is Thursday and I have stuff to do, stuff that will take my mind off things, which is the good news.

"The good news." That was a Kat-ism. "The good news is that Will may have old-fogey hobbies like jigsaw puzzles, but he loves you and has a decent job." "The good news is that the cancer may have spread, but at least it's not in the lymph system. Or my pea brain."

I drive all the way to Scottsdale because also good news is that unemployment means my schedule is my own. Plenty of time for a skinny iced chai tea latte and a wander through the art-gallery-infested Old Town. Rule number four of the perpetual diet: If you snack, snack while in motion. Please.

I leave the Honda parked in front of the Starbucks and walk over to Fifth Avenue, pausing in front of a jewelry store to scrutinize my profile in the reflection of a dusty plate glass window. This morning my jeans buttoned with difficulty, but they did button. Rule number five of the perpetual diet: Put on something a little tight in the morning, when you are at your thinnest, and you will be less likely to overeat during the day.

Of late, the rules have been swarming around in my brain like fire ants.

Fifth Avenue in Scottsdale is one tacky tourist shop after another, featuring objects I am embarrassed by—do visitors to our state think we all decorate our homes with bronze tabletop statuettes of bucking broncos and stylized pastels of Navajos wrapped in blankets? But two blocks later I halt in front of a different kind of window display. No bucking broncos here. No silver squash-blossom necklaces, no white ten-gallon cowboy hats, no green jars of prickly pear jelly. Just a single wooden easel bearing a single object: a three-foot-square watercolor of the Sacré-Coeur.

I know it's the Sacré-Coeur because I have read a ton of books about Paris. A passage from a guidebook pops into my head: "The basilica of Sacré-Coeur, set atop a hill in Montmartre, was built as penance for the crimes of the 1871 Paris Commune."

Which has always struck me as wrong. The penance part, not the crimes part. After all, look at it. Penitence was never on the minds of the people who built this building. It's jazzy and carefree. It's a wedding dress of a church, a frosted cupcake of a church, a Southern belle of a church. A party church. Not the least bit penitential.

Accordingly, the Sacré-Coeur painting in the window is not only non-contrite but sassy. It vibrates, quivers, shimmers, twitches with joy. It yearns to jump up and do the cancan. Its rose window is askew, its Romanesque arches are lopsided, its smooth, round, shining white domes jig and jag. The sky above the domes is pulsating with pink and blue squiggles, like streamers being tossed from a celebrating heaven. This painter clearly grasped the party-church nature of the Sacré-Coeur.

In college Kat used to say, "Your eye for design rocks, you oughta be an artist." Five years later she was still at it. During chemo, when she should have been fretting about hair loss or fluid retention, she would nag me instead. "You should sign up for a watercolor class," she'd say, and I'd always counter, "Is fiber art not art?"

Because while books and words are my chief obsessions, I also sew, knit, crochet, even macramé. I like to make stuff. Step by step by step, until you have a physical and sometimes beautiful object you can hold in your hands. A real and solid thing that does not die and leave you.

One time Kat persisted. "You're not realizing your potential, Amy. You could do something more than make house-y crap," she said.

This was eighteen months ago, during the second chemo regimen. I shifted in my hard plastic visitor's chair and admired the regular twists of the French-blue shrug I'd crocheted for her during the first chemo regimen. I didn't want to argue so I said, "I'm a housewife, remember? A throwback. A dinosaur. One of the last of my kind. Woo-hoo."

"You loon." Kat heaved a pillow at me. "The minute the economy improves you'll get another job and forget all this domestic goddess bullshit."

Her eyes were bright and sparkling, which was so good to see that I strung her along. "I don't know. Maybe getting canned was the best thing that ever happened to me. Speaking of canned, do you think I should learn to put up jam? Tomatoes?"

"Maybe. But have you heard?" Kat said, wincing as she shifted the arm with the needle. "This is the twenty-first century, for shit's sake. Women have careers."

But I despised my old job. Human resources. Gag.

"Hello! Yoo hoo!" The Fifth Avenue art gallery woman is holding the door open and waving. "Come on in! It's cool in here!"

I do not want to "come on in" and be the sole prey of a weekday-bored, fake-friendly, sales-starved store clerk. But it's a hundred-plus degrees out. My iced chai tea latte is melting all over my wrist, and the waistband of my too-snug jeans is sodden with sweat.

"Just looking?" the saleswoman asks, smiling brightly. She has lipstick on her teeth.

I nod and glance around the gallery. Yup, I am the only customer here. It's April, the winter tourist season is over, and summer is marching toward the unwary citizens of the Valley of the Sun with jack-booted feet. I set my chai on the concrete floor and flip through a stack of De Grazia greeting cards, grateful to the sound system for playing Billie Holiday singing "Mean to Me" and almost but not quite drowning out the labored breathing of the clerk.

Who is not so easily evaded. Who circles around a display of dream catchers and stands there until I am forced to look up at her. "Is there anything in particular you're interested in?"

"The Sacré-Coeur," I say. "The painting in the window."

Just like that. It pops out of my mouth just like that.

"Oh yes!" the clerk exclaims. "It's by Sarah Mae Hooter. Do you know her work?"

"Hooter? No. I do not," I say, keeping a straight face.

The saleswoman trots over to the display window, hikes up her pencil skirt, mounts a stepstool, hefts the painting from its easel, and props it on the edge of the dream catcher table. "Sarah Mae Hooter is one of our newest artists," she says, puffing. It's asthma. I'd know that wheeze anywhere. "Don't you love her palette?" she asks. "So joyous."

It is.

It's still joyous when I pay for it fifteen minutes later. The painting is not an original—it's a *giclée* print, seventy-five dollars without the frame and, with it, only two hundred. Which I have because ever since my layoff three years ago I've asked for ten dollars cash back at the grocery store and five dollars cash back at the dry cleaners every week. Being demoted from independent working woman to dependent unemployed spouse can freak out a person. If this happens to you, I recommend starting a collection of money. Cold cash, crispy green fives and tens, will make you feel less unmoored, less helpless. I always carry a couple hundred bucks with me.

As Kat would say, "You never know."

The delighted saleswoman helps slide the painting into the back of the Honda. I drive it straight home, get out the hammer and nails and level, and hang it in the downstairs guest bathroom, which William never uses. Not that he would object to the picture, or even notice it. Hell, he wouldn't register its presence if I hung it over our bed.

Because William is a numbers nerd, not a pictures nerd. I'm a word nerd, but I like lovely tangible objects, too, art and architecture and furniture. And clothes—I love clothes, maybe more than I should.

Dinner tonight is stracciatella, artichoke salad, sausage tortellini, and cannolis with homemade ricotta. Hard to believe that I can now produce a meal of this caliber and hardly break a sweat. It was all bearable, even funny, while Kat was alive. "What year does Will think this is, 1957?" she'd ask. "You two make Ward and June Cleaver look like the Ozzy Osbournes." She never questioned why I went along with it. She must have known that I was just looking for a regular life, a normal life, a solid life that would stick all the raggedy bits and pieces of me together, and keep my brain and my soul from flying apart in one big messy gooey bang.

"You've turned into a primo chef," William says now. Primo is William's highest praise, usually reserved for things like the latest killer app.

"Thanks," I say. I admire my plate, which is pretty much all I can do—I mean, it's not like I can eat this stuff, not until I reach my goal.

"I have news," he says, unfurling one of the blue pima cotton napkins I wash and iron every Monday. I adore ironing, especially napkins. I know, who irons napkins? But they are flat and square and simple and satisfying. William looks at me across the table and even smiles. "My trip plans have changed."

"Oh?"

He is scheduled to leave for New Jersey on Sunday, less than three days away. I have not forgotten.

"The prototype trials are going till Wednesday, not Friday," he says.

"Oh." I swallow a bite of artichoke heart from which I have scraped most of the vinaigrette. "You'll be gone for only two days then. Cool."

"No. Ten. I'm gonna have to stay the weekend."

I take a slice of Italian bread from Defalco's, slather butter on it, and stuff it into my mouth before I realize what I'm doing. Unbelievable. Ten days is exactly long enough for The Plan. Kat would die laughing. If she weren't already dead.

"What will you do here?" William asks, serving himself a second helping of tortellini. When we were first married he taught me how to make the pasta from scratch, rolling it out into thin, smooth translucent sheets, cutting out rounds, and folding them into perky little hats. Today I did it all single-handedly and had everything ready by the time William got home at six p.m. Rule number six of the perpetual diet: Eat regular meals. Regular meals are what set us apart from the animals.

"I'll be fine," I say. "No problem."

After dinner William retreats to the patio to smoke his cigarette, a habit he picked up in the military and has never been able to break. "The man smokes? For reals?" Kat said when she found out, not long after the wedding. I rushed to his defense, saying, "Just one a day. After dinner. It's his only vice."

I wonder if this is true. Inside, I polish the granite countertop with a microfiber cloth. Outside, William smokes and patrols the gravel landscaping. From time to time he leans down to pluck a white stone out of the black stones, or a black stone out of the white stones. How do they get mixed up in the first place? William could explain, using numbers. William says everything in our universe can be understood through math.

I wish that were true.

I look out at him one last time. His close-cropped head is tipped back to watch an airplane etch a fine white line across the Windex-blue sky. He's probably noting the model and altitude of the plane but, poised there, he looks like an actor waiting for his cue. I could end this impasse and go out and kiss him. I could wrap my arms around his annoyingly flat stomach and bury my face in his warm shoulder. Instead I slip off to the guest bathroom, lock the door, drape a towel over my head like a monk's cowl, and sit on the closed toilet lid, hugging my knees. I used to snuggle into myself like this when I was a little girl, when my mother went on the warpath, which was more or less regularly, and it was just all too much. I peer through a gap in my towel shroud. The only thing I can see, the only thing in my tight little circumscribed world, is the rocking-and-rolling Sacré-Coeur.

When I was six Dad gave me an old record player he picked up at a carport sale. I loved that thing—the hard rubber turntable, the chunky plastic dials, the dusty electrical smell. It came with half a dozen albums from the swing era, one of them "Ella Fitzgerald Sings the Cole Porter Songbook." My mother didn't listen to any music at all and Dad liked only fifties rock-and-roll, so to them the records were worthless.

But on Saturdays while they were out working in the yard, I would drop Ella onto the turntable, place the needle into the groove just right, so it didn't squawk, and play the record over and over. Sometimes I'd tie my old blue baby blanket around my waist and waltz around my bedroom.

My very favorite song from that album was "I Love Paris." Ella loved Paris in the springtime. She loved it in the fall. She loved it in the summer when it sizzles. She loved it in the winter when it drizzles.

At that age I didn't know if Paris was a where or a who or a what. Well, okay, I was pretty sure it was a where. What I was totally sure about, even at age six, was that every single note of that song is about yearning.

About desire.

Paris assumes that if you are not in Paris, whatever, whoever, wherever you are is legitimate cause for dissatisfaction. Because if you are not in Paris, you are nowhere worth being. Because—*mais oui!*— in Paris life is bigger, better, and more beautiful.

Most of all, you can be who you really are in Paris.

Unlike in Phoenix, Arizona, an ugly, makeshift, temporary place, a place that feels nailed together just yesterday, a place of lost losers, a place that has never felt like home. This knowledge felt like a secret and possibly shameful thing I wasn't meant to possess, insider information forbidden to obscure-ish people such as me and my parents, people living in a two-bedroom bungalow in central Phoenix, thousands and thousands and thousands of miles away from sizzling, drizzling Paris.

Eventually I realized how lame the whole thing was. Still, Ella Fitzgerald is the reason I defied conventional wisdom and studied French in high school and college instead of Spanish.

Now high school and college are long over and the faraway Sacré-Coeur quivers on my guest bathroom wall. Whispers, "The Plan."

Whispers, "It's not too late."

But I've got news for you. It is too late. At least as far as I'm concerned. Out in the family room the television blares. Even with the door closed, a fat towel draped over my fat head, I can recognize the commercial for Mexican food. In my head I can see the happy family, the normal family, a mother, a father, a boy, a girl, crowding around a kitchen table set for dinner. I can smell the tacos, overflowing with meat and cheese and lettuce and tomatoes and avocadoes and salsa, taunting, "Crispy! Crunchy! Eat me!"

I am so glad I don't have to do the preggers test until tomorrow.

I stand up, flush the toilet in case William wonders what I've been doing in the bathroom all this time, not that he would, and go out to help him work on the solid blue puzzle sky.

two

THE PLAN. Kat and I hatched it three years ago. Well, Kat did. She had just started her first chemo regimen and was listing all the things she was going to do when pronounced cancer-free.

"For sure I want to go to Tahiti," she said. "Or maybe the Galápagos. Or both. And I wanna go zip lining! And bungee jumping. And, I dunno. Skydiving?" Kat had always been a jock. Before the cancer she frequently put her website design business on hold to train for a marathon in Colorado or fly to Hawaii for the surfing. "What about you? What's on your bucket list?" she asked. "No, wait, don't tell me. It's Paris, isn't it?"

"Do ya hafta ask?"

Kat had never been to Europe either, never had the money. At one time I actually had the money, at age eighteen when I received a sizey life insurance check after Dad died. But he'd made me swear to enroll at ASU as soon as possible after the funeral. Of course, all I really wanted was to go somewhere far, far away, somewhere I could be someone else, or be more me. But a promise is a promise.

Kat was still talking. "I've got the most amazing idea. Let's go. Together. You and me."

I laughed. "That would be awesome."

"No, seriously," she said. "It would be my reward for getting better. It would be a celebration."

"We will definitely celebrate. For sure," I said. "But Paris? Seriously? Besides, Will has never been there either and I think he might like to go. With me. What I mean is he would mind if I went without him." At the time we hadn't been married even a year yet; we were still official honeymooners. And Paris, most romantic city in the world, city of lovers, was a place we should go together. At least that's how I always pictured it. We had never talked about it, but I thought we would always go, eventually.

Kat was shaking her head. "You know, there's a way around that."

"Around what?"

"Him minding. Listen to me." She sat forward in her recliner. Kat always looked well before her chemo treatments and today, the first day of the first treatment, her skin was clear, her honey-blond hair thick and shining, her smile unforced. "Eventually I'm going to get better. And eventually Will-boy is going to take a really big old fat-ass business trip. He'll tell you his schedule, which you know he'll stick to. And meanwhile you and I will go on a little trip of our own. To gay Paree. All we have to do is be sure we get back to Phoenix before he does. He never has to know!" She twirled her free arm like a magician pulling a rabbit out of a hat. "Waah-lah! We'll go to Paris and come back and he'll never even know!"

"Kat," I said. "That's insane."

"No, seriously, think about it. It would work. It's A Plan with a capital A and a capital P."

I got up to look out the window. On the parking lot outside, heat shimmered in chevrons above the cars, heat glittered in puddles on the blacktop. It was the middle of October and still over a hundred degrees out. I was born and grew up right here in Phoenix and oppressive weather in October should not seem weird to me, but it does. Right now, in Paris, it is probably cool and people are probably wearing raincoats. I have never owned a raincoat.

"I should think you would want to go," Kat persisted. "It would give you something to do with all that cash."

I flinched.

"Are you still doing it?" Kat asked.

I turned to face her. "Yeah. I know. What kind of lunatic hoards fives and tens in a Tupperware container behind the cookbooks?"

"You do!" Kat said. "But who cares? The point is, you've got money, money, yummy money. How many times do I have to tell you? Money isn't any good hidden away. Money wants to get out in the world. It wants to play with all the other money. Otherwise it's just a bunch of dirty paper."

She reached up and traced a checkmark across my forehead with the tip of her little finger. She used to do that in college, when we were together. I trembled and stepped back, out of her reach.

"Anyway, you dope. It's obvious," Kat said, pretending not to notice. "Can't you see? It's Paris money. It's money for going to Paris. That's why you never spend any of it. Just keep on saving those fives and tens, little girl, and by the time I get the hell out of CancerLand you'll have enough."

Kat did not give up. For the next three years, through the first mastectomy and the first rounds of chemo and radiation, through the discovery of a lump in her second breast and her second mastectomy, through the subsequent rounds of chemo and radiation and third degree burns from same, through the hair losses, the hair grow-backs, the weight losses, the weight regains, Kat talked about The Plan. I don't remember when I stopped saying, "Forget it, you idiot child, it's out of the question, I could never be that sneaky." I just know that we talked about it so much it took on a life of its own, a reality, like a book you've read so many times that the characters become people you feel you know.

And just talking about it wasn't bad, not really. The Plan provided amusement, diversion, release, comfort. We followed blogs about Paris. Movies set in Paris were automatic yeses for the Netflix list. I read a million books on French history. I didn't bother to argue when Kat suggested we send away for passports because, who knows, someday I might need a stupid passport. After Kat's second remission, it seemed merely festive to buy matching rolling carry-ons. For Kat's twenty-eighth birthday, I gave her a tiny travel hair dryer that folded up and fit into its own darling red leatherette carry case. "Now all I need is some frigging hair," Kat said.

It was Kat who figured out how to handle the phone calls from William. When away on business he used to call me numerous times a day. Whenever he had a few minutes he'd grab his cell and touch base with me, even if only for a couple minutes.

"That's not going to work, not in Paris," Kat said. "We need a way to control when he calls so you can be ready." This was during the third round of chemo. Kat was ashen and skeletal, and her hair was sparse and spiky. "Ask him to call you at a set time. Say you're busy in doctor's offices with me and can't always pick up. It's sort of true." She stopped to take a sip of Seven-Up, at that point the only thing she was able to keep down. "Then all we need to do is to calculate the time difference right so you can be in a quiet place to answer the call. He'll think you're at home waiting for him like a good little wifey-poo and you will actually be talking to him from Paris! He will have no idea! Ha. It's too funny!"

We guffawed so loudly the other chemo drippers in the room glared. And later I did ask William to call me only in the evenings, at six. Why not? It was true about it being more convenient.

three

IT'S FRIDAY. The day after buying the Sacré-Coeur, two days before William leaves on his big trip, and — most important — pee-on-a-stick day.

I roll out of bed and pad to the bathroom. The last time I did a home pregnancy test, Kat, naturally, was the instigator. It was a month after William and I met. "Your skin looks different," she told me one Friday night. "Kind of sparkly. I bet you're knocked up." I insisted not, but we went to Walgreen's and bought a pregnancy kit, giggling like middle-schoolers, and the next morning convened in the tiny bathroom of Kat's condo. "Morning, the first pee of the day," Kat said, "is the best time for taking the test."

It still is. I get the kit from its hiding place in the linen closet and take out one of the two wands. Maybe I should wait another day. The longer you wait, they say, the more reliable the test is. And who knows, my period might show up any moment, making all of this moot.

It's not normal, I realize, to not want to know. But then I am not normal, not when it comes to potential spawning. Or maybe I am normal, or at least less not-normal, and my reluctance to do the test is a sign that I'm not pregnant. Because if I were pregnant, wouldn't magic motherhood hormones be making me all giddy and excited? Wouldn't I be planning what color to paint the nursery? Wouldn't I be breaking out the knitting needles and cranking out baby booties?

However, since the fact of the matter is that knowing and not knowing are equally bad, I rip the plastic packaging off the wand, plop down on the toilet, and proceed. "You know the drill," Kat would say. Afterward I pace back and forth between the bathroom and the bedroom, not looking at the wand lying on the counter like a small space-age kitchen spatula. You are supposed to wait five minutes but I wait ten, as measured by the stopwatch function on my phone.

My reward for being so patient is a negative.

I sink down on the edge of the bathtub, a ripple of I-know-not-what running up and down my spine. Of course I am thrilled to see that little blue minus sign, let me tell you. But it's not that I never ever want to have a baby. It's just that now is not the time, and here is not the place.

I take the wand downstairs and bury it deep in the garbage can out in the garage. William will never see it there. To be honest, a mean part of me is glad William isn't getting what he wants. Why should he, so soon after I just lost what I wanted most in the world to keep? Tears fill my eyes. But my stomach, which starts to rumble the moment I step into the cool kitchen, takes precedence. Rule number seven of the perpetual diet: You should be a little hungry when you go to bed at night and a lot ravenous when you wake up in the morning. If not, you are eating too much.

But right now I am seriously starving. I could eat a dozen eggs, a box of cereal, a loaf of bread. I even pick up a banana and peel it.

However, Friday is also weigh day. Rule number eight of the perpetual diet: Weigh yourself once a week only. Not every day, whatever you do. Daily weighing is for morons. Daily weighing is the path to madness and despair.

So I throw out the banana, trudge back upstairs, pull off my nightshirt, slip off my panties, mount the bathroom scale, rise on tiptoe, suck in my stomach, and exhale, hard. The first time Kat witnessed this routine, in college, she hooted with laughter. "Are you trying to levitate?" she asked. I threw a hairbrush at her and she pulled me off the scale into her arms. We never got around to going to class that morning.

How can the house still stand, the sun still shine, the planet still spin, as if nothing has happened, as if Kat were not gone, for good?

I do not know. When I have emptied my lungs of every molecule of air, I open my eyes and peer down at the LED display. Damn. I have lost no weight at all during the past seven days. Nothing. Nil. Not even an ounce.

I stomp around the bedroom naked. Yes, I know my lack of weight loss, assuming it's not premenstrual bloating, is no doubt a simple matter of rule number nine of the perpetual diet: At times during your diet your body will decide there's a famine, and in a bid for self-preservation it will start to hoard calories. You still police every morsel of food you put in your mouth but you stop losing pounds. You may even gain a few back. It's only the plateau. You must not freak out.

But I still feel like a failure. A big fat naked failure. I pause in front of the full-length mirror mounted on our closet door (rule number ten of the perpetual diet! Hang mirrors everywhere!) and examine my body from every angle. It's not so bad. It's not so terrible. All I have left, really, is this belly pooch.

The truly overweight, the legitimately obese, would not sympathize with my weight issues. Not at all. They would hate my guts, what there are of them.

My stomach rumbles again. I put the nightshirt back on and head down to the kitchen, where I open the pantry to take out my plain shredded wheat, one hundred and eighty calories per serving, summer cereal. But my hand brushes against a jolly red box of Ritz crackers. William likes to have a snack of Ritz and extra-sharp cheddar when he comes home from the gym on Saturday afternoons. Crunchy. Buttery. Salty. Creamy.

Shaking my head, I leave the cereal in the pantry, get a lemon out of the fridge, saw off a chunk, drop it into a glass, add filtered water, and chug it down. That will have to do for breakfast. Because, as awful and cruel and uncompromising and downright un-American as it sounds, no matter where you are on the dieting spectrum you will still always have rule number eleven of the perpetual diet staring you in the face: Abstention is easier than moderation.

Seriously. You should try it.

My eyes again fill with tears. Damn. Friday is also the day I volunteer at the library, and last week some of the other volunteers noticed that I'd been crying. "Are you okay?" they asked. "Your eyes look bloodshot." A normal person would reply, "No, as a matter of fact I'm not okay, my best friend—my only friend—just died and I'm sad and unemployed and hungry and stuck in Phoenix, Arizona, and sort of at a major standstill with my marriage, my husband."

But my mother died when I was eight and Dad died when I was eighteen, and if there's anything I can't stand, it's sympathy. Sympathy scrapes the scab off the wound you're working so hard to create. Besides, I never told anyone at the library about Kat. I wanted a place of refuge, a cancer-free zone where I could pretend that everything was normal, that I was normal. So I smiled and said, "No, I'm fine, it's just allergies." Funny. No one there knows me well enough to know that I don't have allergies.

On my way back upstairs to shower and dress I pause in the door of the guest bathroom to gaze at the Sacré-Coeur. I should tell William about the money and The Plan. I should come clean, relate the whole convoluted crazy scheme, show him the matching carry-ons, still packed, climb onto his lap like a kitty cat, wrap my arms around his fragrant neck, brush my lips against his ear, and whisper, "Will, I'm freaked out right now. I'm sorry. But I want to go to Paris. I think it would be good for me."

"Confide in him," a normal person would advise. That's even what Kat might advise.

But the fact of the matter is that we have German night, Italian night, Mexican night—every night of the week a different cuisine. But we never have French night.

Besides, The Plan and Kat are linked. One cannot exist without the other.

four

AT THE LIBRARY I offer to shelve, making the other volunteers happy because that means they get to read to the children and staff the gift shop. And I never mind working alone, sliding the book trolley through the aisles, scanning the call numbers, slipping each returned volume into the slot where it belongs. I know every stack and shelf and drawer our small branch possesses.

I bend to lift a heavy biography from the lowest level of the trolley, stretch to wedge it on a top shelf, and smile. No way could I move like this in high school.

Experts rant about the dangers of excess weight. Excess weight causes knee troubles, hip troubles, heart troubles, liver disease, diabetes, infertility, insomnia, loneliness, despair, death. But no one mentions the simple discomfort of it. No one discusses how an extra eighty or hundred pounds hinders your every movement. You can't curl up in the corner of a sofa. You can't sit on your feet, or even with your legs crossed. You can't take bubble baths because you don't fit in the tub, or you're too afraid you won't be able to get out of the tub, or both.

When the day comes that you can't clip your own toenails, that you can't tie your own shoes, that you can't wipe your own butt after using the toilet, you shouldn't be surprised. But you will be. You will not have seen it coming. I know. It happened to me.

Just before lunch I spot a book I've never seen before. Mis-shelved in self-help instead of European history, it's heavy and glossy and extravagantly illustrated with woodcuts and engravings and photographs and maps of—Lord God, why are you doing this to me?—Paris. I take it back to the break room, curl up in one corner of the donated brown vinyl sofa, give my toes a squeeze, and let the book fall open across my lap. My favorite way to begin a book is to let the book decide, to let the book say, Here is where you need to be, here is where you belong. Because books can always be depended on. Books are more reliable than people. Don't shake your head. You know it's true.

"Planning a trip to Paris?"

I almost dump my zero-calorie cola over a double-page photo spread of the Tuileries. Rose, head librarian, is standing over me, munching on a bag of Fritos. If Rose only knew how many truly awful jokes Kat and I used to make about her. It started the Saturday morning we ran into her at AJ's Fine Foods on Lincoln and saw her shopping cart loaded with Pepperidge Farm goldfish, Oreos, Blue Bunny pistachio almond ice cream, frozen cheesecake, Reese's Pieces, Lucky Charms, cream sodas. Balanced on top of the pile were two enormous bags of Fritos. Which led to the horribly politically incorrect nickname "Rosie the Frito Bandito." Then came "Rosie the Rotund." Then "Rosie the Unabridged Librarian." Kat, who was a health and exercise—but not dieting—nut, started it. But I admit I joined right in.

"Oh. Hi, Rose," I say now.

The sofa drops three inches when Rose plops down beside me. She does not appear embarrassed. But that's Rose. She wears her weight with swagger. Pride even. She consumes soft drinks and cookies and greasy fast food in full view of all, daring you to disapprove. If you stare, she stares back. If you scowl, she scowls back. You are always the first to look away. "Fat is Rose's superpower," Kat liked to say. "If only they made capes big enough."

One time William overheard us snarking about her and he got really mad. "She's a human being. Give her a break!" he growled later, his chocolate-brown eyes glittering. "I know. You're right. I'm sorry," I said and after that I made a point to be nicer. But I could never be actual friends with Rose. Because skinny friends keep you skinny and fat friends make you fat. Because weight control is like war. You need to pick a side and stay there. That's science. As well as rule number twelve of the perpetual diet.

If this makes me a bad person, then so be it.

I shift to the left, to put a space between Rose's soft shoulder and my bony one.

"Ah, Paris," Rose sighs. "I was just there last year, you know. Nice town. But, Lord in heaven, I can't believe how rude the Parisians are." She presses into my side to peer into the book. "Not only that, the Hilton botched our reservations and we ended up staying in a poky little place on a side street. Gadzooks. There was hardly room to turn around in the shower. And those towels they give you? Not big enough to dry your toe."

I can't help myself. I look down at Rose's feet, planted eighteen inches apart on the worn industrial-grade carpet. Sure enough, a roll of ankle fat bulges up around each sandal strap.

Rose flips through the book and pauses at a photo of the Louvre. "Oh, yeah, that glass pyramid thingie in the Louvre? Impossible to find the entrance. There's a good mall underneath it though. With a fantabulous food court." She lobs a Frito into her mouth.

I clench my jaw. Of course William is right that Rose is a human being worthy of compassion and regard. But which is more revolting? The stench of Fritos? Or the fact that said stench makes my mouth water?

In high school, I created a private taxonomy of fat people, lumping them into two categories. Category One fat people are fat locally. They have a potbelly, or saddlebags, or a bubble butt, but the rest of them is normal, even slender. These are the pear-shaped women with swan-like necks, the beer-bellied men with toothpick legs. Category Two fat people are fat globally. Everything is puffed—knees, ankles, wrists, elbows, fingers, toes. It's as if someone shoved a bicycle pump into their mouths and pumped them up.

When I was fat, I was a Category Two. Like Rose.

But this is never going to happen to me. Not again. Not if it kills me.

"Anyway, if you ever do go to Paris, be sure and talk to me first!" Rose says, slapping the book shut. "We spent two whole days there." She pops up off the sofa with unexpected ease. "Fat people are stronger than we are," Kat said once, "because they're always lifting weights." Fortunately, William was not around to hear that one.

At the door Rose turns. "A trip would be good for you," she says. "You need to get out of your comfort zone. Live a little. Try new things."

The book slides off my lap, onto the floor. It's as if Rose knows about The Plan.

five

BUT THAT'S CRAZY. There is no way Rose can know about The Plan.

I leave the library early, drive straight home, and yank my Tupperware container full of cash-back savings money out of its hiding place behind the cookbooks. I don't need to count it. I know I have exactly two hundred tens and one hundred ninety-six fives, which comes to two thousand nine hundred eighty dollars. Paris dollars, according to Kat.

But I also know this money is no good to me. It can never get out in the world; it can never play with all the other money. If I buy something with it William will wonder why he isn't seeing a charge on the Visa. If I deposit it in the bank he will wonder where it came from. William is OCD about keeping tabs on our finances. Which I guess is not a bad thing to be OCD about.

I dump the contents of the Tupperware container out onto the kitchen counter. What we have here, ladies and gentlemen, really is just a pile of dirty paper. A pretty sizable pile. A major chunk of change. Money to burn.

Now there's a thought.

A basket of matchbooks resides in the bookcase. William likes to use real matches to light his cigarettes, and collects them from the few restaurants and bars that still give them away. I choose a sweet little box of wooden matches and then dig out our largest stainless steel mixing bowl—the one I use for bread dough, which seems appropriate—and heap the money into it. I strike a match.

The phone rings. I blow out the match.

"Hey," Will says.

"Hey," I say, letting the still-glowing matchstick fall hissing into the kitchen sink.

"I'm calling to ask if you would pick up my blazer at the cleaners," he says. "I forgot."

"Oh. Yeah. Sure."

"I didn't want to wake you this morning to ask."

"Right. Thanks."

"You're welcome."

After five more minutes of this kind of talk we hang up and I gather up all the money and put it back into its Tupperware container. Because it is not as easy to incinerate nearly three thousand dollars in cash as you might think. And because I am not crazy. And because I might need this money, eventually. You never know.

But first I have to start the salsa for the enchiladas. (It's Mexican night. Olé.) I yank open the louvered pantry door, steeling myself against the siren song of the Ritz crackers, and survey my rows of canned tomato products. Diced tomatoes, stewed tomatoes, whole tomatoes, tomato purée, tomato soup, tomato sauce.

Un-effing-believable. No tomato paste.

I make menu plans and shopping lists out the ying-yang. But it happens at least monthly: I lack a key ingredient. I either neglect to put it on the shopping list, or I put it on the shopping list but neglect to buy it.

"What you should do," William likes to say, "is organize your list in the order you encounter items in the store. There's an app for that."

I concede the logic here. But I compose my menus and lists on good old-fashioned paper. No app needed or wanted. "I am not that compulsive," I once told Kat. "Ya think?" she said, waggling her eyebrows. Kat could be pretty annoying sometimes. Maybe if I concentrate on her bad qualities I will miss her less.

Maybe. I slam the pantry door shut. Anyway, today it doesn't matter about the tomato paste because there's some in the emergency food rations.

Stockpiling food was William's suggestion. "Not a two-year supply, like the Mormons," he said. "But people should keep emergency provisions in case of a disaster." Phoenix doesn't have earthquakes or floods or tornadoes, but I agreed preparedness is a good idea no matter where you are. I downloaded instructions for building a disaster kit from the Red Cross website.

At first we kept the emergency food in the broom closet. It looked good there. Organized, mature, provident. Every time I took out a mop or a dust rag and saw the translucent bin filled to the brim with cans of water-packed tuna and bags of whole-grain pasta, I felt safer, calmer, solid-er.

It was six months ago that the whole arrangement spun out of control. Kat received a terminal prognosis and she, as part of an ensuing flurry of activity, asked me to empty her rented ministorage locker. She had kept one for years, using it to store her surfboard, her skis, her mountain bike, her camping equipment, her golf clubs, the Noritake china that her grandmother left her and that she hated, and everything else that didn't fit into her tiny one-bedroom condo. She gave me the key and I promised to sell or give away everything and to cancel her rental agreement. She would not have to sort through stuff she'd never get to use again and feel bad.

But on my first trip over there I stopped off at the grocery store on the way and as I stood in the check-out line clutching my five-pound bag of apples and quart of skim milk a display of Coca-Cola, the full sugar kind, the real thing, caught my eye. Before I knew what I was doing I was lugging two twelve-packs of half-price Coke out to the parking lot.

We do not keep sugared drinks in the house. Nor do we buy pre-fab food like canned soups or frozen TV dinners or margarine. We make even ketchup and mayonnaise from scratch.

Still, this sort of slip-up happens and I always immediately return the contraband, no harm, no foul. But this time I took my purchase to the storage locker and hid it there, taking one of the Cokes to drink, warm, on the drive back home. It was fizzy and fabulous.

I eventually did empty the locker of all Kat's stuff. But at the same time I refilled it with forbidden food. Cases of ramen noodles, cartons of energy bars, cans of hash and SpaghettiOs, bags of sweetened cereals, boxes of sugary cookies, bottles of saccharined tea and coffee. All of it in flagrant violation of rule number thirteen of the perpetual diet: Never ever eat processed food. Processed food, oozing with salt and transfats and fructose and unpronounceable chemicals, is diabolically engineered to stimulate your appetite while never satiating it. Processed food, brought to you by faceless, heartless corporations who care only about the bottom line (theirs, not yours), is the very last thing you should put in your poor defenseless pathetic little body. It is the only rule that comes from William, but it is still a good one.

I grab my keys and, despite the hundred-degree heat, walk to the storage locker facility, only six blocks away on Gilbert Road. It won't hurt me, I'm not pregnant and, who knows, maybe I'll sweat off a couple ounces. When I get there I step into the cool dim space—the facility is one of the upscale kinds, meaning carpeted and air-conditioned—and slam the orange metal door down. Here I am safe, as far from the future, from real life, as I can get. I sit cross-legged on the thin carpet, rest my hands palms up on my knees, like in yoga, and listen to my sweat dry. Here no one can nag me. No one can ask a question, make a comment, suggest I be doing something more productive with my life, criticize, condemn, quibble, cavil, carp. Not Rose, not William. Not Kat. Somewhere on Gilbert Road an ambulance whines. Horns yelp. Brakes squeal. It's hellish out there but here in my secret storage locker it's as cool and clean and cocooning as a freshly laundered sheet. The yoga pants I changed into when I got home from the library are guiltily comfortable. Plus I didn't put on a bra under my T-shirt. "Not that you need a bra," Kat used to say.

I open my eyes and skim my fingers over the smooth plastic wall of a storage bin. Tomato paste doesn't count as a processed food because canned tomato products are actually not that bad, but when I bought a half-case of it not long ago—they were on sale two cans for a dollar—I dropped it off here at the same time I was stashing a twenty-four-count box of Vienna sausages.

At least I think I did. I hardly know what I have anymore. William would track the inventory on an Excel spread sheet, and not in an ironical way either. "Have you ever noticed," Kat said once, "that the man has zero sense of humor?" "That's not true," I countered, "he likes riddles. And puns." Kat just stuck out her tongue at me. They always rubbed each other the wrong way, William and Kat.

I rise to my knees and peer into the box fourth from the bottom. When you kneel, Dad used to say, you should be saying a prayer. Hah. I've done an awful lot of praying of late and I have to say it has not done that much good.

Plus, storage locker carpet is not ideal for kneeling so I get to my feet. The top box is full of a whole bunch of something blue—the heavenly Virgin Mary blue of the macaroni and cheese box. I'd know it anywhere. How long has it been since I've had good old pre-packaged, salty, chemical-y mac and cheese? Too long. And so far today I've had only a glass of lemon water and half a can of diet soda. My stomach is so empty it feels as if it's folding in half, as if it's digesting itself.

I take one of the blue boxes back to the house, boil the noodles until they're soft—no al dente for this girl—stir in the envelope of cadmium orange cheese powder, adding whole milk and a half-stick of real butter for extra creaminess, dump everything into a big mixing bowl, Virgin Mary blue like the box, and carry it and a spoon to the guest bathroom. The Sacré-Coeur judges not. The Sacré-Coeur shimmers and shakes and shimmies and says, Come on, join the party.

If Kat walked in on me right now she'd laugh her head off. She'd be wearing her favorite blue jeans and white peasant top, and her hair would be long, the way it used to be, and the color of honey on whole-wheat toast. "Hey," she'd say. "You gonna eat all that by yourself?"

But where Kat used to live and laugh, there is now a big black gaping hole. Where once she was so real, so here, so alive, so present, she is now so absent. I swallow only two spoonfuls of the mac and cheese before taking the bowl out to the kitchen and running it all down the garbage disposal.

six

"HOW WAS your morning at the library?" William asks, helping himself to a second piece of chili cornbread. I barely had time to get the enchiladas done, and had to resort to bottled salsa and canned black beans doctored up with cilantro and garlic. Fortunately, for once William does not seem to notice.

Maybe because we are eating in front of the TV, in flagrant violation of rule number fourteen of the perpetual diet: Don't eat in front of the television. Or the computer. Or while reading. Or under any circumstances that encourage the mindless consumption of food.

But the D-Backs have an important game and of course William doesn't know about the rules, so here we are. "It was okay," I say, putting down my spoon to rub my burning eyes. "I like the library. Maybe I could get a real job there."

"Maybe."

"Even if only part time," I persist. "They've laid off so many real librarians that now they're shorthanded. It's not unionized. The experience might help me get into grad school."

Citing facts and data, even facts and data you have made up, is the best way to convince William of things. Once Kat asked, "How do you stand living with such an android?" and I retorted, "He's not an android, he's an engineer."

But, truly, sometimes I wonder if they are one and the same.

William nods, his focus on a commercial touting the eternal male verities of trucks, babes, and beer. I know he felt bad about my putting all my savings toward the down payment on this house, the hasty buying of which was part of our whole shotgun-marriage thing. At the time it seemed like the right decision—plus it must be stated that he did contribute the lion's share—but it made grad school for me that much more remote. And that was even before I got laid off. Anyway, the commercial is over and so is the conversation.

I carry my plate to the kitchen and dump the rest of my enchilada into the disposal. Rule number fifteen of the perpetual diet: Not eating calories in the first place is better than eating calories and then trying to burn them off. And when you think about it, a lot less effort. "You never eat something and then, like, throw it up, do you?" Kat asked once. "God, no," I said. "I can't stand throwing up."

"Wanna go for a walk?"

William has switched off the TV and is standing behind me, dangling a pair of green running shoes.

When was the last time we went for an after-dinner walk? Weeks. Months. Years. "Okay," I say.

It is the end of the workweek and there are even people outside. Mothers and fathers returned from work, children retrieved from day care or school.

"Hey." A tanned, thirty-something guy around William's age slams the door of a minivan parked in the driveway next door. "Not a bad night," he says, raising a Dustbuster in salute.

William flashes him a thumbs up. "Gotta take advantage while you can."

The guy nods. We stroll on. Soon it'll be too hot to walk, or do anything, outdoors. Soon people will hurry from air-conditioned house to air-conditioned car to air-conditioned workplace, refer to hundred-degree temperatures as "warm," and say that "it sure beats shoveling snow," even if they never lived in snow country, even if they were born and raised right here in boring stupid old Phoenix.

"Do you know him?" I ask.

"A little," William says. "I've seen him around."

A red Mini Cooper whooshes by, a surfboard lashed to its roof. I spread my arms out, like wings, but stay right where I am. Phoenix, Arizona. The Mini Cooper, on the other hand, is on its way to somewhere new, somewhere fun, California or Mexico. Or Paris. We round a corner and pause to watch an enormous jackrabbit streak across the street in front of us. It stops under an ocotillo and sits, nervous nose twitching, erect ears swiveling, rigid forelegs quivering.

"Look at the bunny!"

"That ain't no bunny," William says. "That's a big ol' jackrabbit."

"Rabbits. Bunnies. Same-same. Right?"

We've had this conversation dozens of times. Just not recently.

William keeps to the script. "Wrong," he says, grinning. "Jackrabbits aren't rabbits. They belong to the hare family."

"Then why do people call them rabbits?" I ask. "Besides, they're cute."

"If you think invasive species are cute."

"Anything furry with floppy ears and a fluffy tail is cute."

We smile at each other for the first time in weeks. William takes my clammy hand in his dry one and we cross the street, shoulders rubbing. A single smoke a day, weirdly, does not make William smell like cigarettes. His own personal aroma of vanilla—like tapioca pudding, like crème caramel—is too resilient for that. I lean into his arm to step over the long handle of a red wagon and to get a stronger whiff.

"Good to see little kids still play with red wagons," William says.

I stiffen and withdraw my hand. So. Not a neighbor-saluting, bunny-admiring, marriage-renewing after-dinner walk after all.

"And good to see they still leave them out on the sidewalk for people to trip over," I say. He leaves in less than forty-eight hours. I wish it were this very minute.

He grabs my hand back and squeezes it. "So whaddya think?"

"Think?"

"About us. About having a kid."

A three-quarter-ton pickup truck roars past and squeals around the corner.

"By my calculations, it's time," he adds.

I fiddle with my silver horseshoe earrings. They used to be Kat's. "You've been calculating?"

"I ran some numbers, yeah."

Numbers. Unbelievable. Unfathomable. I pull my hand free, step off the curb, and turn to face him. "You have got to be kidding."

"How so?"

"How so? Kat just died. And now I'm supposed to bounce back— bada bing—and be ready to move forward? On your schedule? I'm supposed to shrug and say 'that's that'?"

He scowls at me. "No. Of course not. But there is no reason not to start thinking. Planning."

William is a math whiz, a gourmet cook, an aeronautical engineer, and a planner. Last July we went to a couples' baby shower and he was one of the few males there willing—even eager—to hold Robert and Jen's tiny newborn. He made his arms into a nest for the blue bundle and sat quietly, solidly, murmuring chirpy sounds as if he knew all about babies. I was a little surprised to find myself yearning to grab that tiny ham-sized parcel myself, to feel its warmth and to breathe in that weird new-baby wet-pancake aroma, but Jen leaned in and crooned in that simpering voice of hers. "Ooh, how sweet is that? I bet it won't be long before you two have one of your own!" she said and William winked at me and the moment passed. And here I am celebrating home pregnancy tests that turn out negative. It makes me tired to think of it.

"Do you not want to have a family?" he asks now. I feel a little sorry for him. The whole time Kat was sick he never complained. My birthdays ticked by, twenty-seven, twenty-eight, twenty-nine, but William never so much as uttered the words "biological clock."

"You know," I say, stalling, trying not to think of the pregnancy wand hidden in the garbage can in the garage. It's not hot out, not by Phoenix standards, but I've begun to pour sweat. A fat droplet rolls down the flat space between my breasts. "You didn't want me to get pregnant again. Right away. Back then, I mean." I lift my heavy hair off my hot neck and try to stretch the tension out of my shoulders. I feel headachy, and kind of floaty and odd. Maybe my period is starting.

"No. Did you? I wasn't earning enough. We were still living in your old place."

After Dad died I kept on living in that old central Phoenix bungalow. It had only evaporative cooling and a single unrenovated bathroom, but it was paid for. When I got knocked up and we got married, bada bing, William moved in with me while we house hunted.

"Why do you bring that up now?" he asks.

"I just wasn't ever sure. It was really just that you thought we didn't have the money?"

"Money is important."

Please don't let him recite the facts and data. The four years of our marriage have been spent on working, on saving, on buying a house, and on Kat. Facts and data. They drag everything out into the daylight, kicking and screaming.

But they do not save you. They do not fix what is broken, undo what is done.

"Do you not want to have a family?" he persists.

I think I do, maybe I do, someday, but I say, "What I want is to be cut some slack. It's too soon, can't you understand that?"

"I can. But, Ames. It's not like she was your actual sister or anything."

I stop feeling sorry for him. For years Kat was the only family I had. She was the closest thing I ever had to a sister. Ever will have.

Plus, of course, there's this: I worry I might be incapable of loving a child, incapable of feeling the overwhelming transcendent and selfless passion that mothers so famously feel. I worry I might turn out to be like my own mother. Which, trust me, you would not wish on any kid.

"Maybe it's not that I'm so afraid of having a baby," I say through gritted teeth. "Maybe it's just that I don't want to have one with a clueless asshole like you." And then I bolt across the street, just avoiding being flattened by a speeding SUV.

"What the hell?" William shouts after me.

I keep going. Not because of the clueless asshole remark but because William will want to know what I meant by being afraid to have a baby. I've never mentioned it to him before. Not even when I was pregnant four years ago. I miscarried after only three months but was totally panic stricken every single minute of that time.

Even worse, after the miscarriage I didn't feel anything. Not disappointment, not loss, not grief, not even relief. "What is wrong with me?" I worried to Kat. She reassured me. "It's because it was so abstract," she said. "The baby wasn't a person to you yet. Anyway, a lot has been happening. Meeting William, getting pregnant, getting married. All in only a few months." I said, "Maybe you're right," and she said, "Of course I'm right," and I felt much, much better.

For that, and for so many other things, I will always owe her.

seven

BACK AT HOME William does not talk. He pours himself a light beer and settles down in front of the TV with his jigsaw. I trudge upstairs in search of Midol, on the way passing the empty bedroom that William refers to as the nursery. I don't have to go in there to look because I know the matching carry-ons, fully packed, are still standing side by side in the closet, like fat dictionaries on a shelf. They were stored at Kat's as part of the secret of The Plan and when Kat went into the hospital for the last time I claimed them. "What's all this?" William asked when I brought them home. "You going on a trip?" I flinched. Even zipped tight shut, I could smell the lemon verbena, Kat's signature scent, coming from Kat's bag. "They're just things Kat wants me to have," I said, unable to look him in the face. "Wanted me to have."

The next morning I am wrapped in a blanket on the sofa rereading Harry Potter. Last night's headache turned out to be the beginning not of my period but of a summer cold, and my head now feels like a fat balloon ready to detach itself from my neck and float away.

William pokes his head into the living room. He didn't even notice, or seem to, that I spent most of the night on the sofa. "I've gotta go in to work for a few hours," he says, adding, "pre-trip prep." It is Saturday. He leaves tomorrow.

"Okay," I rasp, gasping for breath and fumbling for a tissue. The Nyquil I double dosed on at three a.m. hardly seems to be helping at all.

"Listen," he says, standing in the doorway, keeping his distance from my germs and, maybe, from me. "I wanted you to know. This is my last trip for a long time. I'm being moved to a pre-management track."

I close Harry Potter with a thunk and sit up, shading my eyes from the fierce morning sun blazing through the front window. "Management? Seriously?" I say. "That's great."

He squints at me. "Yeah," he says after a moment, and turns away.

I jump up, swaying. Ugh. The Nyquil zombies. "Let's cook out tonight," I call, staggering forward a few steps. "Barbecued ribs? Would you like that? Will?" I have been bracing myself for Thai night but William loves ribs and I feel I sort of owe him.

But it's too late. He's gone.

I shuffle to the kitchen and mix up William's grandfather's favorite cold remedy: the juice of a whole lemon, a spoonful of honey, and a shot of bourbon in very hot water. I use my favorite cobalt blue mug. Rule number sixteen of the perpetual diet: Boldly colored dishes make food taste better, and when food tastes better, you eat less of it.

At least that's the theory. This is why my plates are tangerine orange, my bowls are cherry red, and the handles of my flatware are lime green.

Whether it's the blue mug, or the lemon juice, or the honey, or the booze, I am suddenly wide awake. William's last trip. In my head, my enormous echoing empty head, Kat's voice hisses, "The Plan."

Whatever. I go upstairs and take an extra-long, extra-hot shower, breathing steam through my cottony mouth and down into my congested lungs. I twist my hair into a single long black braid, put on a white eyelet sundress, and swig a dose of cough syrup straight from the bottle. On the bright side, the head-cold-from-hell seems to have killed my appetite. "Don't you ever want to just let go?" Kat used to say. "Haven't you ever just wanted to curl up with a big old box of chocolates and devour it?"

Indeed I have. Dad turned grocery shopping over to me when his MS kept him housebound. We lived on take-out tacos and frozen pizzas and sugary cereals. Even worse, between meals, during his naps, and after he went to bed at eight p.m., I snacked. Triple-layer boxes of chocolates, family-size bags of potato chips, half-gallon buckets of ice cream.

I might've turned into one of those people you see on the evening news who can't get out of their beds and have to be moved with forklifts when they fall into comas, but after Dad died food stopped tasting good. I'd bake a chocolate cake, eat a slice, and throw out the rest. I'd make a tuna sandwich, eat half, and stuff the other half down the garbage disposal. Potato chips went stale in the cupboard, Danishes grew moldy in the bread box. To cut down on waste, I started living on frozen dinners. Lean Cuisine. I chose it because it sounded French. I know, pathetic.

In less than a year the hundred pounds had disappeared. Bada bing. My asthma went away, too. At ASU, where I met Kat, she could not believe I had ever been anything other than slender ("You're a wisp," she said, running her hand over my thigh).

But of course lost weight is never *lost* lost. It's only out of sight. In the last eleven years I've added and subtracted the same twenty or thirty pounds more than a dozen times. Yet no matter how often I lose them they are always waiting, just around the corner, biding their time, tapping their feet, checking their watches, ready to descend once again in ripples and folds and bulges. Fat is vigilant. Fat is patient. Fat is eternal.

I am backing the Honda down the driveway, on my way to Costco for the ribs, when a pink-pantsuited shape appears in my rearview mirror.

"Amy! Yoo-hoo!"

I slam on the brakes. It's Kathryn.

"Hello, Kathryn," I say, lowering my window. "How nice to see you." Though it isn't nice. The last time I saw Kathryn was at the funeral.

"Goodie. I was hoping you'd be home." Kathryn hurries up the driveway, a large cardboard box in her arms. "Otherwise I was going to have to leave this on your doorstep."

"Let me help you," I say, leaping out of the Honda and taking the box, though Kathryn is neither old nor infirm—she's a fit sixty-something, the aunt Kat was named after and Kat's only living female relative, sole survivor of the family's breast cancer gene.

"Thank you, honey. I was just on my way to the airport." Kathryn lives in Ohio. When Kat and I found out about the cancer gene, it changed things. At least for Kat, who said, "It all seems so much less random now." I asked, "Should that make us feel better?" and Kat answered, in a lower voice than usual, "Yes. It means it's not my fault, it means it's nothing I did, or didn't do." "Why," I said, "would you think it was something you did? How is that even possible?" but she fiddled with her practically non-existent hair and wouldn't say more.

Kathryn follows me through the garage and into the kitchen. "Oof! It's surely hot out there!" she exclaims. "My, what a lovely home you have. So neat and tidy. So nice to see nice young people with such a nice household." I plunk the box on the kitchen counter and Kathryn places her pink Kate Spade bag beside it. "I just sold Kat's car," Kathryn says, "and transferred the title to her condo. That's everything."

Kathryn doesn't know about the storage locker, paid up through June.

"But, wouldn't you know," she continues, "I found a few final things I was just sure you'd love to have." She rips a strip of plastic packing tape off the box.

I already have a lot of Kat's things—her hand-tooled black cowboy boots, her fake Navajo rug, her never-used Kitchen Aid mixer, her numbered Ansel Adams print. And her silver horseshoe earrings, which I haven't taken off since the day she gave them to me.

Kathryn extracts a newspaper-wrapped cylinder from the box and unwraps it. "Isn't this darling?" she says, holding up a tall, thin, clear iced tea glass. She unwraps a second glass, and a third. There are eight in all, plus a matching pitcher. Kathryn lines them up on the counter, swooshing the newspaper onto the floor. Kat was the same. She cared only about results, not the messes and upsets caused getting to the results. "All product, no process," William would say.

"And that's not all," Kathryn adds, reaching again into the box and lifting out a large round flat something, mummy-wrapped in toilet paper. "I've been wondering what this was," she says, tearing off the white strips with French-manicured hands. I use some to blow my nose. Right now all I want to do is crawl into bed and stay there. Forever. The toilet paper is making a knee-high pyramid on the floor when Kathryn holds up a large ceramic serving platter. It's shaped like a turkey, green and black and orange and white, and is big enough to hold a twenty-five-pound bird.

"Hmm. Looks antique-y, don't you think? Maybe it's worth something."

I stare at it. Sneeze.

"Gesundheit," says Kathryn. "Kat's cupboards were completely empty except for this. It had a yellow sticky on it, with your name. The iced tea set—that was in her coat closet. I thought, down here in Phoenix where it's so hot, you must drink an awful lot of iced tea."

I blow my nose again and force my eyes from the turkey platter to Kathryn's face. "We do," I say. Kathryn's short, sleek bob is on-purpose gray. The parentheses framing her mouth and the half asterisks bursting from the corners of her eyes also seem on purpose. On TV, she would play the amazing mom. What would she say if I told her about The Plan, about Paris? About William wanting a baby, immediately if not sooner? About my own fat crazy mother, dead and gone so long ago? No doubt something comforting, something wise. She would resolve all of my pathetic neuroses and tie them up with a bow in time for the commercial break. A pink bow.

"Oh, one more thing," Kathryn is saying, fishing in the Kate Spade bag. "I'm the executor of the estate, you know. Were you aware that you are Kat's sole beneficiary? It will take a while to find out how much it comes to. Meanwhile, I also found this envelope addressed to you. I should have given it to you sooner, but it got mixed up in all the other paperwork. I didn't even realize I had it till this morning."

She tosses a manila envelope onto the turkey platter. "Amy," it says in flowing Italic script. Kat took up calligraphy in college, and every birthday card I ever received from her was addressed in just this way.

"Are you all right, punkin?" Kathryn asks. "You look sickly. It's no wonder—you're such a skinny little thing! Do you have the sniffles? Fancy catching a cold in such hot weather. Here, take a load off." She shoves a barstool under me. "You young girls never eat right. Let me fix you something. Would you like a piece of toast with butter and jam?"

Toast, ninety calories. Butter, a hundred for just one tablespoon. Jam, forty-ish. "No. I'm okay," I say. "I guess I shouldn't have skipped breakfast." Or had bourbon on top of cough syrup.

"Dear oh dear oh dear. You need to get some protein in you. Do you have any lunch meat or cheese in the house?" Before I can answer Kathryn is rummaging around in my refrigerator. "Here," she says, finding the stick of William's Saturday afternoon cheddar and breaking off a hunk the size of a plum. She doesn't use a knife. She doesn't even wash her hands first.

But I eat the cheese. "Thank you. I do feel better." Which is a little true. I circle around the kitchen island, putting it between us. This is my kitchen, my house. "May I offer you something? Coffee? Tea?"

"Oh, heavens no. I have a plane to catch! And I have to return that awful rental car. I must be going." Kathryn nods at the iced tea glasses lined up on the counter like soldiers, the manila envelope lying on the turkey platter like an open palm. Her work here is done. In less than a minute she's zipped out the door, hopped in the rental car, and tootled goodbye. I stand in the driveway until the car disappears around a jacaranda tree. Is it wrong to wish it had been Kathryn, not Kat, who got the cancer?

I return to the kitchen. Wrap up the cheese and put it away. Wrap up the iced tea glasses and matching pitcher in the newspaper and return them to the box. Pick up the turkey platter and cradle it in my arms.

"Hey-o," Kat said. It was four months ago. We were going through her kitchen cupboards. "Check out this crazy turkey platter," she said. "You need to own it."

"Good God, Kat. What a hideous object."

"That's what makes it so great."

"Says you."

"Says me. Can't you see? It's turkey shaped! Shaped like an actual turkey!"

"I see that. Ick."

"Snob. Where's your sense of whimsy?"

"Apparently I have none. Where did you get that thing anyway?"

"Garage sale. Three bucks. A bargain at half the price. Ha. Take the turkey platter, take the turkey platter!"

"Not gonna happen."

"Take the turkey platter! Or I will come back and haunt you for the rest of your life."

It was my turn to make a snappy comeback. Those were the rules.

"Oh never mind," Kat said after a long pause. "I'll give it to Goodwill. It's probably a valuable collector's item. Someone'll take it to Antiques Roadshow and they'll sell it for a coupla thou and you'll be sorry."

Alone in my kitchen, I sneeze for what has to be the twentieth time today, put down the platter, pick up the manila envelope, and hold it up to the light. Looks like a DVD. Could be something. Could be nothing. Probably is nothing. But I take it upstairs and insert it into the computer.

It's a video. I press my icy hands to my burning forehead and lick my cracking lips with my cheddar-cheese-furred tongue.

"Amy-girl. Hey." Kat's face has popped up in the video window.

Her skin is waxen and her eyes are like black holes. She's wearing the pink T-shirt she wore constantly during her last weeks. She is completely bald and doesn't have her wig on, or even one of the stretchy turbans I sewed for her. "Cutest alien ever," I used to tease.

"I tried to write you a letter," Kat begins. "But you know me, I'm a talker, not a writer." She pauses. "Nyuk, nyuk," she adds.

"Anyway." She leans forward, her face filling the screen. "A picture is worth a thousand words, right?" She's wearing false eyelashes and her lips are painted strawberry red. "I have three things I want to tell you. Only three! Don't worry, I'm not gonna go on and on." She holds up an index finger, smiling brightly. "First, I want to tell you—to order you!—not to be sad.

"I know, I know," she says, dropping her hand. "It's crazy. You're probably thinking, 'How stupid. Of course I'm going to be sad.' I get that. I do. I guess what I mean is, don't be sad *for me*. I am fine! I'm…not afraid." Three, four, five seconds go by. "Okay, okay, I have been afraid, a lot, through it all. As you know. But now I'm down with it. Really. Everyone has done everything anybody could possibly do. I'm ready now, Amy, I am," she says, lifting her chin. "The only thing I feel bad about is leaving you."

She squeezes her eyes shut and takes a labored breath. "I think to myself how I would feel if things were the other way around. And it kills me to realize how much this is hurting you. Kills me literally, I guess. Har har."

I hit Pause. I jump up, sprint down to the kitchen, drink a glass of water, sprint back upstairs, return to the computer. Kat's face waits, her head tipped back the way she did when she was about to guffaw. I click Play.

She does guffaw. "Sorry. That was bad. But now that I'm, you know, dead, I figure I get to say whatever I want. Anyway, here's thing number two," she says, holding up two fingers in a lop-sided V. "It's maybe weird. But, take a closer look at Will. I don't think you know him as well as you think you do." She pauses again, licks her lips. "I realize I've never exactly been his biggest fan. But maybe I was wrong. I see that now. I don't want to say tons about this. Just do it, Amy. I don't want you to be alone."

I am hunched over the computer, clutching my stomach. Kat is inside the computer, talking, laughing, breathing. So alive. So real. I dry my cheeks with the brushy end of my braid and glance at the timer at the bottom of the video window. Two minutes out of four are over. Already.

"Are you up for thing number three? I hope so. You're gonna like it." Kat holds up three fingers and waves them back and forth like windshield wipers. "Here it is: Go. To. Paris."

Five long silent seconds tick by.

"I told you you'd like it," she finally continues. "And I mean it, girlie girl! You need enabling and I am officially enabling you. I don't care how you do it, when you do it, who you do it with. Just go. This is my official deathbed request. You've been aching to go to Paris, to go somewhere, for, like, forever. You have to do it. You need to do it. I order you to do it."

She nibbles on her bottom lip. "On second thought, I do care when you go," she says, letting her eyes fall shut. She's wearing eggplant purple eye shadow. "Do it soon. It's too easy to put things off and then we just end up never doing them. We never get the thing we really wanted. No one knows this better than me." She opens her eyes. "Take it from one who knows."

Her lips quiver and she presses them together, making a thick red dash in her thin white face. "I know, I'm rambling. Sorree. I'm dead and I still can't shut up! I just want you to get something you really want for once. You deserve it. You've spent your life doing things for other people. Your dad. Me. Will."

The unholy cocktail of bourbon, lemon, and cheese rumbles in my stomach. Kat places her palms together, rests her chin on her fingertips, and takes another wheezing breath. "Okay, I think I've made my point," she says. "Points. At least I hope I have." She gazes thoughtfully into the webcam. I gaze back. I'd crawl inside the screen if I could.

"Can I tell you one last tiny little thing?" she says, dropping her hands. "I always loved you, Amy. Maybe too much. Maybe I've been selfish. Maybe I've done things I shouldn't have done. In fact I know I have. I only wanted to be sure you would be happy. And I'm really really sorry. Please remember that. I don't want to go all sappy here. But it's something I need to tell you and I'm glad to be able to tell you. People never say these things until it's too late. I hate that. Don't you? It's stupid. People are stupid. So I'm saying it now." She slumps back and two shining tears trickle down her face. She swipes them off with the back of her hand. Tries to smile. "I love you. I'm sorry. Don't forget."

A second later the smile widens into a grin. "I guess that was four things. Sorry. You know me. I never could keep to a plan. Turn this off now, Amy-girl. Oh, one more thing," she adds. "Go look in the outside pocket of my carry-on. Bye. Remember—outside pocket."

And then the video window goes black.

eight

"SOMETHING TO DRINK for you, *madame*?"

The flight attendant smiles even though I am easily the two-hundredth person she's said this to.

"Um. Sparkling water, please," I say.

I am on an airplane.

I am being addressed as *madame*.

I am implementing The Plan. Without Kat. Without William. With only myself. Because this morning after watching Kat's video four more times I went to the spare bedroom that William calls a nursery, unzipped the outside pocket of Kat's still-packed carry-on, the one that smells like lemon verbena, and found an envelope with two blue plastic cards inside. "Okay," read the enclosed note. "It's not a fancy presentation. But these are airline gift cards. One should get you to Paris. One should get you back. Now you have no excuse. Go! Hugs, Kat."

The next hour went by like a bag of M&Ms. It took only twenty minutes to locate a flight on Air France, LA to Paris, and to redeem the cards. Fifteen to reserve a spot on Alaska from Phoenix to LA. The hardest part was writing a three-line email to the Hôtel du Cheval Blanc, chosen long ago as a not-too-expensive-yet-ideally-located place to stay. Finally I clicked on Send, grabbed my wallet, hopped in the Honda, and vroomed off to Costco for the ribs. A reply from the Hôtel du Cheval Blanc was waiting when I got back. "You have *chance, madame*," it said. "We happily have a cancellation for the nights you name. We would be pleased to welcome you on Monday next."

And now I am on my way. I take a deep breath through my mouth, because my nose is still completely plugged up, and survey my realm. My carry-on is stowed in an overhead compartment across the aisle, my tote bag is stuffed under the seat in front of me, and my money belt is strapped under my brand new skinny jeans, which are way too tight. But the skinny jeans are mandatory. They are part of The Plan.

Just twenty-four hours ago William and I barbecued ribs together on the patio. He ate heartily but said little. I too was mostly silent, unable to think about anything other than my reservation on Air France and my packed suitcase and the fact that oh-wow-oh-God-I'm-actually-doing-this.

After dinner he didn't turn on the TV and didn't work on his jigsaw puzzle and didn't refer to last night's conversation about babies. Instead, he fiddled with his packing, rifled through his briefcase, and went to bed early. We did not make love. I popped a decongestant and lay rigid as a chopstick beside him, reviewing the schedule for the next day. Drive William to airport. Drop him off at Terminal 4. Return Honda to house, catch shuttle bus reserved earlier, head to Terminal 2, board Alaska flight to LAX, wait two hours, board Air France flight, non-stop from Los Angeles to Paris. "Slick as snot," Kat would say.

Even so, I might never have gone through with the whole insane scheme if it hadn't been for the first Daily Phone Call.

I was still at Sky Harbor, waiting for my connecting flight to LA and for William's six o'clock call in the quietest place I could find—the ladies' room on the lower level of Terminal 2. This level is always deserted except for, or maybe because of, a display of black and white photographs of historic Phoenix. Historic Phoenix. Now there's an oxymoron for you. I shut myself into the handicapped stall and fished my phone out of my purse. Five fifty-five p.m. Perfect. I paced back and forth in the small space and tried to calm the bang-a-langing of my heart.

At six-fifteen he still had not called. William, Mr. Reliable, is rarely late, with calls or in person. If delayed he texts. Plane crash, traffic accident, terrorist attack, cardiac arrest, kidnapping—one by one I ticked off the possibilities and then resolutely pushed them away, like second helpings of mashed potatoes. "Maybe he's run off with a waitress," Kat said the time we got our wires crossed and William forgot to pick me up from the car mechanic's. "No, he's not like that," I said, even though I'd only known him a couple weeks. Kat stuck out her tongue. "What do you know what he's like?" she said. "You don't know anything about him. He could be an axe murderer for all you know!"

William turned out not to be an axe murderer.

Six-twenty. My stomach churned. To a lot of people, going to Paris would not be a big deal—just hop on a plane and jet off, woo-hoo—but in my whole life I've only been to California a half dozen times and Nogales one time. And that was in the company of either Kat or William. Going all the way to France, alone? What was I thinking? It may as well be the frigging moon.

Besides, am I really this deceitful?

I was about to grab my carry-on and get on a shuttle and go back home to my knitting when William's smiling image popped up on the screen of my phone. I almost dropped it in the toilet.

"Hey," William said.

"Hey," I replied, trying to keep the tremor out of my voice. In William's mind I was curled up in the corner of our white leather sofa, watching the latest British import on public television. He doesn't like to face up to problems. If he's unhappy about something he's more the silent treatment sort of person. Once I tried to talk with Kat about this but she jammed her fingers in her ears and sang, "La la la! Don't tell me! I don't want to hear about trouble in too-good-to-be-true land!"

Anyway, problems with William usually do blow over in a few days.

"What's up?"

"Not much," I said. Only standing in a toilet stall, lah-di-dah, waiting to board an airplane to Paris, France. Good thing this isn't a video call. I licked my dry lips. "What's up with you?"

"Not much."

Another pause. "How was your flight?" I finally asked.

"Uneventful."

I studied the rust and sage and cream and ebony wall tiles. "Good. That's good."

"Just got back from dinner with Bob Wallace," he added.

"Oh. Sounds great. What did you have to eat?" Stupid question. I knew it would be high carb, high fat, and high salt, topped off with something high sugar. I slid my hand along my ribs, which I can now count despite the fact that my stomach still has a small but persistent pooch.

"He's being transferred to D.C."

"Who?"

"Bob Wallace."

"Oh. Good for him. I'd love to live on the East Coast," I said.

"What?"

I sniffed and cleared my throat. "What I mean," I said, "is that it would be fun to move somewhere else. To a new place. Change can be good."

Several more silent seconds slipped by. Then he yawned. "Guess I oughta turn in," he said. "Gotta get up at oh-dark-thirty."

Locked in the handicapped stall, phone clamped to my ear, I was suddenly not ready to say goodbye. "Will?" I said, wracking my brain for a way to confess, Will, I was just about to do something awful, I was going to go on a trip, a trip all the way to Paris, without telling you, but I'm not going to do that, that would be sneaky and awful and kinda wrong and probably stupid. "William, wait."

But he had hung up.

In the deserted hallway outside the ladies' room I paused to blow my nose in front of a poster-sized black-and-white photo of a 1907 Arizona ostrich farm. I had pulled it off, the first Daily Phone Call. And nothing I said was an actual lie, technically.

nine

"FIRST TRIP TO PARIS?" The woman seated next to me is peering at me curiously.

"Yes. It is." I wipe my watery eyes and choke back a sneeze. I probably shouldn't be flying in my condition.

"Ours too. We've been saving up for years." She gestures toward the dozing man beside her. "A second honeymoon! I can't believe it's actually happening."

If Kat were here, she'd chat the whole nine hours with this couple and arrive at Charles de Gaulle Airport with their names, occupations, email addresses, and life stories. Kat collected people. She had two thousand Facebook friends, three hundred of whom attended her funeral. I shouldn't have been annoyed, but I was. I was annoyed when people singled me out for special condolences. I was annoyed when they didn't.

The woman beside me opens a magazine to a dog-eared page where the words "Six Ways to Sex Your Mate" scream in inch-high blood-red letters.

Yikes. You never know about other people. What they're capable of. I myself, for example, didn't know I was so capable of so effectively deceiving my very own mate until just a couple hours ago.

The plane jutters and yaws. So does my stomach. But it's too late to change my mind, to push Undo on The Plan and go back to the way things were before. Even if the minute I arrived in Paris I got on a flight straight back to Phoenix, things could never be the same. Not without Kat, to make me laugh, to be there as my ballast, to explain me to myself.

I plug in my earbuds and take out the book she bought me for my twenty-seventh birthday two years ago. *French for Travelers*. It falls open to the chapter entitled "At the Café," and my stomach performs a queasy little backflip. I have never eaten in a restaurant alone before. Starbucks, yes. McDonald's, yes. But not a real restaurant. "Live a little," Rose said. Hah.

Four rows up a baby erupts into a high-pitched wail. Poor baby on an overseas flight. Poor mother of a baby on an overseas flight. Two nights ago, on the baby walk-and-talk, William said, "You'd make an amazing mom," as if it were an axiom, as if he knew it for a scientific fact. I wanted to ask, "Why do you think that? How can you be sure?" but by then the conversation had turned into a confrontation.

"William wants kids," I once told Kat. It was six months after the wedding and five months after the miscarriage. Ages before anyone thought of cancer and dying.

"Who cares what Will-yum wants? What matters is what you want."

We were lying on the pool deck at the north Scottsdale apartment she was renting back then, drip-drying after a midnight swim. William was on a business trip and I was spending the night. "What do you think?" I said, wanting to change the subject. "About having children?"

"Me? You don't wanna know."

"I do," I said. "I want to know."

"We-ell," she drawled. "I just realized one day that I think puppies and kittens are way cuter than babies."

"Ha. Meaning?"

"Meaning I don't think that makes me very maternal."

I pondered for a moment. "Maybe it has nothing to do with being maternal. Maybe it just means puppies and kittens are in point of fact way cuter than babies."

Kat snickered. "You could be on to something."

"What I'm trying to say is," I continued, bunching up my towel to make a pillow, "it's the fluff factor. Anything fluffy is automatically cuter than anything that's not. Picture puppies and kittens with all their fur shaved off."

"Gack. Definitely less cute."

"Definitely."

"I suppose that's the reason humans wear clothes. To hide our lack of fluffiness."

"Clothes are actually nothing but a fluff substitute."

"So true."

"What's amazing," I concluded, "is that humans can bear to take their clothes off long enough to mate."

"Now you're going too far," said Kat, half rising. "Look at you! Who wouldn't want to mate with you?"

I rolled over and sat up.

"Just because you had a miscarriage, you know," Kat said, reaching over with her foot and stroking the side of my calf with her big toe, "doesn't mean you can't ever have a kid."

"I know that."

"And just because your mother was a neurotic mess, it doesn't mean you would be one, too. There's no reason you just can't, as they say, have it all. The perfect husband and the grad school and the cool career and the non-fluffy baby."

For a moment I focused all my attention on a trio of lawn chairs convening at the far end of the pool deck. "I know that, too," I finally said. But did not believe it.

The pool aerator came on, spraying us with a mist of water and the scent of chlorine. I shivered, though the July night was ovenlike, and my head throbbed. When I was a little kid, my mother had frequent migraines and left the child rearing to Dad, except for bedtime stories. "Reading me stories was the one thing she would do," I told Kat in college, when we were telling each other everything. "But when I turned five she pushed me away, off her lap, and said, 'You're too heavy, you need to learn to read by yourself.'" Kat, eyes popping, had asked, "What did you do?" I said, "I learned to read by myself," and Kat said, "You're a tough nut, kiddo."

The pool aerator turned off. I stood up, wrapped my towel around my waist, and looked down at Kat. "So why do you think William wants children?" I asked, in spite of myself. "I mean, really."

"Oh, I don't know." Kat was sitting cross-legged, stretching her arms above her head. Kat had beautifully sculpted arms, courtesy of hours at the gym. "He's just a red-blooded American boy, I guess," she said, yawning. "It's the biological imperative." She jumped to her feet. "You know how a lot of only children have crazy romantic ideas about big families? Maybe it's that."

"You're probably right."

We gathered our stuff and padded barefoot up the warm concrete stairs to Kat's apartment. Kat snorted.

"What now?" I asked.

"Maybe the trick is to have a baby and pretend it's a puppy or a kitten until your maternal instinct kicks in."

I had to grin. "Maybe."

We fooled around that night, just a teeny tiny little bit.

"This didn't count," Kat said the next morning. "It was just for old time's sake."

I didn't answer because I knew that to Kat it did count.

The four-rows-up baby is now shrieking like the lead in a death metal band. Disgruntled passengers crane their necks to see what, if anything, the mother is doing about it. If it were a puppy yipping or a kitten mewing would they be any less annoyed?

People around me begin to lower their tray tables. A food cart is inching down the aisle. Dinnertime.

I unwrap a cough drop and pop it into my mouth. I know I won't like what's being served. Rule number seventeen of the perpetual diet: Be a picky eater. Picky eaters eat less. Picky eaters are thin.

ten

"SLIDE UP YOUR SHUTTER," the woman seated beside me says, jostling me awake. "Let's see what there is to see."

We have been crammed into this metal tube for nine hours and now it's happening. Paris is mere minutes away. I rub my eyes and open my shutter.

But I do not see Paris, City of Light. I see farms, ordinary Midwestern-looking farms with barns, tractors, pastures, and cows. A yellow and green patchwork quilt of fields, punctuated by occasional villages, billows to the horizon. No Notre-Dame, no Eiffel Tower. No Sacré-Coeur. Something has gone wrong.

Our still-fresh-as-a-daisy flight attendant, however, is not in the least bit ruffled. "*Bonjour, mesdames, messieurs. Bienvenue en France,*" she announces, plopping covered plastic trays in front of us.

Fruit cup, croissant, bread roll, strawberry jam, butter, a slice each of cheese, ham, and turkey, a pale leaf of lettuce, a single cherry tomato, water, orange juice. My first meal in France is ice-cold, odorless, and tasteless, but I eat every morsel. Rule number eighteen of the perpetual diet: Do not allow yourself to get so famished that you mindlessly devour whatever's put in front of you.

Too late. I lean back in my seat and groan.

"Are you all right?" the woman next to me asks. "You don't look too good. Of course, nobody feels human after an overseas flight. I'm Roseanne, by the way."

"A Rose by any other name," Kat would crack. "You can't make this stuff up." Kat loves coincidence. Loved.

"Not much longer now," Roseanne says. "Aren't you just too thrilled?" She smiles at me as she slathers her croissant with butter. "Is anyone meeting you at the airport, darlin'?"

"No." I sip my orange juice. Delightful, delectable, forbidden juice. Rule number nineteen of the perpetual diet: Fruit is good, but fruit juice is not good. Eat whole fruit. Drink plain water. Eschew the juice.

But, unlike water, OJ cuts the parch of my throat.

"No," I say again, working to keep the quaver out of my voice. "I'm traveling alone." I blow my nose as unobtrusively as I can. The seatbelt sign is on so I can't go to the back of the plane and shut myself into a bathroom, which is where I've been trying to give vent to most of my coughing, sneezing, and nose blowing. But, like William, Roseanne has not mentioned my cold symptoms. Don't ask, don't tell.

"Well, bless your sweet little heart," says Roseanne. "Aren't you brave! Bob, this young lady is coming all by herself to Paris. Honey?" She shouts to be heard over the howl of the death metal baby, who started shrieking the moment the plane began its descent, but Bob is asleep. Truly asleep, mouth cocked open, head rocked back. How could anyone nap now? When the plane is about to land. In Paris. Or near Paris. Now, that's brave.

Roseanne shrugs. "Where are you staying, hon'?" she asks me.

"A little hotel. Not far from the Bastille."

"The Bastille." Roseanne nibbles on her bright red lower lip. "I've heard of that. We're at the Hilton. According to our travel agent, it has modern American-style bathrooms and queen-size beds. We're keeping our fingers crossed."

The flight attendant collects our breakfast trays, and the plane buzzes with arrival energy. I force my new black boots over my swollen feet and suck in my stomach to reposition the money belt under my too-tight skinny jeans. The money belt is vital. It holds my passport, return ticket info, my two thousand nine hundred and eighty Tupperware dollars, and my old single-girl, still valid, credit card.

Roseanne keeps up a steady flow of chatter as we shuffle through passport check, baggage retrieval, and customs, where we have *rien à déclarer*. I stay glued to her side as we get some euros at the money change window, and follow them into an echoing hall full of people. People carting carry-ons and lugging luggage and bearing backpacks, people jostling and elbowing and shoving, people speaking many tongues, people reeking of incense and salami and cologne, people who know nothing about me, about Kat, about William, and who could not care less.

I've read shelves of guidebooks and megabytes of travel blogs—I of all tourists should know what to do and where to go—but I am still pondering the overhead signs, which are in both French and English, when the crowd squirts us through an automatic door. Just like that we are outside, in the fresh air. The fresh French air.

"Taxi, taxi, we need a taxi," Roseanne chants. "Let's share," she adds, squeezing my arm. "What do you say, darlin'? You'll fit in with no trouble, you're such a skinny little thing."

People would never say, "Wow, you're so fat, how do even you fit into a chair!" But skinniness is okay to remark upon. Worse, they often add, "You're so lucky to be thin," as if thinness were an accident, as if thinness were a quality you either have or you don't. But there's nothing accidental about thinness. Nope. Not in twenty-first-century America.

Of course I am no longer in America. I grip the handle of my carry-on so hard my knuckles ache. "Okay," I say. "Sharing a cab. Good idea."

We join a taxi queue. Outside in the fresh French air it's cool, cold by Phoenix standards, so I button and belt my fingertip-length black trench coat, the first raincoat I have ever owned, and pop the collar. It feels like a costume, a uniform, a disguise.

"Glory be, just look at all this blessed humanity," Roseanne says, squinting up and down the queue.

A Middle Eastern–looking family with five children and four luggage carts pushes past us. In Phoenix people don't push. And they don't stand so close together. In Phoenix people's faces don't seem to say, You need to be sharper here. You need to be smarter. You need to be alert and pay attention, because here so much more could go wrong.

I take mental inventory of my purse, money belt, tote bag, and carry-on. Check, check, check, and check. While we were waiting at baggage retrieval Roseanne sighed. "Oh, honey child, I do envy you your one little bag, traveling so light, so free and easy. But the older you get, the more of a support system you need!" She cackled as Bob stacked two suitcases, two garment bags, a filled-to-capacity duffle bag, and a canvas tote onto a battered metal cart. I had to look the other way to hide my smile.

I am so efficiently packed because Kat and I spent two years shopping for the perfect travel wardrobes. My goal was to travel light, like an experienced world traveler; Kat's was to look fabulous, whatever it took. One morning I arrived at her condo to drive her to the outpatient clinic and she was still in bed, laptop teetering on her bony knees.

"Hey, I found this amazing site all about what Frenchwomen wear," she announced.

"And?"

"And you wouldn't believe the shoes. Four-inch heels."

I snorted. "To walk around those bumpy cobblestone streets? Get out."

"But! I looked further. Low-heeled boots are okay if your black jeans are skinny enough and your black top is hip enough."

Wardrobes based on black had been our first travel decision. "What hipsters we are. No one wears black in Phoenix," I said for the millionth time.

"I know. Yay us," said Kat. "We will not stick out like hick tourists. But," she added, snapping her laptop closed, "what about an accent color? Don't you think we should have accent colors?"

"Probably."

"I'm thinking pink."

"You would," I said.

From the start Kat bought big time into the whole breast-cancer-awareness pink thing. It was surprising, and even annoying. I considered for a moment. "I'm going for white. Black and white. Like a classic movie from the forties."

"You would," Kat said.

By the time we finished we'd each purchased a black blazer, two pairs of black skinny jeans, a pair of black boots, two long-sleeved black tees, and five blouses in varying styles, pink for Kat and white for me. Also, sweaters—a black woolen cardigan for me, a pink hoodie style for Kat—ordered from a company in Canada, where people know about keeping warm. Finally, and best of all, raincoats.

"You are pathetically easily thrilled," said Kat, who had chosen a hot pink vinyl slicker. "Do you think we need little black dresses?" she added. This was months later, just after her final surgery. "In case we want to go somewhere fancy? I've always wanted an LBD."

Two weeks after that the doctors told Kat she had to do an extra round of chemo so we had plenty of time, when Kat was not barfing her brains out, to look for the dresses. We also got new underwear, money belts, silk scarves—Frenchwomen wear scarves—and folding umbrellas. I'd never owned an umbrella either. Mine was black. Kat's was pink with white polka dots.

"We are gonna be so hot!"

"Are we still young enough to be hot?" I asked. We were twenty-eight. "I'm thinking the best we can do at this point is to be formerly hot."

"Speak for yourself, *chiquita*. We're the youngest we're ever going to be!"

eleven

"MESDAMES, MONSIEUR?" A man with a halo of dark curls hurries us toward a gray sedan with a lighted sign on the roof saying "Taxi." In seconds our luggage is stowed, somehow, into the tiny trunk and Bob, Roseanne, and I are lined up in the back seat like chickens on a skewer. In this quieter, calmer, smaller space, my heart begins to settle. I lock my door and verify the alignment of my arms.

Rule number twenty of the perpetual diet: When you sit, check to see if you can feel the flesh of your waist on the insides of your elbows. If you can, you weigh too much. It's how I know I've put on pounds before anyone else does. The elbow test. Never fails.

"Bonjour." The cabdriver twists in his seat to look at us, raising an eyebrow. He probably thinks we're a family—father, mother, failure-to-launch loser adult daughter visiting *la belle France.*

"Hilton!" Roseanne cries, handing him a scrap of paper with an address printed on it.

The taxi lurches away from the curb. Like everything else in the past two days it happens with ease. In fact I can't remember when any sequence of events has gone quite so smoothly. Maybe meeting and marrying William. That went along as if we'd been greased. I wish for an instant that William's firm shoulder were pressing against mine instead of Roseanne's cushiony one.

"You should tell him," Roseanne says.

"Tell him what?" We are passing a green bottle the size of a house. Not a bottle made of glass—it's wooden or something and is set at an alluring angle by the side of the road. Drink me, the giant bottle seems to say. If my French were as good as it should be I could ask the cabby, What is that all about? He would say, Oh, that? It's an advertisement for sparkling water, been there for years. Or, This is a very important bottle, it commemorates a battle fought near here in 1848. Or, Bottle? I do not see a bottle.

"You should tell the driver the name of your hotel," Roseanne says, jabbing me with her surprisingly sharp elbow. "Go ahead, honey. It can't hurt to try."

I turn from the window and lean up between the seats. "*Monsieur?*" I say. "*S'il vous plaît?*"

"*Oui, madame.*"

"*Pourriez-vous—*" My voice cracks and I have to cough and begin again. All night on the plane I mentally rehearsed the name and address of my hotel in French. "*Je voudrais...aller...à l'Hôtel du Cheval Blanc, numéro vingt, rue des Mauvaises Filles, s'il vous plaît.*" I'd like to specify "after you drop off this couple at their hotel," but I don't know how to say that in French.

"Hilton," he says. At least that's what I think he says. He pronounces the word "Eel-ton."

"*Oui,*" I agree. "*Pour...*them. But for me, I mean, *mais pour moi—Hôtel du Cheval Blanc, numéro vingt, rue des Mauvaises Filles.*"

Am I saying it that badly?

His black eyes inspect me in the rearview mirror.

"*S'il vous plaît,*" I add.

"Hilton," he repeats.

Roseanne scoots forward—no one is wearing seatbelts. "You need to take I and my husband to our hotel and then this young lady to her hotel," she shouts into the cabby's ear. "Do? You? Understand?"

I cringe.

"Hilton. One stop," the cabby says, lights a cigarette, rolls down the window, and turns up the radio.

"We'll sort it out when we get there, Amy. Don't you worry," says Bob. It's the first time I've heard his voice.

The cabby drives with his right hand draped over the steering wheel and his left hand dangling out the window. He swerves around a delivery van, inserts our taxi between two diesel-fume-spewing tour buses, cuts off an eight-wheeler, tailgates a sports car. Other drivers lean on horns, pump fists out windows. Roseanne opens her mouth but closes it again when Bob places a hand on her knee. No one says a word as the traffic thickens yet we continue to hurtle down the freeway, one time veering up onto the shoulder to overtake and pass a shuttle van, my window coming within inches of a graffiti-covered concrete wall.

If we were in an accident, if I got hurt here, or died here, no one would ever know what happened. No one would have any idea where to even start to look.

But before we perish in a fiery freeway crash we decelerate onto an exit ramp and turn right onto a wide tree-lined boulevard. Roseanne releases a long loud sigh and I press my cold hands to my hot cheeks. I'm here. I had to lie and cheat and steal to do it, but here I am. In Paris. "Cowabunga!" Kat would say.

We glide past a bakery. This could be my bakery, the bakery I visit every day. We pass a butcher shop, a bookstore, a luggage store, a laundry, a shoe store, a wine shop, a yarn shop, a mini-market with plastic bins of fruits and vegetables stacked on each side of the open door.

We pass a store selling computers. Funny how the buildings are so old, so formal and ornate and kind of eternal, yet the shops inside are so mundane, so modern. There's an appliance store displaying washing machines in the windows. A short, slender man in a leather coat emerges from another bakery—there's one every few blocks—carrying a baguette. He pauses under a spindly leafless tree, tucks the baguette under his arm, lights a cigarette. He is not posing for a postcard. He is picking up breakfast.

Or lunch. I dig my cell phone out of my purse and power it up. It takes ages. What if it doesn't work here in Europe? What if William is not able to reach me for the Daily Phone Call? What if—yes. Yes. The phone takes longer than normal to boot up and when it does it says "SFR" where it usually says "AT&T," but it has bars.

"I have 12:05 p.m., local time," Bob says, adjusting his wristwatch. "What does your phone say, Amy?"

"The same." Noon. Lunch then. Monday lunch. I lick my dry lips.

Afternoons in chemo, mornings in doctors' waiting rooms, nights when Kat couldn't sleep and phoned me to come over—we talked about this moment. Arriving in Paris. "The minute we get there, we'll drop off our bags at the hotel and head straight for the Eiffel Tower or the Champs-Elysées or the Latin Quarter," Kat said. "We won't waste a single second."

"It's mostly your dream, you know," she remarked to me in a waiting room one day. We were early for an appointment with the plastic surgeon to talk about reconstructive surgery, back when we thought there was going to be reconstructive surgery. "You should be the one to set the itinerary," she said.

"But no. We'll decide everything together," I said. "We'll vote."

"Okay, I vote for lots of shopping."

"I vote for cathedrals. And museums."

"You're such a brainiac," Kat said. "We're really polar opposites, you know."

"No. No way." Kat and I had been a team since freshman year. Classmates, confidants, lovers, then inseparable friends.

"You say no. But, really, we are. We're kind of like an accident. Or at least I am. That's me, an accident waiting to happen." A nurse's aide called Kat's name. Kat stood and, before she disappeared into the examination room, turned and added, "You'll see. You'll manage great on your own one day. You will." She was gone before I could argue.

The taxi glides by yet another bakery and turns off the wide boulevard into a side street. The tall-by-Phoenix-standards buildings enclose me, embrace me. Everything feels so right, so familiar. It shouldn't. I have never been anywhere, certainly not anywhere old like this. But these golden buildings, this crooked street—I feel as if I have known them all my life. And now, today, on a Monday lunch hour in April, they seem to know me, too. To recognize me. Oh yes, it's you, they seem to say. Here you are. You made it. You came. At last.

We pause at a red light beside a sidewalk café where a woman with shoulder-length honey-blond hair like Kat used to have is sitting at a table for two, tilting her head back to look up at the sky. I follow her gaze. The sun has disappeared behind fluffy meringue-white clouds, clouds that in Phoenix you'd take the day off for, just to celebrate the novelty and wonder and glory of a sky that is not blue.

"Aren't you just too thrilled?" Roseanne asks.

I nod. A light rain begins to fall, the drops glittering on my window like rhinestones. Roseanne chatters to no one in particular. Only five days ago William announced his business trip and now here I am. In Paris. Slick as snot.

I have got what I always wanted.

twelve

THE FIRST TIME I got what I always wanted I was seven.

In those days, what I wanted was to have chin-length hair, like Anna Fetzer, the prettiest and most popular girl in second grade. Anna's shining bob jounced when she jumped hopscotch squares. It fell in a beguiling fringe across her tawny cheeks when she hunched over her arithmetic worksheets. All the boys, and most of the girls, were in love with Anna.

My own heavy black mane hung to my butt. My mother braided it every morning into two thick ropes that Scott Rasmussen, the boy who sat behind me, yanked whenever he got the chance. "Giddy-yup, horsey girl!" he'd hiss. "Get along, old paint."

I begged my parents to let me get my hair cut like Anna Fetzer's but my mother refused. "A girl's hair is her crowning glory," she said. "You should be proud to have so much of it." My father just grinned and said, "I'm staying out of this." I pleaded. Pouted. Whined. I clipped out photos of magazine models with bobbed hair and left them on my mother's nightstand. I resisted getting it washed until Dad pointed out that short hair has to be washed more often than long. I refused to eat the tamales my mother worked so hard to make at Christmastime, even though I love tamales.

"You were a handful when you were little," Dad liked to say later, when it was just the two of us. "A real firecracker." He never seemed to notice how well my mother had managed to crush the fireworks out of me, and how well they managed to stay crushed.

One January Saturday morning she went to the grocery store. Dad was home but a neighbor lady knocked at the seldom-used front door. Her car battery was dead. Could she get a jump? "I'll just be across the street," he called to me. "Don't leave the house."

I lifted my head, put down my book. I had no intention of leaving the house. The place was mine, and I knew exactly what I would do.

I headed straight for my mother's sewing basket, took out the shears, carried them to the bathroom, wicked blades pointed down, and carefully placed them on the white tile counter. Then I dragged the kitchen stepstool out of the broom closet, shoved it to the bathroom sink, closed the door, and turned the key in the old-fashioned lock. When Daddy returned he wouldn't question the locked door. Not at first.

At that age I adored cutting paper dolls, snowflakes, daisy chains, bits of magazines for collages, and I owned two pairs of plastic blunt-tipped scissors, little-kid scissors, for this purpose. But I had stopped loving them the summer before, the instant I touched the cool, smooth stainless steel of my mother's sewing shears. "Put those down!" she snapped and I withdrew my hand, but the sparkling blades twinkled at me. Here we are, they said. Aren't we gorgeous?

If I stood on the top step of the stool I got a good view of my upper body in the medicine cabinet mirror. How much smaller the toilet and bathtub and sink seemed from up here. This must be the way the world looks to adults. Smaller. More manageable. I lifted the shears and worked the blades. Snick, they whispered when they opened. Snick, they whispered when they closed.

My cumbrous mass of hair was hanging loose that morning. "Fix her braids," my mother had called as she slammed the back door. Dad and I exchanged glances. We knew no hair braiding would be taking place that day, not until my mother got back and did it herself. Hah, is she gonna be surprised. No more braiding. Ever. I giggled and pressed my bare knees against the cool edge of the bathroom counter and wished I'd thought to bring a comb. But my hair is stick straight. Sometimes, for special events, like a distant cousin's *quinceañera,* my mother tried to curl it but the waves always fell out even before we left the house. I picked up a strand of hair, studied it. A few practice cuts might be a good idea—just to get the feel—so I opened the heavy jaws of the shears, placed the strand between them, and squeezed. Snick. A lock of hair dropped into the sink, making a black comma on the white porcelain.

Oh yes. I could do this.

I used my fingers to part my hair down the back of my head and bring the two heavy halves over my shoulders. Surely I could cut just as straight and true as my mother did when she sewed the giant muumuus she always wore.

"Amy?" Dad's voice was loud and surprisingly close. "Are you all right in there?"

"Y-yes." I teetered, catching myself by placing a palm against the mirror my mother had cleaned just that morning. "I'm. . .busy." I was going to get in trouble for making a handprint on the mirror. What was he doing back so soon?

He rattled the doorknob. "Amy, why's the door locked?"

"Da-a-ad-eee!" Normally I didn't bother to even close the bathroom door. Not when it was just the two of us. I thought hard. "I'm...pooping!"

"Well, excuse me, Your Miss Royal Highness," he chuckled. "Don't take all day in there."

"I won't."

Lying to my father shouldn't be as easy as lying to my mother. But I had no time to think about that now. I grabbed the shears and positioned them just at the place where the neatly scissored ends of Anna Fetzer's shining bob grazed her flawless jaw. The metal was cool, smooth, soothing, and my heart thumped as I grasped a long hank of hair, my mother's pride and joy, and placed it between the blades. I looked myself in the eye and squeezed. Snick. Twelve inches of black hair fell into the sink.

Wow. I felt lighter already. I cut a second hunk, then a third. In minutes the sink was half full of hair and I was starting on the other side. Cutting hair is fun. I could do it all day.

The back door slammed. "Art? Amy?"

Uh-oh. I'd have to speed it up. I seized bigger handfuls of hair and frantically sawed the scissors back and forth.

"Art?" My mother's voice was getting shriller and harder as her heavy footsteps came closer. "Where is everybody? Amy?"

Faster now. Faster.

"Amy?" She was outside the bathroom door. "Are you in there? What are you doing? Open this door immediately."

I kept cutting. It was all I could think to do. The hair was no longer landing in the sink but falling onto the floor, over the toilet seat, into the tub.

The old lock on the bathroom door broke on the second try. Even twenty-two years later I can still see the glitter of my mother's small black eyes as the door exploded open and she took in the scene—the stepstool, the forbidden shears, the hair everywhere, and my head, one side trimmed at more or less Anna Fetzer length and the other a ragged mess, looking, as Dad would say later, as if I'd "gotten caught in the lawnmower."

I felt the shears being yanked out of my hand and watched them fly into the bathtub. I heard my shoulder pop as my mother dragged me off the stepstool, across the hallway, through the living room, and into the kitchen.

From then on it was war between my mother and me.

"Oh my God. But what happened after? To your hair?" Kat asked when I told her the story in college.

I sighed. "What do you think? She drove me straight to a barber's and had him cut it short short short, like a boy's. Using a straight-edge razor. It hurt."

"Harsh," Kat murmured.

When the shears hit the bathtub that day, they made a thumb-length gouge in the porcelain. Every time I took a bath from age seven to age twenty-five, which is when William and I sold the house, I rubbed my big toe over it. Every time, I remembered my mother's words as we left the barbershop.

"Are you happy now? You got what you always wanted."

thirteen

I TURN the brass key in the lock and lean on the door. I made it. I am here, in my very own hotel room, in Paris.

Brr. My very own hotel room is glacially cold. I look around. The window, a tall six-paned double casement French window like you see in photographs, is wide open, that's why. I close it, sit on the bed, and give in to a prolonged session of coughing and sneezing and nose blowing. It was so dry on the airplane I didn't want to take a decongestant. I find one now, and swallow it with a handful of water from the bathroom sink.

I did end up going to the Hilton with Bob and Roseanne. The cab driver could not be convinced to do otherwise. But once there Bob hailed me a new cab, placed my carry-on in the trunk, told me to take care of my cold, and handed me into the backseat, like a gentleman, like Cary Grant. "*Au revoir!*" Roseanne shouted as Bob slammed the taxi door. Actually, it sounded more like, "Orr ray-vorre." She did not say, "We should get together, while we're here." I was half surprised, half relieved, half disappointed.

"Three halves. Not doable," William would be sure to point out.

Because William values precision in thought and word and deed. "More proof he's an alien life form," Kat snarled the time I tried to explain this to her. She never truly understood why William was the first male to make me fall crazy in love. "It's true what they say. Love really is temporary insanity," I confessed to her the night before the justice-of-the-peace wedding. "Boy meets girl, girl goes cuckoo, boy gets girl," Kat replied, smiling tightly, "what could be more perfect, what could be more normal?"

It even started out normally, at the company Christmas party. Or, as HR insisted on calling it, the holiday get-together.

"Shrimp?"

I looked up at him. He was tall and lean, and stood soldier straight. "Sure," I said, no longer wishing I had stayed home with a book. "Thanks." Shrimp, low in fat, high in protein, is one of the few good choices at buffets. When not deep fried.

"Do you know what those are?" He pointed to another platter.

"I think they're crab cakes." Also known as calorie bombs.

"And the orange stuff?"

"Probably sauce. Apricot? To go with the crab cakes."

Months later I wondered, Was he testing me? William surely knew what a crab cake was; he grew up cooking everything in his grandfather's restaurant. I have never asked because I want to think it was just the weirdest pick-up line ever.

He stacked five patties on his plate and ladled sauce over them.

"Wow," I said.

He grinned. "I haven't eaten all day."

"Good for you," I said before realizing how abnormal that might sound. But he only laughed.

"Let's go find a place to sit," he said. "I'm Will Brodie, by the way." I expected his eyes to drop to my chest but his gaze held mine.

We talked only to each other the rest of the evening. "Can't believe we've never met before," he said. But in a relatively large consulting firm it wasn't that surprising, he in Engineering Design up on the third floor and I in Human Resources down in the basement, never the twain shall meet. I recognized his name, of course, from the personnel files because I was familiar with every file cabinet Human Resources owned. I knew he was from Minnesota, had an advanced degree in mechanical engineering, and was single, six years older than I, and an Army vet.

When the party wound down and it was politic to leave he asked me out for a drink. I said no. All I knew was his file, really. Since I spent all of my free time in high school caring for Dad my first real date was as a college freshman, with a short pudgy guy from my gender studies class. Stupidly, I assumed that because he was pudgy he would be harmless. He asked me to a dorm party, I said yes, drank three and a half beers, and went with him back to his room. I woke up at four a.m. when he shoved me out of bed. "You gotta leave now," he mumbled before falling back asleep. A week later I met Kat. It was easy, safe, comfortable, and fun to hook up with her. We stayed hooked until two weeks before graduation, when Kat ran into me having coffee with a guy from my research methodologies class. "You think you can chart a middle ground," Kat ranted later. "But you can't. Not with me."

We remained friends though, best friends, exclusive friends, and it was almost as if nothing had changed, except for the sex of course.

After the holiday party William waited three days and then asked me to lunch. Mexican food. He related his whole life story, born in Minnesota, which I already knew, raised by his grandfather after both parents died in a car crash when he was three, which I did not know.

"Does your grandfather live in Sun City?" I asked, nibbling on a shard of quesadilla.

"Nope. No old folks' ghetto for him. He's still toughing it out back in snow country. But that's good because he has all his friends there, and I get up to see him pretty often."

I soon learned that "But that's good because" was the way William started out a lot of his sentences. "I broke my leg snowmobiling when I was sixteen. But that's good because during my six months in a cast I discovered how much I love math." Or, "I couldn't find a job in Minnesota. But that's good because it brought me to Arizona, where I met you."

He'd had one long-term relationship before, with a woman who left him to sing in a bluegrass band. "I seem to go for the arty types," he remarked as he paid the bill.

"Do you mean I'm an arty type? Or that you're glad I'm not an arty type?" I asked. Back then I wore tailored pants suits and kept my hair in a bun. Not arty-looking at all.

"I'm thinking it's too late either way."

Later when I told Kat this I said, "I practically swooned right there in the front of Garcia's." Kat's eyes glittered. "Tell me more," she said, "tell me everything."

On the way out to the Mexican restaurant's parking lot William popped a peppermint in his mouth and grinned at me. "Are you busy on Saturday?" he asked, lifting his aviator shades to look into my eyes.

I was. I was signed up for a class at Home Depot, "How to Install Ground Fault Interrupters in Your Home." I wished I were inventive enough to make up something more fabulous sounding but the truth turned out to be better.

"Hey, that's impressive," he said. "A lot of women wouldn't even attempt such a job."

A lot of women don't own 1920s stucco bungalows with 1920s wiring. William attended the class with me and the next weekend we went to see the Christmas luminarias at the Desert Botanical Garden. Over New Year's we drove up to Sedona. By the end of January, William was spending more time at my bungalow than at his Scottsdale condo.

By Valentine's, we had told each other almost everything.

By Easter, we were married.

fourteen

AFTER BLOWING MY NOSE for the thirtieth time I pull off my boots, get up, and pad to the window. Below me a turquoise and white city bus puffs to a stop, disgorges a dozen passengers, and lurches away with a snort. Moments later a second bus pulls up, and then a third. I open the window and lean out to study the street. Great. Just great. My hotel room is right smack above a busy bus stop. No wonder I found a vacancy so easily.

I close the window and wrap my arms around my middle. April in Paris? Chestnuts in blossom? Not so much. It feels like winter here, at least like a Phoenix idea of winter, and the diesel fumes from the buses are making me sick to my stomach. Here I am, in Paris, but what good is it doing me? Every joint in my body aches, even my teeth ache, and if I sneeze one more time I'm going to pass out. I turn away from the window and crawl into bed still wearing all my clothes, including the trench coat.

Kat would adore this room — the bedsheets are hot pink, the quilt is printed with enormous crimson poppies, the carpet is deep fuchsia, and the wallpaper is a massively insane riot of scarlet cabbage roses the size of dinner plates. Even the ceiling is covered with it. "It's like a giant Valentine's Day present," Kat would say. "It's like being *inside* a present!"

I squeeze my eyes shut but cannot block out the pink.

The next thing I know it is dark and my cell phone is dingling. I leap out of bed, stubbing my big toe on something hard. "Ow. What the—?"

Paris, I'm in Paris, in my hotel room. My purse is on the floor next to the armoire, and my phone is in my purse. I grab the phone on the fourth ring. William's face fills the phone's display.

"Ames? Hey there, babe! You napping?"

How long have I been sleeping? "Of course not. I wasn't napping. I was—doing yoga."

"Well, you have on your sleepy voice. What's up?"

"Oh. Nothing much." I place my purse on the bed. Must keep better track of that. "I was meditating," I say, clearing my throat. "Deep meditation." Think. Say something that sounds normal. "How are you?" I ask, rubbing my throbbing toe.

"Just got back from dinner. Italian. I gotta say, New Jersey has the best Italian food." His voice is loose, relaxed. He must have had wine. Or beer. Or beer and wine. He sounds so close. I have flown all the way to Paris yet William, my present, my future, is right here next to me, in my ear.

I limp to the window and lean my burning forehead against the pane. "Whadyu have to eat?"

"Lasagne. With sausage. About a pound of cheese. I gotta say, the portions here are huge. Big enough to feed a dozen Amys."

"Sounds great," I say, though food sounds disgusting to me right now. The plus side of having a cold.

He tells me about his day. The trials are not going as hoped. Geoff the lead engineer is pissed. Frank the program manager, who wasn't supposed to arrive till Wednesday, came early and is redefining the protocols. They will have to recalculate all the tolerances.

"Bummer," I say. Sugar and fat and salt are bridging the gulf between us. For now.

"So how about you?" he asks. "How was your day?"

"Well," I say, turning to look at my rumpled pink bed, "I washed the sheets."

"You did? On a Monday?"

Oops. At home I wash sheets on Wednesdays. "Yes. I had—I had an accident."

"Huh?"

"What I mean to say is—is that I spilled a cup of coffee all over the sheets," I babble. "I was treating myself to breakfast in bed and got sloppy, I guess."

It's easier to lie to William than I thought it would be, but it doesn't matter because he is not listening.

"Babe," he begins, his voice catching, "are you really busy right now?"

Outside a bus wheezes to a halt. I retreat into the bathroom. "No," I say, closing the door without making any sound. "I'm not doing anything."

"What do you have on?" William says.

I'm not cold anymore, I'm warm. Too warm. I'm hot. And dizzy. "Yoga pants," I say, looking down at my black trench coat, rumpled and flecked with pink sheet lint. "With my turquoise top." His favorite. He bought it for me on my twenty-ninth birthday last September.

"Mmm. Nice. I'm lying down right now. On the bed. Comfortable."

"I'm lying down, too," I say, leaning against the door.

"You know, I think you should lose those yoga pants. I think you'd be a lot more comfortable."

I gaze at my reflection in the speckled mirror above the sink. My face is gray, my nose is red, my hair is flat on one side and puffy on the other side. I look like the madwoman in the attic. Just crazy enough to go through with this.

"Tell me you're...comfortable," William murmurs.

With my free hand I flap the lapels of the trench coat to make fabric-rustling noises. "I am," I say, "getting there."

William is groaning. It never takes him long. For the first time, I'm glad I'm by myself in Paris. No way could I pull this off with Kat barely smothering her guffaws in the next room.

"Ames? How far are you?"

I fake a soft moan. "Yes," I whisper. "Yes."

Five minutes later William is half asleep. "G'night, Amy baby," he murmurs. "I love you."

"I love you, too," I rasp and wait, crushing the phone to the side of my face. Maybe he'll say something amazing, something to make it possible for me to confess, "William, I've got a surprise for you. I'm in Paris. I so wish you were here with me."

But he has hung up. "That was stupid," I say to the speckled mirror.

I put the phone down and yank open the bathroom door. If Kat were here she'd be plenty turned on right now. It'd be hard to say no to her. I struggle out of the trench coat, fling off my T-shirt, pace around the room in my bra and jeans. I spot my tote bag and fish out the potato chips, unauthorized against-all-the-rules potato chips left over from dinner on the plane last night, and eat them all, though they scratch my sore throat.

Yet another bus is idling below my window, belching diesel fumes and passengers. Over the last four years of love and marriage, I have omitted telling William a number of things. The cash-back savings. The Plan. Over-and-done-with activities with Kat. But I have never flat-out lied to him. And now I have to continue lying—by commission, not omission—until I return to Phoenix on Sunday.

Unless I never do go back. It would solve so many problems. Maybe all my problems. I wouldn't be thinking of Kat every five minutes because there is nothing here in Paris to remind me of her. I would never have to deal with the baby thing. I wouldn't have to cook stupid three-course dinners every stupid night. I wouldn't have to lie to Will, or anyone, ever again.

I renounced lying, as penance, after my mother died. "Plus it's easier," I once told Kat. "It's too much of an effort to keep everything straight otherwise."

"So you're saying that you, Amy, are honest because you're lazy?" It was two a.m. William was on a trip and I was again spending the night at Kat's. To keep her company, that's all.

"That's what I'm saying."

Kat smiled, but not with her eyes. "Sometimes, though," she said, "lying is necessary."

"Why? When?"

"To protect someone."

"To protect yourself, you mean."

"Sometimes," Kat continued, "it's safer to lie than to tell the truth."

"Safer," I echoed.

"Yes. Safer for both parties." Kat looked away from me. "You know what I mean?"

"Not really. What do you mean?"

We were standing on opposite sides of Kat's kitchen island, the white Corian countertop a flat shining void between us. It was after Kat's third and final chemo regimen. She was bloated and bald, had given up on her hair, and was in her turban and giant hoop earrings stage.

"What do you mean?" I repeated.

"What I mean," Kat said, wadding up a dish towel and throwing it at my head, "is that life is a game you get to cheat at. You may think that by obeying all the rules you are superior. And that being superior makes you safe. But it doesn't. It doesn't make you safe. It just makes you a superior rule-obeyer, that's all."

Maybe that's true. Maybe being a rule breaker is the way to go. Breaking the rules is how I got to Paris.

I dig a clean T-shirt out of my carry-on and slip it over my head. There is no chair in the room but if I roll the carry-on to the window, I can sit on it. I look around for my phone to check the time. Three-thirty a.m. My first twelve hours in Paris have been wasted on being sick and on sleeping and on lying to William. But there are still five full French days ahead of me. Maybe I'll feel better tomorrow. A van rolls up to the bus stop sign below and ejects a tall skinny guy with yellow dreadlocks, a beat-up guitar, and a Canadian-flag patch on the sleeve of his ragged denim jacket. He lopes across the quiet street, props himself against a plate glass window, and brings his arm down in a dramatic strum.

"Day-oh!" he sings. "Day-yay-yay-oh!"

He lifts his face to the sky—a midnight-blue French sky—lights a cigarette, shifts his gaze upward, and seems to look straight at me. I lean back from the window but keep my position. I am safe and snug in my own room, in Paris, in a tacky crazy bower of flowers, a room of my own, a room with a view. Of a bus stop.

fifteen

GET OUT. Get out of this room.

Last night after the phone sex—the lying, deceitful, fraudulent phone sex—I couldn't get back to sleep so I sat on my carry-on at the window listening to the day-oh guy. He only knows the one song. Sunlight was drowning out the streetlights when I retreated into the pink bed, again freezing cold. The day-oh guy went home, or wherever he goes, and I dropped into a deep sleep, helped on my way by a triple dose of cough syrup.

And now it is past noon. I am showered and dressed. I am again buttoned and belted into my lovely fingertip-length black trench coat. I have strapped my travel purse crossways over my chest and stocked my tote bag with umbrella, hat, and scarf.

Someone pounds on the door.

I grab at the wall for support. What if it's William? Come to demand, "What are you doing here?" Come to ask, "Why, Amy? Why?" I look around for somewhere to hide but the armoire is too small, the bed too low, the window too high, the bathroom too obvious. I am trapped, like a wasp in a jar. What an idiot I was to think I could just walk away from my life, my responsibilities.

But of course it can't be William. That's impossible. I crack open the door and am both relieved and crestfallen to behold the hotel maid, who mumbles, "*Femme de ménage,*" as she pushes her way in. She makes the bed, glaring. The maid. Not William. William doesn't know where I am.

No one knows where I am.

Just as the maid pulls the door shut behind her my cell phone pings the arrival of a text. Where is that damn phone? Where has it gone to this time? I locate it on the table next to the bed, my stomach flipping like a hooked carp. But it's only from Rose. "Library to hire fulltime assistants!" it says. "Gadzooks! You should apply!"

I need to get out of this room. I need to walk through that door, descend the stairs, and go out into the waiting streets, the glorious streets, of Paris. Instead I open the window and take a deep breath of the cool damp air. It feels good on my dry throat. Paris is here and I am here and for a moment it's almost enough to just look down at it all from my window, taking it in like oxygen, like food.

It is raining.

I lean out to get a better look. The wet black pavement shines like patent leather. The wet roofs of passing cars flicker like signal mirrors. Everything is sparkly and glittery. That's what rain does. Rain is the miracle that washes away dust and sweat and sin. Dad used to let me stay home from school when it rained. "Wet days don't happen so often in Phoenix," he would plead with my mother and we would wander our inner-city neighborhood together as long as the precipitation lasted, jumping in every puddle we could find. When we got home, gloriously damp, maybe even shivering, if it was below sixty degrees, we'd change into dry clothes and make hot chocolate. Sometimes hot chocolate was already made for us. Sometimes the cookies that my mother rarely admitted to keeping in the house were set out on a flowered china plate. There were times like that.

Hot chocolate. Cookies. God.

Below me yet another bus shudders to a halt. Passengers exit and scatter. Every single person down there knows where to go, what to do, and how to do it. A litter of teen-aged boys tumbles out, smoking, jabbing, jostling. They pause to gawk at a mini-skirted girl crossing the street. She skips over a puddle, pretending not to see them, pretending not to notice she is young, beautiful, thin, and munching a foot-long hotdog.

Okay, here's a plan. I will go out into the sparkly glittery streets of Paris and find some food, any food. And water. I blow my nose one more time, for luck, grab my tote bag, and hook it over my shoulder. Before my brain can manufacture objections or concoct fears I stomp out of the room, clomp down the creaking wooden stairs of the Hôtel du Cheval Blanc, and stride into the tiny smoky lobby.

"*Bonjour*," says the deskman.

"*Bonjour*," I answer as I pass. Just outside the glass front door, there's a giant puddle. I step into the center of it. I am wearing boots. I am invincible.

I pop open Kat's pink polka dot umbrella, cross the street, dodge a bicyclist, skirt the spot on the sidewalk where the day-oh guy spent the night—though it's being washed clean now—and head for the red-and-white-striped awning of the nearest bakery, the location of which I have been acutely, painfully, exquisitely aware ever since my cab passed it yesterday afternoon. How long ago that feels. The bakery has not gone anywhere though; it is still here, waiting for me, on the corner where my quiet street intersects with a busy boulevard. I come to a complete stop in front of the large display window, my jaw dropping.

Tarts. Ruby raspberry, golden lemon, amber apricot, emerald kiwi, garnet plum—as tempting as unguarded platters of jewels.

And cakes. Tall triple-layered white vanilla cakes and brown chocolate cakes, showcased like favorite children on fluted white porcelain pedestals.

Also light-as-air cream puffs. Flakey layered napoleons. Perfectly piped meringues. Precisely molded madeleines. Plain puff pastries in the shapes of pinwheels and hearts, glistening with sugar. And bread. Baguettes, of course, a yard long, but also round breads, ovoid breads, braided breads, regular bread-shaped breads. When I left Phoenix I never wanted to see food again, never again wanted to chop, slice, mince, sauté, braise, roast, sear, but this food, here, is ready to eat and so, so magnificent. I take a deep inhalation of yeast and butter and sugar, snap Kat's umbrella closed, and follow a pair of black-clad teenage girls into the bakery.

The baguette sandwiches are the first things to catch my eye. The length of your forearm, stacked like firewood, lavishly buttered, and stuffed with chicken, ham, pâté, cheese, lettuce, tomato, they are displayed out in the open, uncovered, at mouth level. Rule number twenty-one of the perpetual diet: If you do let yourself get completely empty, which you should not (see rule number eighteen) don't then turn around and gobble down something sweet. Go for protein. It will steady you, strengthen you, settle you. Sugar is always a bad choice but it's an even worse choice on an empty stomach. It turns you into a lunatic. More of a lunatic.

"*Madame?*"

The counter girl is thin and unsmiling.

Kat would say, "Order a cake! Order a tart! Order a cake *and* a tart!" But as the counter girl looks at me, every single one of my eight years of straight-A French fly out of my head. The girl is saying "*Madame?*" a third time before I finally manage to blurt, "*Tarte? Petite? Framboise?*"

"*Bien sûr,*" she says, rolling her eyes at the person in line behind me. She lifts a perfect raspberry tartlet out of the display case and swiftly enfolds it in a pyramid of stiff white paper. "*Vous désirez autre chose, madame?*"

Do I desire anything else? Ha. When do I not? I should get one of those yummy-looking chicken sandwiches. Chicken is "*poulet.*" But how do you say "sandwich" in French? I should know. I probably do know, somewhere in the echoing caverns of my food-deprived brain. It's probably in *French for Travelers*, but I cannot check because I left it in the hotel room.

"*Autre chose?*" the girl repeats.

"*Non,*" I say. "*Non, merci.*"

I pay, scurry back to my hotel, mount the creaking wooden stairs to my room two at a time, dump the dripping umbrella on the fuchsia carpet, unwrap the raspberry tartlet, and bite into it.

When I was fat I ate constantly. But I never enjoyed my food. I never felt full or satisfied or content. Eating was like pushing an elevator button over and over yet the elevator never comes. This tartlet deserves to be savored, to be consumed with care and attention and love and gratitude, but I barely pause for breath between bites, completely disregarding rule number twenty-two of the perpetual diet: Don't be a gulper. Gulpers are fat. Whatever you eat you should take small bites, count to five between bites, and chew each bite thoroughly.

Not this time. In less than twenty seconds all that's left of that heavenly little raspberry tart is a constellation of crumbs scattered over the carpet. I bend to pick them up.

I make it to the toilet with barely a nanosecond to spare.

Five minutes later I'm back in the pink bed, curled like a shrimp. I never throw up. Is my head cold turning into the stomach flu? Or am I being punished for gulping down the tartlet, throwing sugar onto the cough syrup sloshing around in my otherwise empty stomach? I pull the sheet over my face and close my eyes, but don't fall asleep, or relax, or die, because hunger will not let me.

"You wimp," Kat would say. "Are you going to spend your whole time in Paris being sick in a frigging hotel room?"

I would like to disagree. I would like to argue. But that's the problem with the dead. You can't fight with them, you can't reason with them, you can't prove them wrong or yourself right, beg them to choose you, to stay with you, to love you more than death. They are gone. They have left only a big black ugly gash where their beautiful vibrant selves used to be. They no longer give a shit.

I allow myself to lie there for fifteen minutes. Then I throw off the pink bedclothes, grab Kat's umbrella, and leave the hotel a second time, returning to the bakery with the red-and-white-striped awning.

Where the stack of baguette sandwiches is gone.

But not to worry. Just across the busy boulevard is a market, a convenience mart like a Seven Eleven at home but darker, smellier, and with only a single aisle. No one speaks to you here, no one even looks at you. You are free to just pluck things off the shelves and toss them into your hand basket, like at home. Actually, better than at home, because this is food shopping in Paris.

I study the small open dairy case. Milk, cream, cheese, eggs. There must be something bland and settling here, something to soothe a treacherous tummy, something like cottage cheese. But they only have yogurt. Though normally I like yogurt, just the thought of it now makes me want to heave.

Wait a minute.

Here's a cottage cheese–sized container. Not cottage cheese, though. It's labeled "*riz au lait*." Hmm. *Riz* is rice. *Lait* is milk. I am a fan of both those ingredients. Both those ingredients are harmless, good for you. I drop the container into my basket.

I am grocery shopping in Paris. Like a real Parisian. If I lived here, if I stayed here forever, I would shop like this every day, buying just what I need for my own simple meals thrown together in fifteen minutes or less. Roasted vegetables. Poached salmon. Fresh fruit salad with quinoa and almonds.

For now, though, I don't have a kitchen so I add a bag of trail mix to my *riz au lait,* along with a bottle of Evian, a Valrhona chocolate bar, and some crackers. Not to stash away in the food storage locker but to eat here, right away. Food, incredible, awesome food, is everywhere. It's not evil. You don't need to shun it or hoard it or hate it or fear it. It's just food and it will always be there for you.

My plan is to head straight back to my hotel room, to be near its reassuringly nearby toilet, but my stomach calls out to me so insistently that I find an empty doorway to stand in, tear open the package of crackers, and eat two of them, chewing thoroughly, swallowing carefully, counting to ten between bites. They are the most amazing crackers—salty, buttery, and sweet at the same time. I eat five more, watching the cars and buses and bicycles and people rush past, and then crack open the bottle of Evian.

"So what was your first meal in Paris?" Kat would ask.

"Well, basically, bread and water," I would answer. "Har har."

But already I feel stronger, calmer, clearer. Rule number twenty-three of the perpetual diet: When you are sick, eat what tastes good to you. Dieting while ailing is a wicked effective way to drop pounds. But of all the weight-loss methods I know, and I know them all, it is the most stupid. You just get sicker.

I cannot resist peeling off the foil lid of the container of *riz au lait* and sniffing the contents. Huh. It's nothing more or less than rice pudding. Good old rice pudding. Dad used to make it for me from scratch when I was home sick from school. He'd bring it to me in bed, set up the portable TV on my battered oak dresser, and let me watch reruns of "Little House on the Prairie" in the middle of the afternoon. Rice pudding settles tummies. Rice pudding has healing powers. There's only one problem. I don't have a spoon.

A spoon. A small simple ordinary thing. Kat would find a way to get her hands on one. She would locate a store that would sell her one. She would go to a restaurant and get them to give her one. She would steal one.

I lean out of my doorway and peer up and down the busy boulevard. The rain has stopped and the sky has lightened to a bright shining pewter. Funny. My mental image of Paris has always been in black and white, like an old movie, like a 1940s Robert Doisneau photograph. And now here it is—black streets, white sidewalks, black wrought iron balconies, white clouds tucking everything in like a puffy eiderdown quilt.

I hook my tote bag over my shoulder and set forth. This wide avenue—dazzlingly wide compared to the baguette-thin street my hotel is on—has tons of shops and businesses. I pass bakeries, cafés, a Laundromat, a dry cleaners, a bookstore, a travel agency, a sushi bar, a cobbler's, three dress boutiques, four banks, two pharmacies, five shoe stores, a school, a church, a Chinese deli. Shops selling chocolate, cheese, flowers, wine, fruit, vegetables, meat, eyeglasses, shoes, cameras, DVDs, appliances, bedsheets, blankets, baby clothes. Every human need could be satisfied on this street. You could live your whole life on this street and never need to go anywhere else.

Here's a china shop. Unlike any china shop I have ever seen, it sells only white dishes. White dinner plates stand in the aisles in leaning towers as high as your waist. White tea cups and white coffee mugs and white soup bowls and white salt and pepper shakers and white tureens and white pitchers crowd every inch of the shelves. My mother wouldn't have approved of the clutter. "An accident waiting to happen," she'd say.

What else is new. I slip into the crowded shop. It has spoons, chunky white porcelain ones most likely meant for Chinese soup, stacked beside some weirdly huge coffee cups the size of cereal bowls. Naturally, I can't remember how to say spoon in French, but I don't need to. I just watch the cash register to see the amount due, hand over a silver five-euro note, and accept my change, hoping it is correct. Voilà. No talking equals no humiliation. It is certainly not what Mme. Dupont, my high school French teacher, had in mind for her star pupil. But it does the job.

When I leave the shop I continue in the opposite direction from my hotel. Because why not? If I stay on this same street I can walk as far as I want. When I get tired all I have to do is turn around and retrace my steps.

Note to self: next time don't leave the map in the hotel room.

A well-dressed, well-shod, well-coiffed woman walking a white dog with a black head steps out of a wine shop in front of me. She is wearing a black-and-white plaid Burberry raincoat. And so is the dog. What must it be like to live a life where you and your dog wear matching designer raincoats? Kat and I would get hours of conversation out of this. How can I be alive, existing on the planet, eating, sleeping, breathing, walking, talking, boarding airplanes, buying spoons, encountering elegant women on the streets of elegantly black-and-white Paris, and Kat be gone? So very much not here? It's wrong. It's evil. I follow the elegant woman until a mass of smelly elderly tourists pouring out of a smelly idling bus separates us. How many times have I forgotten that Kat is dead and picked up my cell phone to call her and tell her some stupid thing like, "Hey, I just saw a woman and her dog wearing matching outfits"? The night of Kat's funeral, the person I most wanted to talk to about it was Kat.

Two blocks farther on, a flower shop breaks all the Paris black-and-white rules by displaying buckets of red and pink and orange roses in front of the door. They've even strewn rose petals over the pavement. Kat said, "I don't want flowers at my funeral. I want food. And booze. I want people to eat and drink and get happy." People did. They chatted and laughed and nibbled and sipped as if they were at a cocktail party. I wanted to kill them all. I wanted to murder every single one of them.

The neighborhood of myriad tiny shops transitions to a busier, noisier, grittier district of multi-level department stores. The sidewalks grow more crowded, the traffic more congested, the ambience more corporate. There's an enormous Starbucks, and a McDonald's. And a Foot Locker. And, incongruously, a Subway sandwich shop. A sharp wind kicks up and the rain starts again, falling in fat heavy drops. A taxi shoots past, splashing dirty water all over my shiny new boots.

I sneeze and turn around. I have food shopped. I have spoon shopped. I am quivering with urban energy and my head is throbbing and I am starving and I am solo in Paris, where food is only one of the many awesome temptations you are invited to surrender to.

sixteen

"UNE OMELETTE, s'il vous plaît," I say to the waiter.

It is a frigging miracle. I am sitting at a table by a window in a café in Paris, speaking French to a French person. And being understood.

It's not even that scary because I am not the only lone female in the place. Two tables away a woman with expensively cut silver hair sips coffee and works a crossword puzzle. She's wearing pearls and a dove-gray Chanel-style suit. Probably not a tourist. A mini-skirted Japanese girl huddles over a table by the door studying a fold-out map of Paris. Most likely a tourist. Another woman who could be fifty or seventy or a hundred sits at the bar clutching a goblet of white wine in her left hand and a schooner of beer in her right hand. In addition to a matted gray overcoat, she's wearing pink fuzzy bedroom slippers. Definitely not a tourist.

"Madame." The waiter sets a steaming plate in front of me. My omelet, accompanied by—who in the world could ever have seen this coming?—French fries. Fries at ten in the morning. Even more heinous than white wine and beer at ten in the morning. At any time of the day fries are a major no-no, of course, but for breakfast they are simply beyond the pale.

However, I myself am way beyond the pale. The pale has been in my rearview mirror for a couple days now. And since this is my first hot meal since dinner on the plane, I inhale the perfume of egg and potatoes and flip a mental middle finger at rule number twenty-four of the perpetual diet: It's okay to eat protein and vegetables together, or starch and vegetables together, but never protein and starch together. Protein and starch together are harder to digest, meaning they stay in your body longer, meaning they have more time to turn to fat.

Within minutes I've devoured every single morsel, in addition to the basket of bread the waiter also gave me, which I did not order but which I consume as if I had. As I put down my fork and look up, the sun steps out from behind a cloud, warming my face. The nature gods are giving their blessing. I smile. I, Amy, have traveled to Paris, ordered a meal in a restaurant, and eaten it. It was a no-brainer. Even the menu was a no-brainer, organized into *"Les Omelettes," "Les Salades,"* and *"Les Sandwichs."*

Oui, Mme. Dupont. I remember now. The French word for "sandwich" is *"sandwich."* And the plural for *"sandwich"* is *"sandwichs."* No *e*.

I unbutton my Canadian sweater and contemplate the corbelled and corniced buildings across the boulevard. From the taxi on Monday the buildings lining every Parisian street were a solid golden-hued façade but now, really looking at them, I can see they are individual structures set close enough to touch and varying substantially by height, width, and, slightly, by color—cream to toffee to custard to butterscotch to caramel to toast. I lean back in my chair and cross my legs. My nose has stopped running, my cough is almost gone, and my stomach is content for the first time in what seems like a decade. I could sit at this table forever, gaze out at these delicious buildings forever. "You're being a piss-poor tourist, girl," Kat would say.

But maybe this café, this table, this window are the reasons I came to Paris. Maybe it doesn't matter what I do. It only matters that I am. I have all the time in the world to figure out who I am.

I run my tongue across my dry lips. One thing the waiter didn't provide was a glass of water. In Phoenix water—ice water—is automatic, is practically required by law. Come to think of it, the waiter hasn't come back to check on me at all, to ask if everything is okay, if I need anything else. No, he's leaning against the bar, laughing and chatting with the bedroom-slippers lady. Funny. She looks like an unwashed street person. You'd think they'd throw her out, but she is obviously an accepted regular, a fixture even.

In my hotel room a half bottle of Evian is standing on the nightstand but I can't leave the café until I pay and I can't pay until the waiter comes. What we have here, Dad would say, is a Mexican stand-off.

"I beg your pardon." The woman with the expensively cut silver hair is peering at me over her reading glasses. "Might I help you?" she asks in bell clear British English.

"Oh. Hello," I say. "Thank you. Yes—I was wondering, how can I get a glass of water?"

"Ah. You simply ask for it."

"I would like to. But the waiter isn't coming back."

"You must beckon to him."

I look at the waiter, now puffing on a cigarette and sipping an espresso. Am I supposed to yell *"Garçon!"* like in old movies?

The woman smiles, lifts her head, says, *"S'il vous plaît,"* without even raising her voice, and the waiter puts down his espresso and hurries over. *"Pourriez-vous apporter un carafe d'eau pour cette jeune femme?"* she says to him, indicating my table. Her English is *Masterpiece Theatre* but her French is effortless. She turns back to face me. "Would you like anything else?"

"Yes! Tea, please. I would really love a cup of tea." Tea is good for colds, Dad always said.

"Et un thé au lait," the woman tells the waiter. "I assume you take it with milk?" she says to me.

No. But then I've never tried it that way either. "Of course," I lie. "Thank you."

"My pleasure," says the woman, returning to her crossword puzzle.

I guzzle two glasses of the water—room temperature, not a sliver of ice to be found—and linger over the tea. Which is not bad with milk. Which is excellent, actually.

The waiter left my bill when he brought the water and tea. Fifteen euros—more than twenty dollars. A major rip-off, William would say. But this is Paris. I reach over my right shoulder to unhook my purse from the back of my chair.

My purse is not there. I twist to the left but it isn't on that side either. I jump up and scan my surroundings. My purse is not on the floor. It's not under the table. It's not on the other chair.

It's not anywhere.

I sit down. Then I stand up. Then I clamp both hands over my mouth and race out of the café at warp speed, just barely making it to the street before spewing the omelet, the fries, the bread, the tea, the water, everything, into the gutter. This cannot be happening. Not here, not on a public sidewalk in front of a restaurant. Not in Paris. I place my hand on a nearby parked car for support but it begins to shriek,

"Whoop! Whoop! Whoop!" so stridently and loudly that I stagger and stumble in my own vomit.

I am starting to sob when the woman with the perfect silver hair and the bell clear British English is suddenly beside me, her mouth moving. I shake my head and point to my ear and then to the car, which is garishly red and freakishly small in addition to horrifically loud.

"It's an alarm. A car alarm," the woman shouts, her voice barely audible over the din.

"I know!" I shout back, and feel my chin quivering. I can't stop it, and I can't stop the hot tears streaking down my cheeks. I am raising my arm to slam my fist onto the roof of the car when the whooping stops.

"My word. Let me be of assistance," the woman says. Cupping my elbow, she firmly leads me back into the café, past the waiter standing at the door with his arms folded, past the Japanese girl holding her hand over her mouth and giggling, past the bedroom-slippers lady double fisting her wine and beer and muttering to no one in particular.

"Would you care to join me?"

I ignore her, plopping down in the first chair that presents itself, slumping forward, and resting my hot cheek against the cool table. What is wrong with me? Stress, jetlag, the cold, a flu, not enough food, too much food, the wrong kind of food? If I didn't know better, I'd think it was morning sickness.

The Englishwoman clucks and moves to retrieve my coat, which I left sprawled over the black-and-white checkerboard tile floor. She shakes it out, arranges it around my shoulders, smooths my hair back from my face, and takes a seat across from me.

"I'm Margaret," she says, speaking as crisply as if we were being introduced at a garden party. For a second I flash on Harry Potter. "And you are?"

"Amy," I mutter. "My name is Amy."

"How do you do, Amy? I think you'd better drink a little something," she says, gesturing to the waiter to bring water. "Not too quickly, mind you."

I don't much want to but I sit up, dry my wet cheeks with the tissue she is holding out to me, and take a sip. "Thank you," I say.

Margaret studies me. "For a moment there you looked rather peaky," she says, "but your color is better already. Are you visiting? Is your hotel nearby? Perhaps you ought to go and have a lie-down."

I glance over at my abandoned table, where the fifteen-euro bill for my omelet and French fry breakfast, now splatted into the gutter outside, still waits. "Yes—I—but my purse is gone. Someone took it." My head throbs and a ring of pain circles my skull, like some kind of evil enchanted tiara.

Margaret arches her perfectly penciled eyebrows. "Oh my goodness. Oh dear. Where had you left it?"

"I hung it on my chair. Like this." I gesture to the back of my chair.

"Oh, but you must never place your handbag where you can't see it, my dear," she tsks, shaking her head. "Not in Paris. Not in any big city."

But the café isn't even crowded. For a short while two men were seated at the table behind me but they finished their coffees and left fifteen minutes ago. Was it them? Was it the Japanese girl? The bedroom-slippers lady? The waiter?

Was it Margaret? I study her pearl necklace, her diamond-encrusted watch, her Louis Vuitton handbag held firmly on both stockinged knees. No, not Margaret.

"I hope you didn't have very much in it," Margaret says.

What was in that damn purse? A pen, some Chapstick, Kleenex, eye drops, a tube of Kat's lemon verbena hand lotion, and money—not a lot, just what Dad would call walking-around money. The bulk of my cash is in my money belt and so is my credit card. Thank God for that money belt.

But my phone. My cell phone was in my purse. I cover my mouth with both hands even though I have nothing left to throw up.

"Amy?"

I choke down a mouthful of bile and do not answer. Why did I ever come to Paris, what made me think I could pull off a thing like this? Kat, are you happy now?

seventeen

"DON'T GIVE A THOUGHT to your bill," Margaret says, patting my arm with her cool smooth fingers. "I would be more than happy to take care of matters." She opens the Louis Vuitton purse with an expensive-sounding click.

"Oh no! I can pay. I have other money." I jump up from my chair, reeling. Wait. Should I have shared that? Too much is happening too fast.

"Wait," I say. "I mean, excuse me. Please."

I dash to the back of the café toward a lighted sign that says *"Toilettes."* The waiter, again planted at the bar with a cigarette, indicates a steep spiral staircase with a jerk of his head. I clump down carefully—you would never see such a treacherous staircase in a restaurant in the States—and collide with the raincoated backside of a man standing in front of a urinal. He is peeing. Peeing, right out in the open.

"Excuse me. *Excusez-moi,*" I say, keeping my eyes averted as I slink past him. At the end of the dim corridor I find a broom closet–sized room labeled *"Dames,"* lock myself in, stand as far as I can get from the gaping maw of the toilet, which is not far, take a deep breath, unzip my jeans, and peel them partway down. The money belt, holding my credit card, passport, return flight info, and cash, is still there. Of course it is. I still have everything I need.

Everything, of course, except my phone. I lean against the tiled wall, feeling hugely ill in every cell of my body.

Last night, during the third Daily Phone Call, things with William were almost normal. No phone sex this time, thank God, just a brief recounting of his day with Frank the program manager. He did not seem to want to discuss anything more personal, leaving me no opening to say, "Oh, Will, by the way, did I mention that I'm in Paris?" And so I listened and commiserated, and when he ended the conversation with a perfunctory, "I love you," I said only, "I love you, too."

I meant it but I also wondered, Maybe he wouldn't care that much if I just disappeared, here in Paris. In fact, maybe after a while he wouldn't even notice I was gone. He is always so wrapped up in his work. It doesn't seem possible that we've been married only four years. It seems like twenty. It seems like a hundred.

When I remount the spiral staircase ten minutes later the waiter is setting the tables with scalloped paper placemats. I walk straight over and hand him my credit card. "*Merci*," he murmurs, swipes it through a portable card reader, and waits. And waits. I don't use that card very often. If the charge is refused I will have to rely on cash and that won't last very—but it does go through, finally. Thank God.

"It's a good job you didn't put all your eggs in one basket," Margaret remarks. She was watching the transaction from our table.

I sit down opposite her and try to smile. The skin of my cheeks feels tight because, after making sure the peeing man was gone, I rinsed my face at the filthy dirty sink in the corridor and let it air dry.

"I know you may feel this is the last thing you want right now," says Margaret, "but I would recommend that you eat a little something. Just a bite. To soothe that poor tummy of yours." She raises her hand and the waiter appears at her side. "*Puis-je vous demander une tranche de pain de mie grillée?*"

"*Mais bien sûr, madame,*" he says.

Before I can say yes or no or maybe, a plate holding a slice of toast materializes in front of me. Middle-aged women are always trying to feed me toast. It looks delicious though.

"Not too fast," Margaret cautions.

I slather the toast with butter, because naturally I am starving again, and bite off a corner. Crispy. Crunchy. Eat me. Margaret was right. It's soothing on my throat and the fist of my stomach unclenches a little.

"Would you like a sweet? It will freshen your mouth," Margaret says, extracting a white peppermint from her handbag. Kat would approve of Margaret. Her hair, her accent, her pearls, her spectator pumps, her distinctive but not overpowering scent of Shalimar, her masterful way with the waiter.

"Have you been in Paris long?" Margaret asks.

I roll the peppermint around in my mouth. "Not long," I say. It is Wednesday. I've been in Paris less than forty-eight hours and I haven't done much more than sleep and barf. Kat would definitely not approve.

Margaret nods. "Which sights have you seen so far?"

Of course, I'm supposed to be seeing sights. As part of The Plan, Kat and I made a detailed day-by-day itinerary and printed it out, but it is still crammed in the bottom of my suitcase. "Not many," I admit. "I just got here really. Yesterday I took a long walk and came across a lovely park. Perfect grass. Daffodils. A statue of a man on a horse."

Pathetic. I have just described every park in Paris.

"Near here?" Margaret says, brightening. "That would be the place des Vosges. It's quite the nicest park in all of Paris."

Quite the nicest park. People really talk like this.

"Have you visited," Margaret continues, "the Ile Saint-Louis?"

"No." I know about it, of course. Paris is divided by the Seine and in the Seine are two islands—the Ile de la Cité, where the Notre-Dame stands, and the Ile Saint-Louis. "Not yet."

"I have an errand to run there. Would you like to accompany me? It's not far and it's a lovely day for a stroll."

I could go back to my hotel room. I could do more aimless wandering. I could freak out over the lost phone. Or I could go on an errand to the Ile Saint-Louis with elegant English Margaret, a person I have just met. "Yes, I would like to," I say, gathering up my coat and tote bag, "very much."

"Splendid," Margaret says.

My barf is still on the street outside the café, behind the no longer shrieking and still impossibly tiny automobile. "What a small car," I say.

"It's a Mini Cooper."

"Seriously?" I pause to look closer. "I'm pretty sure the Mini Coopers at home are larger than this."

"Of course they are," Margaret laughs. "Everything is bigger in America!"

Is she making fun of me? We pass the mini Mini Cooper and turn left into a shadowy street where the buildings seem to lean in over your head, the kind of street that on my long wander yesterday I didn't dare to enter but that today with Margaret feels like just a street. It can't be more than twelve feet wide—I picture two Williams lying head to toe—and the sidewalk is so narrow we have to walk single file. Single file Indian style, Dad used to say, though I told him over and over that people don't say that kind of stuff anymore. It's chilly on this street, cold actually, and I shiver, shoving my hands deeper into my coat pockets and quickening my step to keep up with Margaret, who sets a brisk pace. But we both stop short when a massive bottle-green door swings open in front of us and a cocoa-colored poodle bounds out onto the sidewalk. The poodle is followed by a man who murmurs, *"Pardon,"* as he brushes past.

My mother would say "Don't be a snoop," but it's impossible not to reach out and grab the door so I can peek around it.

Whoa. I had expected to see a dingy hallway but instead I am blinking into a sunlit cobblestone courtyard. In the middle of the courtyard someone has carved out space for a rectangle of grass. About the size of a parking spot, the rectangle is bordered by tall red tulips and shaded by a white flowering tree. Under the tree is a stone bench and under the bench is a stone rabbit, sitting up on its haunches and looking straight at me.

If I lived in this building, I would pass through this courtyard every day. I would sit on this bench to eat my morning croissant. I would know this stone rabbit by name. "Wow," I say.

Margaret is peering around my shoulder. The spicy scent of her Shalimar fills my nostrils. "You'll find that Paris has many secret gardens," she says. We gaze into the sunlit courtyard for another moment and then Margaret slips her elbow through mine and indicates a sooty building next door. "Do you mind if we pop in here?" she asks. "I have a parcel to post."

"Sure. No problem." This is what you do on a normal Wednesday afternoon in Paris. You head for the Ile Saint-Louis to run an errand and on your way you pop into the post office. "You're English, aren't you? Do you live here? In Paris?" I ask.

"Yes. For going on thirty years now. I came when—"

The rest of her explanation is drowned out by a deafening barrage of gunfire.

I am bolting for the post office door, the only possible haven on this shop-less and restaurant-less street, when Margaret grabs my arm. "Here they come!" she cries, an enormous smile spreading across her face. "Whuh?" I gasp and try to pull away. But she holds me fast, clamped to her side.

I stop struggling when I realize that the deafening sound is not gunfire. It is hooves. Horses' hooves. Twelve horses, to be exact, now thundering past us, only inches away.

Which would be sufficiently weird all unto itself, but riding the horses are cavaliers. Actual cavaliers like in a storybook, wearing shining silver helmets and spotless white breeches and peacock blue jackets lined with crimson and trimmed with golden epaulettes and braids. They ride in four precise rows of three, filling the width of the tiny street, backs straight, elbows tucked, heads erect. I feel my mouth sag open.

After the last horse's tail has swished past Margaret releases me and claps her hands like a child. "Oh, you lucky girl!" she cries.

"What—what *was* that?" I say, wiping my eyes. Not that I had been crying, exactly.

"The Garde Républicaine. A marvelous sight."

"The who?"

"The Garde Républicaine," Margaret repeats as the clatter of hooves dies away. The street is again silent. "Part of the French military. They've been in existence for, I don't know, forever. Hundreds of years." Her face is bubblegum pink and her eyes are twinkling. "These days their role is mostly ornamental of course."

"They looked like something out of a fairy tale," I say. "I could hardly believe what I was seeing."

"Yes, isn't it lovely? Their quarters aren't far from here. Fancy—horses kept right in the heart of Paris! Very occasionally we are treated to the spectacle of their comings and goings. You really are extraordinarily lucky, my dear."

Lucky? Lucky people don't lose their parents, their job, their best friend. Lucky people don't go to goddamned Paris alone because they're too spineless to come clean with their goddamned husband. Lucky people don't get their purses stolen on practically the first day.

But maybe my luck is about to change.

"A lovely day. Your lucky day," Margaret says, squeezing my arm and leading me down the street. She seems to have forgotten about her parcel. Come to think of it, she isn't even carrying a parcel. "Ah to be young again. Your whole life ahead of you."

A walnut-sized lump swells in my throat, but I don't need to speak because Margaret launches into tour guide mode. "A remnant of the twelfth-century medieval wall," she says as we pass what to me looks like a rough rock flying buttress. "Foundation stones from one of the towers of the Bastille," she notes as we cross through a tiny park where daffodils nod their heads beside a cluster of eroding stone blocks. "The Seine," she remarks as we enter a broad boulevard.

"The Seine? Seriously? Where?" I break away from Margaret's grip to peer over the waist-high stone balustrade we are walking beside. It turns out we are not on a boulevard at all. We're on a bridge.

I have seen tons of photos of the Seine. It's always gray and flat, like the Papago Freeway. But the Seine in real life is not flat and not gray. "That's funny," I say. "The water is humpy and bumpy, and thick-looking. And really brown."

"It carries a lot of mud this time of year," replies Margaret, who has joined me at the balustrade.

We stand side by side and watch the roiling water below. "Huh," I say. "The Seine. Who knew that in real life it would look like—chocolate milk?"

Margaret tosses back her head and laughs. "How delightful! Seeing Paris through your eyes is like seeing it again for the first time!" She retakes my arm and we continue the rest of the way across the bridge. It would be weird for women to walk arm in arm in Phoenix, at least for straight women, but in Paris it just feels very cool. At the next corner Margaret pauses. "*Et voilà*," she announces. "The Ile Saint-Louis."

"Already?"

"We keep everything close to hand here. So we don't misplace it."

Is Margaret teasing me again? We enter another urban canyon, oddly empty for a street in the center of a huge city, but soon the blank shuttered buildings give way to bright shops and busy cafés and a sidewalk stand whose sign, no lie, announces it as a "*Sandwicherie.*" We pass an outdoor restaurant where a man and woman are eating lunch— roast chicken, golden brown and crispy, his accompanied by a mountain of French fries, hers by a tangle of the thinnest of thin green beans. I can't help it. I stop to stare.

Rule number twenty-five of the perpetual diet: Feast your eyes first. Seriously, really look at your food. It's hard to believe, but if you concentrate, looking at food can be as satisfying as actually eating food.

Sometimes when I'm hungry and I don't want to eat I sit and look at the pictures in my cookbooks. It fills me up.

Kind of.

For a while.

"Which reminds me, it's nearly lunchtime," Margaret says. "How is that tummy now? Are you feeling at all peckish? I know it's a bit early but there's a lovely spot just along this street."

"Yes, I would like that very much," I say before remembering that my mother taught me to always refuse invitations at least once—you're supposed to wait for them to be repeated. But this is a day for saying yes to things.

Within minutes we are seated at a window table in a hushed mahogany restaurant. Shining copper plates polka-dot the mahogany-paneled walls. Mahogany chairs flank chessboard-sized tables draped with damask. Even the coffered ceiling is a dark, almost black, mahogany. My mother would say that I shouldn't be here, that I shouldn't be allowing myself to be befriended by a complete stranger like this. But my mother isn't here. I am. I am in Paris. On my own. And starving.

The waiter, resplendent in a white apron that goes all the way to his ankles, hurries to our table and places a small earthenware platter between us, murmuring, "*Bon appétit.*"

The platter holds four small round golden pastries. "*Gougères,*" Margaret explains. "Cheese puffs. A specialty of the *maison*. And complimentary."

I have a recipe for cheese puffs in one of my many cookbooks so I know what goes in them, and let me tell you they are not diet food. Of course Kat would say, "Gift food doesn't have calories," but Kat never counted a calorie in her life.

We have two *gougères* each—I make up for mine by specifying the green beans, not the fries, with my roast chicken. "*Poulet rôti!*" Margaret exclaims. "Lovely old standard. Haven't had it in years." When it arrives, Margaret picks up her knife in her right hand and her fork in her left. "*Bon appétit,*" she says, adding, "Are you traveling alone, Amy?"

Should I admit to being in Paris by myself? Would it be wise? Years ago I once told Kat, "I've learned it's best to err on the side of discretion. What I mean is, I've seldom regretted not telling people things, but often regretted telling people things." Kat said, "Really? Me, my life is an open book." I said, "Really?"

I set down the fork I had just picked up. "Yes. I mean, no," I say. "I'm not alone. Not exactly." After all, Kat is with me, in my head and in my heart, always. My dad is with me. William, too. Even my mother is still a very real presence in my brain. But I can't tell Margaret that. That's crazy-sounding.

"Girls are so frightfully independent these days," Margaret is saying as she tears a piece of bread in half. "My daughter has traveled all over the world by herself."

"Oh? Where is she now?" Good. Let's change the subject.

"Berlin. She followed her heart. A man."

In Phoenix you might follow your heart and a man to, say, Tucson. Or, at most, LA. Here in Europe you touch down in another world capital.

"Love turns your—" I hesitate. I was going to say, "brains into oatmeal."

"Love transforms you," I say instead.

"Oh, yes, it does indeed," Margaret sighs.

As we eat she recounts the exploits of the well-traveled daughter, who seems too good to be true. I listen and nod, from time to time glancing out the window at the people hurrying past. Always people. An endless supply. And since this is Paris, they are all thin people. Even wrapped in coats, even swathed in scarves, you can tell they are thin. Thin and self-assured, darting through traffic, murmuring into cell phones. Everyone in Paris has a cell phone. Everyone except for me. At least tonight I won't have to lie to William. "What did you do today?" he asked last night on the third (and now last?) Daily Phone Call. "I went for a nice long walk," I said, managing to lie and be perfectly truthful at the same time.

I eat all of my meal, instead of only half as I originally intended. Resistance is futile, William would say. The chicken is dropping-off-the-bone tender, the green beans toothsome and almost sweet. It is simple food, simply prepared, but it bursts with honest flavor and life.

After the waiter refills our glasses—Margaret ordered an entire bottle of Brouilly for just the two of us, insisting, "Wine gives strength. Besides, you're in Paris, you should celebrate!"—he removes our empty plates and Margaret leans across the table toward me. "I am watching my waistline," she confides, "so I limit myself to a nice *café-crème* after lunch. But you, my dear, should most certainly have pudding."

"I'm good," I say. "I mean, thank you. But I'm not a huge pudding fan."

Margaret giggles. It was she who drank most of the Brouilly. "Pudding is what we Brits call all desserts," she says. "I'm afraid you Yanks find us terribly peculiar."

"No, no, not at all." More like terribly adorable. "I'll just have coffee with you," I say. "That lunch was a lot more than I usually eat." At home I am able to watch William consume enormous meals while eating hardly anything myself, but here it seems impossible. Here it is all I can do to say no to dessert.

The *cafés-crème* are accompanied by sugar cubes individually wrapped in yellow paper, like tiny birthday presents. Margaret tears open both of hers and drops them in her cup. I unwrap one and consider it. A cube of sugar averages fifteen calories. After a moment's hesitation, I stir it into my coffee.

"How are you feeling now?" Margaret asks.

The coffee is sweet and rich and thick. "Better. So much better. Thank you."

"Is Paris living up to your expectations?"

"Oh yes. Totally."

We sip our *cafés-crème* in companionable silence, as if we lunched together in this elegant yet cozy restaurant every week, as if we were old friends. Or aunt and niece. Or mother and daughter.

When Margaret finishes her coffee, she sets down her cup with a mannerly clink. "I need to spend a penny." She rises and smoothes her gray wool crepe skirt. "The loo," she adds, winking.

"Of course," I say and watch her weave to the back of the restaurant and disappear through a frosted glass door marked *"Toilettes."* I sigh and toss the other sugar cube into my tote bag. I stir my *café-crème* just to hear the trill of silver on china. I lean back in my chair and undo and redo my long ponytail. One of a trio of businessmen across the room looks over at me and smiles. I flutter my lashes, arch my neck, and turn away. I do feel better, freakishly better. My sore throat and headache are gone. My congestion too.

To think that only a couple hours ago I was puking in the street. Now I feel strong, stronger than I have in years. And fit. My skinny jeans are comfortable despite the huge lunch I've just wolfed down. Crazy. I should be fat and bloated right now. Instead, I am firm, limber, alive, and pulsating with vitality. I take a long deep breath through my nose, rest my chin on the heel of one hand, and gaze out the window. The never-ending stream of thin and confident pedestrians flows by. If I wanted to, if I chose, I could with a single effortless bound fly to the gray mansard roofs of those buildings across the street. I could flit from dormer window to dormer window, on tippy-toe. And then I could float down to the sidewalk again, light as a cheese puff, landing right in front of that ice cream shop across the way.

I raise my face to the cobalt blue sky. Close my eyes. I could soar over the city. I could orbit the earth. I could sail to the sun.

eighteen

ON THE NIGHT Kat died, three weeks and four days ago, I experienced this same monstrous potency.

I wasn't with her at the actual moment of parting. I intended to be. I had been camping on the sticky vinyl-upholstered chair in her room, only stepping out to go to the toilet or to grab a snack from the vending machines down the hall. But on the third day at ten minutes before seven my stomach growled so loudly it could be heard over the beeping of the machines clustered around her bed.

"Get out of here," Kat said in a low voice. "Get something decent to eat. I ain't going nowhere." I smiled in spite of myself. Kat was still Kat. The cancer had metastasized to the brain, but when her doctors suggested opening up a port in her skull so they could pour the chemo right in, she told them, "No way. Forget it. I know when I'm beat."

I did not go far, only downstairs to the cafeteria to purchase a stale muffin and a Styrofoam cup of tepid tea, and when I returned fifteen minutes later the machines were still beeping and buzzing. But Kat's head was thrown back, her mouth was open, and her hands were flung out off the bed, palms up, fingers curled. She lied. She did go somewhere. She tricked me into turning my back so she could sneak away and leave me on my own, alone, forever.

A nurse glided in. "I'm sorry, you'll have to go now," she said after a stilted moment. Most of the nurses and nurse's aides had been hugely sympathetic—Kat was "so so young," they all crooned. Except for this one. She was frosty and stiff and her sympathy was perfunctory. "She phones it in," Kat liked to crack.

So I did not go. I stood like a stone statue by the side of the bed, my senses magnified beyond human ability. I could hear birdsong from the eucalyptus trees five stories down. I could smell the beef stew the cafeteria was serving up in the hospital basement. I could see right through the hospital sheets to Kat's long thin flat scarred beloved body.

There might still be a chance. It might not be too late. I grabbed Kat's hand and gazed with all my being into her stiffening face, trying to shine the intense life force flooding my body into hers.

"I'm sorry," the nurse said, more loudly this time, "you have to leave. There are things I need to do. Please."

She reached across me to unhook the morphine drip but I ignored her, laced my burning fingers through Kat's cooling ones, and concentrated harder. Surely some essence of Kat still lingered, a capillary, a nerve, a blood cell, an errant wisp of protoplasm, something that needed only my vital animating touch to kindle it. I squeezed Kat's hand. Kat did not squeeze back.

The nurse was getting ready to say something else when Kathryn, who had arrived in Phoenix two days ago to handle all the things that were going to need being handled, tapped me on the shoulder.

"You can go now, honey," she said, not unkindly. "Go and get some sleep."

"No," I said. "Not yet."

The nurse, glaring at both of us, started to roll away the machines.

"Amy," Kathryn said. "I'll call you tomorrow. Go now. There's nothing you can do here."

Nothing I can do. Of course she was right. I took a last long look at Kat's now abandoned body, and ran out of the room.

I don't remember taking the elevator down to the lobby and leaving the building. I know that in the parking lot the cars looked smaller than cars usually do. The palm trees bordering the sidewalk seemed shorter than on my many other visits to this hospital, and the sky was oddly lower, too. I slid behind the steering wheel of the Honda and glowered at the blooming pink oleander grazing the front fender.

Both flowers and fender cringed. I flexed my fingers. If I cared to, I could cremate each poisonous pink blossom with a mere glance from my laser-lethal eyes. If I willed it, I could shatter the windshield of every vehicle in the vicinity with just a thought from my murderous mind.

But before I turned into Godzilla, clomping through Phoenix, chomping on city buses and telephone poles, I texted William, taking care not to crush the cell phone in the might of my grasp. He called back five minutes later.

"Will?" My voice sonic boomed in my ears. "I'm leaving the hospital."

"Leaving?" he said after a pause. "I see."

I could hear his brain whirring, deducing the sequence of events that would logically lead me to not only call him for the first time in days but to leave the hospital.

"Yes," I said.

"Are you all right?" he asked, his voice husky.

"I'm fine." I was more than fine. I was all-powerful. I was omnipotent.

"Where are you headed now? Should you be driving?"

Prudent question. Very William.

"I'm still at work," he continued. "Why don't you come here?" William's office was ten minutes from the hospital. Our house was all the way across the Valley, an hour's drive away. It was rush hour and I hadn't slept in more than 72 hours but he didn't realize that now no harm could possibly come to me.

Whatever. "Sure. All right," I said.

"Are you hungry? We can get a bite to eat."

"Okay." I had thrown the tea and the muffin into the trash can and now—how is it possible to want food at such a time?—I could eat a cow, an elephant, a house, the planet.

"I'll wait for you out front," he said. "Just park in the visitor's spot and we'll take the Jeep." He wasn't going to make me come into the building, to wait in the lobby where I might run into Jackie or Robert or Heather or whoever. That surprised me a little, his sensitivity.

"Okay. Thank you."

When I got into the Jeep beside him he didn't seem to notice anything amiss, anything altered, about me. We drove to a nearby business hotel where the bar is never crowded. I had a margarita and a plate of mini-tacos and chips with guacamole and a chimichanga. Then another margarita. Then a third. Then more chips.

"La," I sang. "La la la." I licked the coarse salt from the rim of the margarita glass and then, because William was paying more attention to the basketball game on the TV above the bar than to me, I licked the side of his face.

"Whoa," William said. "I'm going to have to cut you off."

"I'm already cut off. I'm cut up. I'm cut. I'm cute." I licked his cheek again. It was rough and warm and salty. Edible. Devourable.

"You are. Cute, that is." He drained his margarita, also his third. "We shouldn't attempt driving home." He was right. In Phoenix the police arrest you first and ask questions later.

"We can fly."

"You probably could."

"And you. Too. You could ride on my back. You could be the navigator who figures out the victors."

"Vectors," he corrected.

"I knew that," I said. "I was just testing you."

We did not fly, or drive, home. William booked a room at the hotel, just the way they say you should do in the don't-drink-and-drive commercials.

"I love this room. It is amazing. It is a room like no other. And I love this bed. It is amazing. It is a bed like no other." I dove into the pillows and popped up out of them like a prairie dog. I flailed my arms and legs until all the pillows flew to the floor, stood up on the mattress in my bare feet, and started to bounce. I was never allowed to bounce on the bed as a child.

"Not as amazing as you," William said and tried to catch me, to take me into his arms, but I bounced out of reach, off the other side of the bed, and landed on my butt on the floor.

"I'm okay!" I sprang to my feet and twirled to the window, my arms cupped over my head like a ballerina. We were twenty stories up. Phoenix, dull soulless inert Phoenix, was stretched out below, flat as a board game, brown as the bottom of your shoe.

"I love being up high."

"High, that you are."

"I love being on top of—everything." I pressed my nose against the dusty window. I yearned to burst through this glass, to shatter it, to fly away, to be free, to be above all this, to be gone. Away. Forever.

When Daddy died, in a final merciful bout of pneumonia, I forgot about my car in the hospital parking lot and walked the whole ten miles home, and then walked the whole ten miles back to the hospital to retrieve the car, not the least bit tired though then too I had been awake for days on end.

"I don't care," I said out loud. "I never wanna sleep no more."

"Huh?" William was sprawled cattywampus across the bed, watching me through slitted eyes, the back of one slender hairless hand resting on his forehead.

"I said, I do not need sleep. Ever. I have evolved. Into a new life form."

"You have evolved," William mumbled, "into pure energy and light."

"Yes! I'm going flying." I stretched out my arms, ran around the bed and out of the room, and was halfway down the hall by the time he caught up with me.

"Wait up, Ames."

A miracle. William wasn't dragging me back. He wasn't telling me to behave, settle down, grow up. He was going along with my craziness. It had been a long time since his love had felt this unquestioning, this unconditional. I flushed hot from head to toe, hot with power and wonder.

"Onward!" I shouted.

"Downward!" William roared.

We took the stairs, stomping down all twenty stories to the lobby and bursting through the revolving doors to the parking lot outside, searching for William's Jeep but never finding it because we turned right instead of left at the ocotillo. By the time we found our way back to the hotel bar we were thirsty again. The bill that later appeared on the credit card showed we managed to be served two more margaritas apiece. I don't remember that or anything after that. I am pretty sure we managed to have sex, though it doesn't seem likely. Or even possible.

But it is always temporary, this I-am-not-dead euphoria. The next morning I could barely move. Or see. Or hear. When Kathryn called to discuss funeral plans I just let her rattle on. When she hung up I stayed lying in bed, curled into myself like a stillborn kitten. William was there, of course, stuck to my back like a cocklebur, his heavy arm wound tightly around my shoulders. It was all I could do not to pull away.

nineteen

"MY DEAR, are you in your cups?" Margaret asks as we leave the restaurant.

"Uh, excuse me?"

"Your cheeks are the most delightful shade of pink. And you are weaving. Perhaps you're not used to wine?"

I'm not new to wine, just not to two glasses of it at lunch.

Margaret giggles. "I confess to feeling a bit tiddly myself. What did you have planned for this afternoon, Amy?"

"I was thinking of visiting the Sacré-Coeur." Just like that. It pops out of my mouth just like that.

"Super. Why not?" Margaret links her arm in mine. "You can easily get there via direct Métro from Cité," she says. "Which is not far. I'll accompany you to the station. The walk will do us both good."

Walking always does some good, if only to burn off a couple stray calories. We approach a second bridge, where people have circled to watch a boy juggle flaming torches and ride a unicycle at the same time. "Lovely! This busker is one of my favorites," Margaret exclaims. The juggler catches the last torch, leaps from his unicycle, the people applaud, Margaret tosses a coin into his basket, and we walk on, again crossing the chocolate-milk Seine, frothy and delicious. My surge of impossible horrible power begins to fade.

"What color is the river usually?" I ask. "When there is no spring runoff?"

"Dark. Greenish. I imagine you would say jade."

"Jade. That's nice."

We pass an old man playing a tiny piano on wheels—tin bowl set out to invite coins—and start down a long straight street with souvenir shops on the right and a high black ironwork fence on the left. Margaret steers us to the fence side. Apparently, souvenir shops are only for tourists, not real Parisians like Margaret. And me. Anyway, supposing I do go back to Arizona, who would I buy souvenirs for? Not William. He must never know I have done this. Rose? The other volunteers at the library? Nope. For better or worse, right or wrong, Kat was my everything. You don't just pick up another best friend at the corner drugstore. You can't order one off the Internet. You get one per lifetime, if you're lucky.

We reach the end of the ironwork fence and I glance back over my shoulder. Holy crap on a cracker. All this time we have been walking beside the Notre-Dame. The most famous cathedral in Paris, in the world. I pause to get a better look but Margaret presses on, puffing and paying our whereabouts no heed. The Notre-Dame—to real Parisians it's no big deal, it's an everyday sight, ho hum.

"The horse chestnuts are flowering early this year," Margaret remarks as we enter a leafy tunnel of trees. I glance back at the boxy towers of the cathedral winking through the greenery. I will return, not to worry. The Notre-Dame is not going anywhere. It will wait for me, just as Paris waited for me. There is no hurry, no rush. At the far end of the tree tunnel we veer right and jaywalk across a busy street to an open square, where Margaret makes a beeline for a vacant bench.

"Oof!" she says, plopping down. "I would accompany you but I have an appointment for a pedicure. Anyway, nothing could be simpler. All you need do is take line number four in the direction of the Porte de Clignancourt, go nine stops, and get off at Barbès-Rochechouart." She fishes a small red booklet out of her handbag, opens it, and displays a map.

"When you come up out of the Métro," she continues, flipping to a new page, "look for a store called Tati. T—A—T—I. It's enormous, several streets wide, you won't be able to miss it. Keeping the store on your right, follow the boulevard until you reach the rue Steinkerque. Do you see? Here." She taps her scarlet manicured nail on a faint blue line. "Turn right. You'll see trees at the top of the street. Carry on and you'll soon spot the Sacré-Coeur itself. You can't miss it," she says again. "You do have a plan, don't you?"

A plan. Do I have a plan? I used to.

"A map, I mean," says Margaret.

"Oh," I say. "Yes. A map. Of course." I dig through my tote bag and extract a green Michelin guide.

"Oh, one of those big fold-out things," Margaret says, shaking her head. "Here, take mine. Don't worry, I have another one at home. This is the kind of map Parisians carry." She holds up the red booklet, riffles through the pages. "You see. Very handy. No big awkward sheet to unfold and refold. Each page is an *arrondissement*. There's a Métro map in the back."

The Métro. Knowing the Paris Métro is knowing Paris. In *Charade* Audrey Hepburn took the Métro. So did Audrey Tautou in *Amélie*. I have watched movies and read novels and followed blogs and studied guidebooks and there, just twenty yards away, my very first Métro station, "Cité," awaits me.

However, I venture down into the bowels of Cité only because Margaret comes along.

"You do have an umbrella, don't you?" After helping me buy a packet of tickets, she entered the tunnel with me to wait for the train. "It might drizzle later."

I nod and look around. We are standing on a black asphalt platform. Above our heads the white tile ceiling is reassuringly high, and white pendant lights the size of beach balls glow like harvest moons. But at each end of the asphalt platform black D-shaped holes gape like hungry mouths. Riding the Métro means entering one of those mouths.

"Yes, I—" A turquoise and white train bursts out of the mouth on our left, roars up to us, and screeches to a halt. "Yes, I do have an umbrella," I shout.

All up and down the train, doors fly open. Okay. Time to hop on the Métro, like a real Parisian, like a true world traveler, like a grown-up woman who knows where she's going and what she's doing. But the soles of my new black boots seem glued into place.

Margaret hugs my shoulders. "Right then," she says, shoving me into a car. "Off you go. Enjoy the Sacré-Coeur. Beware the string men."

Did she say "string men"?

Too late. The train lurches forward. Margaret is smiling and waving but I don't wave back because I can't move my arms—a crowd of teenagers burst in just as the doors were sliding shut and has me wedged into a corner. I try to shrink, to be thinner, smaller, but it doesn't do any good. The less space I take up, the more space they take up.

Margaret disappears from sight. I am alone again, friendless again. I cling to a smooth metal pole and try to look French. At the next stop the teenagers spill out, sweeping me with them off the car, but before I have time to panic a new mob of passengers piles on, sweeping me back onto the car. It takes me three more stops to learn to withstand the outward and inward sucking rush of humanity. It takes four to notice that the names of the stations are posted on large blue signs on the tile walls of the tunnels. And it takes five stops to get used to the eerie one-note wail the train makes when closing the doors. Like a lonely elephant calling for its mate.

Nine stops from Cité, the train pulls into the station called Barbès-Rochechouart. What an ugly mouthful of a name. This time I allow myself to be carried off the car, up an escalator, through a revolving turnstile, and into the outdoors, where I pause to take a deep breath of fresh air and look around. The first thing I see, on the opposite corner, is a big red plaid sign saying "Tati." All right, maybe this is doable.

But just as I step off the curb to cross the street a man leaps in front of me.

"*Mademoiselle!*" he cries, brandishing a coil of leather belts.

I start to step around him but five more guys rush up and surround me, waving cellophane packages of cigarettes, perfumes, watches, shirts. One man dangles a plastic-wrapped Louis Vuitton—looking handbag in my face.

I grit my teeth. Despite my regulation black coat, black jeans, and black boots I apparently have "gullible foreigner" written all over me. I push through the clamoring vendors, avoiding eye contact and shaking my head, and hurry across the street to the store called Tati. In this *quartier* the sidewalks are much more crowded than in the neighborhood where my hotel is. The people are different, too. Women in Islamic scarves paw through cardboard boxes overflowing with colorful loose blouses and trousers. Bearded men in leather jackets, eyes black like their jackets, stand around and stare at the women. A teenage girl in an orange ankle-length skirt and green turban steps in front of me and forces me to bump against a man dressed in a long white caftan and a red-and-gray striped skullcap. No one around me is speaking French. I don't know what they're speaking. I pause and glance back toward the Métro station. I should turn around, get right back on the next train, and go back to my hotel. To my own neighborhood. How important is it, really, to see the stupid Sacré-Coeur?

But the Sacré-Coeur is the reason I came to Paris. Or one of the reasons. Besides, there's the street sign Margaret told me to look for—the rue Steinkerque. Another name that doesn't sound terribly French. Nevertheless at the corner I turn right, promptly colliding with a tall figure dressed head to toe in long flowing white robes, like a character out of a children's Bible story.

"Oh sorry!" I say. "*Excusez-moi.*"

The tall figure slowly turns.

I back into a table of I Love Paris T-shirts.

The tall figure is a woman wearing a blue mask. No, not a mask. Tattoos. The woman's entire face, only inches from mine, is covered with thin wavering blue tattoos. Blue parentheses frame her mouth, blue commas outline her chin, blue periods march up the bridge of her nose, and blue dashes run down her sunken cheeks as if she is weeping blue tears.

"I—um—excuse me," I stutter.

The woman raises her eyebrows, diffracting the blue ellipsis that bisects her forehead. Will she speak? Scream? Spit? I sidle along the table, knocking a stack of T-shirts to the ground. "*Fais gaffe!*" someone behind me yells. The tattooed woman blinks, slowly.

Oh, this can't be for real. Her eyelids are tattooed, too. With tiny blue question marks. We stand for a long moment, staring at each other, and then the woman snorts, whirls around, snaps her Biblical skirts against my legs, and disappears into a fabric store.

I don't stop to help pick up the T-shirts. I turn and charge up the middle of the rue Steinkerque, which turns out to be an all-pedestrian street teeming with people snapping photos, studying guidebooks, speaking English, and—most of all—shopping. As if someone has flipped a switch, I am in Touristville. Here everything that the word "Paris" can be affixed to is for sale. Paris scarves, T-shirts, sweatshirts, hats, bags, key rings, postcards, placemats, coasters, aprons, sunglasses, coffee mugs, thermometers, barrettes, umbrellas, refrigerator magnets, music boxes, boxer shorts, baby clothes, chef's hats. And most horrific of all: flashing electric miniature Eiffel Towers.

Yet I push my way up the street because ahead of me, just as Margaret said there would be, are the trees.

I am halfway to the trees, pausing to let a tour group pass me, when I feel something poking me in the stomach. I look down. A band of children is ringed around me and the tiniest one, a round-cheeked raven-haired girl of about five, is shoving a battered square of cardboard into my abdomen.

"Hey." I try to move away but the children, teeth flashing, eyes glittering, hold me captive. Some words are scrawled in blue ballpoint pen on the cardboard. "*J'ai faim.*" Which means "I'm hungry." Is this little girl with round cheeks and chubby fingers hungry?

"Hey," I say again and then—hah—there it is, the professional tip-tip-tap of fingers on my thighs, butt, torso. These children are trying to rob me. These are street children, pickpocket children, urchins, like characters out of Dickens.

I laugh out loud. Finally, I'm a step ahead of the game—or so far behind that I'm ahead, because I have already been robbed today. The only things I have left of value are in my good old money belt, under my trench coat, under my jeans, under my underwear, and no way are they going to get to that. "Sorry, kiddos," I laugh. "Somebody else beat you to it."

The Dickens children look at me as if I am a lamppost that suddenly started to speak, and then melt away. The smallest girl, the last to leave, smiles at me as she sticks her plump thumb into her mouth and drags the cardboard behind her. "I want a little girl who looks just like you," William said on our honeymoon in San Francisco, four years ago. A girl with shiny black hair and cornflower blue eyes, like this. I watch until she has toddled out of sight and then I continue up the rue Steinkerque, pausing at a corner to stare at a man dressed as a Subway sandwich and handing out flyers. This is the kind of job I would have to get if I wanted to stay in Paris for always. Which, let's get real, is an insane idea. Insane.

I finally reach the top of the street, step around a hot dog stand, and freeze. There it is. I'd know it anywhere. Womanly, worldly, white as the blazing desert sun at high noon in June, riding the crest of a steep grassy hill like a fairytale ship, the real and the true Sacré-Coeur.

"Where you from?"

Another man is blocking my path. Not again.

"Where you from?" he repeats. This one is brandishing not a knock-off purse or stolen watch but a fistful of long colored strings.

"Forget it," I say, and start to circle around him, putting out a hand to ward him off.

Which is a mistake because, quick as a cat, he grabs my arm and starts to twist the strings into a bracelet around my wrist.

"Ten dollar," he says, nodding and grinning as he works.

"What are you doing? No, stop, I don't want that." I wriggle my wrist out of the bracelet.

"Five dollar!" he says, undaunted, and grabs my hand again.

"No!" I yank away, breaking one of the strings, and lunge past the man to a concrete ramp that leads to a white stone stairway that curves left into a path that ends at the base of more white stone steps. Many more. But I zip up the stone steps two at a time like an Olympian and when I reach the top of the hill, wheezing and sweating, I find myself the tallest member of a Japanese tour group. They part to let me pass. I find a low wall to sit on and blow my nose and wait for my heart rate to go back to normal. Thankfully, up here, in the very shadow of the Sacré-Coeur, there are no string men, no Dickens children, no street vendors, no Subway sandwich human billboards. Just stupid tourists. As stupid, let's hope, as me. I stand up, redo my ponytail, wipe my eyes, join a queue, and enter the building.

Inside, finding an empty place takes no time at all because no one here has come to sit and pray. No, they have come to "do" the Sacré-Coeur, to consume it like any other material good. I settle into a smooth wooden pew, close my eyes and bow my head. Our Father. Who art in heaven.

"Isabella!"

I look up to see a topless little girl streaking down the center aisle, pursued by a puffing red-faced woman.

"Isabella!"

The little girl makes it all the way to the base of the golden altar before the woman, frantically waving a blue cotton T-shirt, catches her, grabs her sticklike little arm, gives her an angry shake, and forces the T-shirt over her head.

Will Isabella remember this when she grows up? Will she spend the rest of her life trying to say and do the exact opposite of everything her mother said and did? I close my eyes again, rest my forehead on the smooth lip of the pew in front of me, and plug my fingers in my ears. These heathen hordes, milling around and snapping photographs and shooting videos, don't belong here. They don't know how to pray. When I was a little girl like Isabella Dad took me to Mass at St. Mary's on Third Street and Monroe every Sunday morning. It was he who taught me the Lord's Prayer and the rosary. Our Father. Who art in heaven. Hallowed be thy name. I used to think that hallowed meant you have a halo. Good people have halos. I do not have a halo. I am not good.

I squirm in the hard pew. My stomach is still full, contravening rule number twenty-six of the perpetual diet: In addition to going to bed a little hungry (rule number seven), you should be a little bit hungry all throughout the day, too. If not, you are eating too much. People who claim you can diet without hunger are wrong. It's simple—losing weight involves eating less food than your body needs to go on living. So you are going to be hungry. All the time. Deal with it.

I straighten up and look around. I am in the Sacré-Coeur, the real and the true Sacré-Coeur, and yet everything in my life is exactly the same. Kat is still dead. Food is still the enemy. My future is still a big fat question mark. William is still far away, now in miles as well as sympathy, and with my phone stolen he is even farther. William will call me tonight, as per usual. When I don't answer he'll frown, puzzled, and dial again. Still no answer. He'll be worried, will have trouble falling asleep, and will be groggy tomorrow morning. He'll get up in front of a roomful of engineers to give his presentation and go blank. Or he'll trip over a computer cable and break his arm. Or he'll stumble down a flight of stairs and break his leg.

Or something even more horrible will happen, something I could never imagine or predict will happen, and it will be all my fault.

twenty

"PUT THAT BACK!" my mother shouted on that day. That day when something horrible happened, something I could never have imagined or predicted, and it was all my fault.

"No! I want her. I want her," I shouted back, slithering out of my mother's grasp. I plopped down hard on the dirty linoleum floor of the toy aisle, hugging a cellophane-wrapped carton to my chest.

"I told you no," my mother said, her cheeks scarlet, "and I mean no. Get up. We're going." She stalked a dozen steps away, stopped, turned, and scowled. "I mean it, Amy. I'm leaving this store. Right now."

"Good. Go. You're mean. I hate you."

My mother's face turned pale underneath her year-round tan and she glared down at me, black eyes narrowed to slits. "Stay there then," she said, adding under her breath, "I don't care." Then she stabbed on her red plastic wraparound sunglasses and walked away as rapidly as her weight would allow. I licked the salty tears from the corners of my mouth, watched my mother's round form disappear behind a display of folding lawn chairs, and listened to the clicking of her plastic sandals fade away. I knew she'd be back. And I knew I wouldn't get the City Style Classique Collection Barbie doll I was clutching so dramatically, or any other Barbie doll for that matter, so I lined up all the different styles and models by hair color and took my sweet time looking. The one with the red ponytail and the wide-brimmed white hat was my favorite.

And, oh, the clothes. So adorable. Color-coordinated with tiny matching high heels and tiny handbags and tiny luggage. But I would never own any of these exquisite things, much less a Barbie to put them on. I was supposed to be satisfied with what I already had at home, a fat ugly baby doll that cried "Mum-mah" and wet her diaper if you fed her with a special bottle filled with water. "You're too young for a Barbie," my mother told me on my eighth birthday last September, then at Christmas, and now again today, on a white-hot Wednesday in July.

"Hey. You. Little girl. Where's yer mudder?" A man whose necktie and nametag said he was the manager of the store frowned down at me.

"She's here. Somewhere." I tossed my head—not my hair, it was still too short—and held my ground.

The man looked at the dozen boxes spread across the floor, shrugged, and strode off. I spent another good twenty minutes sorting the Barbie sets by ones I would die for and ones I could take or leave. Then I returned everything to the shelf as neatly as I could. My mother did not reappear. Normally she would have been back long before now, impatient to get going. I know I was. I stood up, brushed the floor dirt off the backs of my bare thighs, gazed down at the glittering and now orderly array of Barbies, at the beauty and glamour and sophistication I would never possess. It wasn't fair. Not fair at all. But maybe Daddy would buy me one next Christmas. Sometimes, not often, he did overrule my mother. Right now I was hungry, and thirsty, and had to go potty.

This store was one I knew well. The toy aisle was next to the school supplies aisle. Which was next to the magazines. Which were next to the heating pads and foot powder. Which were next to the pharmacy, where we went more and more often these days.

But my mother wasn't at the pharmacy counter. She wasn't in the cosmetics aisle, either, comparing colors of fingernail polish, also forbidden to me, or in the photo department, picking up pictures. I walked the whole width of the store, peering down each aisle. Nada. I cruised past the row of cash registers, but my mother was not standing in line, face set, glaring. I followed a chattering Mexican family through the automatic doors into the 114-degree heat, but my mother was not out on the blindingly hot sidewalk either, squinting, sweating, angry, ready to paddle my skinny behind.

No, she was sitting in the car. I could see her there, parked in the skimpy shade of an olive tree. We had circled the lot for fifteen minutes waiting for this spot to open up. The best spot. I looked both ways before stepping off the curb, in case she was watching, not that it would help—waiting in a hot car was guaranteed to make her even madder. My mother hated the Phoenix heat, grumbled about it every year from the beginning of April to the end of October. But she didn't say a word to me when I opened the passenger door, climbed in, and fastened my seat belt without being told. She didn't even look at me. She just sat there behind the steering wheel, staring straight ahead.

She was still wearing the red wraparound sunglasses and the upper half of her face was concealed. "Mama? You asleep?" No response. I shrugged. The silent treatment never lasted long. I knew what was coming and I did not care. I opened my door and dangled my foot out. Not that it was any cooler outside but hot air, even very hot air, was better than the smell of my mother's cigarettes.

A pickup truck belching black smoke rumbled past. A mockingbird landed in the olive tree and bounced from branch to branch, peering at me through its golden spectacles. Mockingbirds can sing like any other bird, Daddy once told me. They can even meow like cats. I wished the mockingbird would meow like a cat. Or that a fire engine would roar by, sirens wailing. Or that something big and loud and exciting and new and different would happen. I had a library book, here in the car, wedged in the space between the seats. Why not reread it while I waited for my mother to calm down, or to wake up, or to scream bloody murder at me and give me the licking I no doubt deserved?

I'd sit and read. That would show her. That would show her I wasn't afraid.

I yanked at the book, bumping my mother's dimpled elbow. I held my breath. Waited for her to turn in her seat and deliver a stinging slap across my face. But that's not what happened. What happened was that my mother slumped forward onto the plastic steering wheel, knocking her sunglasses off and revealing her eyelids to be open. But she wasn't seeing. Her lips were parted, but she wasn't breathing. She wasn't doing anything.

A massive stroke, the doctors said. "She never knew what hit her," they and everyone at the funeral repeated over and over until I wanted to scream. Kat said it, too, the night I told her the story in college years later.

"But I never thought that," I said.

"What do you mean?"

"That it was a stroke."

"What do you think it was?"

"I think—I think I made her so mad that her brain exploded."

"Poor baby," Kat said, cradling me in her arms, "poor, poor baby."

twenty-one

IN THE SACRÉ-COEUR, the real and the true Sacré-Coeur, somewhere someone drops something heavy on the bare stone floor.

The cavernous space goes silent for a beat, and then a woman laughs and everyone starts talking at once. I open my eyes and look around. Everyone in the Sacré-Coeur is with someone. Everyone is slotted into a couple, or a family, or a tour group. Everyone has someone and that someone knows where he or she is.

No one in the whole wide world knows where I am.

Except for Margaret, and who is she really? A stranger. A foreigner, unreachable, unknowable, unaccountable. The Japanese tour group files past, noses in guidebooks. Isabella and her frazzled mother light a candle together in one of the side chapels. A guy around my age three pews ahead murmurs into his cell phone. His curly hair is dark and he's wearing a black leather biker jacket, but something about his neck, the way it curves above the collar, is familiar. My stomach tightens. William's hair is not dark or curly but his neck is long like that, fragile, vulnerable, with that same elegant arch. Tonight William will call me on my stupid cell phone. I will not answer. He will leave a message on the voice mail and wait for me to call back. I will not.

Our Father, who art in heaven, hallowed be thy name. In the Sacré-Coeur, the echoing tumultuous Sacré-Coeur, I lace my fingers together the way Dad taught me, clenching them so tightly my wedding ring carves into my flesh. Hallowed be thy name. I can't remember the rest. This is crazy. I know this prayer the way I know the recipe for pancakes. I stare up into the apse of the basilica at an enormous mosaic of Jesus Christ, but he doesn't help me with the words. He just stares straight ahead, arms spread out like a school crossing guard, bland, unsmiling, indifferent.

However, the man in the biker jacket is now looking straight at me, a delighted grin spread across his face. The instant our eyes meet, he springs up and heads over. A jolt of alarm skitters up my spine. I came to the Sacré-Coeur because it had summoned me. I came to think, to pray, to rest, to light a candle and add it to the fluttering racks of other beseeching candles lined up along both sides of the nave, filling the air with the sweet aroma of burning wax and supplication. I came to ask for forgiveness, for myself, for Kat. To ask for the strength and courage to go on without her, to face whatever happens next, to welcome what is *supposed* to happen next. But now there's no way that's going to happen. I leap up on wobbly legs and hurry toward a swinging door marked "*Sortie.*"

Outside the sky has clouded over and it's begun to sprinkle. I speed down five flights of white stone steps, coming to an open space partway down the hill where tourists gather to pose for photos and peer through telescopes. Safety in numbers. Legs still wobbly, I head over to an oatmeal-colored stone balustrade and lean my poochy stomach against it. Below me Paris spreads out to the horizon like a choppy sea. Paris the way it's always been, black and white and elegant and at arm's length. Paris, ever elusive, ever remote, ever distant, even when you are here in person, trampling its streets, breathing its diesel fumes, enriching its thieves. If I had my damn cell phone, I could take a damn photo.

I turn from the panoramic view to gaze up at the Sacré-Coeur. The plump-as-breasts domes of this real Sacré-Coeur are not pearlescent like the ones in the painting still hanging in my guest bathroom back home. The hazy sky above the domes is not filled with festive pink and blue streamers wafting down from a jubilant heaven. This Sacré-Coeur is not sassy, not yearning to jump up and do a cancan. Nope, it's the color of dirty dishwater and it just squats there and glares down at me. It doesn't care about me at all.

"*Mademoiselle?*"

The man in the leather biker jacket is beside me, smiling his delighted smile. He is close enough that I can see the hazelnut flecks in his irises. For an instant his aroma—like vanilla—pins me in place, like an insect in a collection. His grin widens as he holds up my tote bag, dangling it from his grimy thumb.

"Mademoiselle. Votre sac."

My tote bag. I must have left it in the pew. God. What am I going to lose next? I snatch the bag, mumble *"Merci,"* and hurry away but he falls into step alongside me. The sprinkle thickens into ropes of rain.

I accelerate, trying not to inhale the intoxicating scent of the man's cologne. Or is the aroma his own? His own personal innate perfume, like William's?

The man bumps shoulders with me. *"Tu es toute belle, chère mademoiselle,"* he croons in a voice like buttermilk. I notice that an appliqué on the breast of his jacket is embroidered with a blue and green robot and the words, "Half everyday be a happy day." Half? If Kat were here, we would just laugh at this skeevy guy with his ridiculous jacket and his toothy grin and his talk of beauty. If William were here, this wouldn't be happening at all. Four years into a marriage, you forget what it feels like to be prey. But maybe all this is my fault. Maybe this guy sensed that random flash of desire back in the pews. Maybe I am only getting what I deserve.

"Toute belle," he repeats, and wraps his cool hard fingers around my wrist.

I stand motionless.

He nods as if, yup, this is what he expected, this is no more than his due, and steps closer. I am still unable to move. The embroidered robot breast patch is now wet from the rain and has turned a darker blue. Half everyday be a happy day.

He is leaning in—is he seriously going to try to kiss me, in front of all these people, in front of the watching Sacré-Coeur?—when a gust of wind grabs my long thick ponytail and smacks it across his eyes. He flinches, steps back, blinks.

Dear Lord. His eyelids are tattooed with blue question marks, too.

"Get away, get away!" I yell, the spell broken. I yank free and charge down the remaining flights of white stone stairs. It is raining in sharp hard pellets now. My new black boots, boots Barbie herself would envy, land in the very center of each stone step, as if I have run this course many times, as if I know the Sacré-Coeur steps the way I know the stair steps in my own house in Phoenix. If William were here he'd count them. There must be two hundred at least. Three hundred. Why isn't William here with me? I'll never know how many there are now.

At the base of the hill I set off an explosion of pigeons, break up a cluster of string men, and plunge into the rue Steinkerque. Hideous name for a street. The Dickens children scurry out of my path and I keep running at full tilt, somehow not spraining an ankle on a slippery wet cobblestone and sprawling flat on my face.

At the bottom of the street I duck behind a row of postcard racks and look around. People are staring at me. The biker jacket guy is not among them but just to be safe I cross to the other side of the wide boulevard, take my scarf out of my tote bag, and tie it over my head. I fit right in. Lots of women around here are wearing scarves on their heads.

This side of the boulevard turns out to be quiet, tranquil, and free of strident street vendors and the terrifyingly tattooed. Still, I hustle right along. I will go straight back to my hotel, and get a grip. The Barbès-Rochechouart Métro stop is only a few blocks away. In fact, there's the sign already, a big yellow M in a circle. But when I reach the steps that would take me down into the earth I slow to a stop. Even though I have tickets the Métro feels impossible now, without Margaret to usher me into the netherworld, to push me onto a train, to say "Off you go!" I will probably never see Margaret again. Meeting her was just one of those exciting exotic encounters that always seem to happen to other people but that, this time, today, happened to me. I walk over to a wedding dress store and pretend to look in the window. The rain is letting up, almost stopped. It's still broad daylight. I'll just walk back to my hotel. Why not? Paris is a city conceived for foot travel. I don't need to go underground ever again.

Margaret's map book is still turned to the page showing the streets around the Sacré-Coeur. I study the crazed tangle of blue and red lines. Phoenix streets were designed by someone like William, using a ruler and a compass. Paris streets were designed by someone who'd drunk too much red wine, using a wad of tangled string and a leaky pen. But wait, there's a familiar word. Magenta. A boulevard de Magenta, only two blocks from here. "Think pink!" Kat liked to say, even before she got sick and bought into the whole breast cancer awareness pink thing. Is Kat sending me a message? The boulevard de Magenta runs straight as an arrow, William-like, to the place de la République, where all I will have to do is locate the boulevard du Temple, which will take me to my neighborhood. Two long straight shots. I can do this. Cowabunga. All those years of poring over Paris guidebooks, Paris blogs, and Paris maps are finally paying off.

I skirt a jalapeño-green garbage bin and begin to walk. All I have to do is match the pace of the other pedestrians, all I have to do is blend, disappear, and let Paris absorb me. Biker jacket guy has probably forgotten about me by now and is accosting some other hapless female tourist. Or he's gone home to his wife. "Men," Kat would say, "think with their dicks." What is William doing right now? Thinking with his dick, chatting up some skinny-ass waitress in New Jersey? I try to stage this scene in my mind. I can't.

"What you see is what you get," Kat always used to say about William. She started it not long after that first wonderful three-day Sedona weekend. It was late on a Wednesday night, past midnight. She showed up at my house, banged on the kitchen door till I let her in, sprawled across my bed, and ranted about men in general and William in particular. "He buys his jeans at J.C. Penney's," she complained. "He does crossword puzzles in ink. He lets you do his laundry. And he was in the Army. Aren't you afraid old Sarge is going to go all PTSD on you?"

It was weird. At first Kat had ignored William, the way she ignored all the guys I'd casually dated since graduation from college. I lay back with my eyes closed and barely listened, because I had to go to work the next day and because when Kat drank she never did make much sense. For one thing, William wasn't a sergeant in the military. He was a specialist, in electronics. He never even had to fire his weapon.

But ever since that night the phrase, "What you see is what you get," sticks in my mind because Kat repeated it over and over, as if it were some kind of unfixable flaw.

twenty-two

RULE NUMBER TWENTY-SEVEN of the perpetual diet: Exercise helps you lose weight only if you don't then use it as permission to pig out later.

Which is why after the two-hour hike from the Sacré-Coeur I munch down only one handful of trail mix before crawling into my pink bed and falling into a dead sleep. I do not eat any of the Valrhona chocolate bar. I do not wake up at three a.m.—nine p.m. New Jersey time—the time William surely tries to phone me and receives no answer and worries and wonders and puzzles and calls a second time and probably a third and maybe a fourth and thinks God knows what.

Nope, I sleep peacefully all night long just as if I deserve to and when I wake a pear-yellow sunlight is streaming through the white lace curtains. A pigeon flutters onto the wrought-iron railing outside, folds up its wings like an umbrella, and peers in at me, bobbing its shining iridescent head. I roll out of bed, limp to the window, look down, and watch a bus huff by. My feet feel like raw hamburger.

I know what I have to do next. I have to get my hands on a phone and call William and allay his worries. No matter what else happens, I need to let him know what's going on. Last night as I walked back from the Sacré-Coeur I passed a ton of phone stores, and one of them is actually not far from the bakery with the red-and-white-striped awning. I stretch and draw in a long deep diesel-fume-y breath. I don't deserve it, but this morning, Thursday, my third full day in Paris, my cold is completely better. The sore throat is gone. The congestion is gone. The headache is gone.

And my stomach? My stomach is rumbling with hunger. Good old hunger, my steadfast companion, my loyal tormentor. Hunger pushes me into jeans and a fresh white blouse and propels me out of the Hôtel du Cheval Blanc and onto the street. Not a cloud in the sky today, yet not warm. Cool, actually. Later I might need the trench coat I folded and stuffed into my tote bag but not now. Now is perfect, now I am in Paris, alone and untethered and free. I don't deserve it, but I've got it, for as long as it lasts.

"Amy! *Coucou!*" It's Margaret, standing in the door of the same café as yesterday, the Café de la Poste, and waving a white lace handkerchief. She is wearing a different Chanel-style suit, a different pair of spectator pumps, and the same pearls.

She looks gorgeous.

I jaywalk across the street to join her. "Margaret. Hello! Good to see you." In college, before we became inseparable, before we became everything to each other, Kat and I met every morning at a coffee shop off campus, at first seemingly by accident, like this, and later by design. Kat's design, and then mine. It's true. She didn't force me into anything.

"*Bonjour, ma chère amie!*" Margaret takes me by the shoulders and lightly kisses first my right check, then my left, the way French people do in movies. "Fancy," she says. "I looked up from my puzzle and there you were. Do you have time to join me?"

"Sure," I say without missing a beat because I am hungry, so hungry. And because eating something before braving the phone store seems like a smart thing. Like the adult thing to do. We enter the café, where Margaret's coffee and newspaper are laid out on the same table as yesterday.

"How are you?" Margaret begins. "How was the Sacré-Coeur?"

"It was not what I expected, I—"

"*Madame.*" It's the waiter, same one as yesterday, but his eyes are neutral, his face expressionless. As far as he's concerned, yesterday— the purse theft, the public vomiting—never happened.

Here goes nothing. "*Bonjour,*" I say. "*Je voudrais un grand café-crème et un croissant. S'il vous plaît.*" Take that, French waiter guy.

"*Bien sûr, madame,*" he murmurs, and melts away.

"Bravo," says Margaret. She slides her crossword puzzle into her handbag and winks at me. As if we meet at this café every day, as if we always will. I relate the saga of the Sacré-Coeur, the tattooed woman and the Dickens children and the biker jacket guy, trying to make it sound like a madcap adventure. "It's funny. I'm not anti-tattoo. I have one, on my ankle. But I don't think I really belonged there, in that area. It didn't even seem like Paris."

Margaret shakes her head. "I should've warned you. Of course, you could be accosted anywhere—a pretty girl like you, all alone—but that *quartier* is rather dodgy. Nearly all Arab now. I am not surprised by any of it," she says, "except for the Romany children with the cardboard— that's a trick I haven't seen in a very long time."

The waiter changes the subject by placing a fragrant croissant and a steaming cup of milky coffee in front of me. I rip the nose off the croissant, pop it into my mouth, and close my eyes. Crispy. Flakey. Buttery. Our Father who art in heaven hallowed be thy name oh yeah.

"*Bon appétit,*" says Margaret.

I open my eyes. "*Merci,*" I mumble. After a sip of coffee, I add, "Margaret, if I wanted to call the United States, what would be the best way?"

"You don't have a mobile? I thought all young people did nowadays."

"A cell phone, you mean? Yeah, I had one. It was in my purse. Would it be really expensive here to buy a new one? One of those pre-paid things? Or is there, maybe, a phone booth somewhere?"

"Right. Dear me. Public phones are practically extinct in Paris, I'm afraid. And don't try ringing from your hotel, whatever you do. The charges would be ruinous." Margaret places a forefinger to the side of her nose, the way a character in a play would do to show thinking. "Whom do you need to phone?"

"My husband," I say, and bite my lip. I haven't mentioned to Margaret that I have a husband. Not that it's a secret. Why would it be a secret?

"Ah." Margaret arches her perfect brows. "Your husband. You are worried that perhaps he is worried."

"Yes. Yes, I am." Of course William is worried. He is no doubt lying awake in his hotel room right now and wondering why it is his damn wife isn't answering her damn phone. I stare into the flakey white interior of the croissant. How many calories are in this thing anyway?

"I have a suggestion!" Margaret says, clapping her hands together. "Join me for lunch, *chez moi,* and you can use my telephone."

"Your—? Oh no. I couldn't. Thank you, but I couldn't."

"Why ever not? It would be my absolute pleasure. And the call wouldn't cost me a single *centime*, I assure you. I have one of those phone plans with unlimited free minutes to twenty-seven countries, including the U.S. My daughter set it up for me."

The last thing I should do is accept another one of Margaret's lunch offers. It would be an imposition, it would be forward, and my mother taught me not to impose or be forward. And I hardly know Margaret. And I really should be able to solve a simple phone problem on my own. I'm going to be thirty in September. Thirty.

"Do come," Margaret urges. "You would be doing me an enormous favor. Truly. I am in possession of a new box of Godiva chocolates. I can't very well eat it all by myself, can I? I haven't anything else to do all day," she adds.

I touch the tip of my finger to a flake of croissant on my plate and lick it off. Butter explodes on my tongue and travels straight to my thighs. "Well," I say, "if it's not too much trouble. If you have the time."

"Time! I've got nothing but!" Margaret laughs her bright silvery laugh. "But I must warn you, you will work for your victuals. We'll need to do a bit of shopping first and then I will expect you to toss the salad and lay the table."

"Of course. Of course. I would love that." My mother never let me help in the kitchen. I would be sure to ruin or break something, she always said.

"Right," Margaret says. "When you've finished breakfast we'll be off to the fishmongers."

I pop a piece of croissant into my mouth to keep from giggling. Fishmonger. Kat would get a major kick out of that—Kat, who wouldn't hesitate to accept Margaret's invitation to lunch and offer of a phone. She would jump at the chance. But Kat is not here to do any jumping, to tell me what to do, as she always did, to nag me, to take the lead, to grab at the brass ring of anything exciting, anything adventurous. Kat is not here but I am. The new and improved Amy, the Amy who says yes, Amy 2.0.

At the fishmonger's Margaret chooses a dozen oysters, still in their shells, and two whole trout, still with their heads on. At a produce market—greengrocer in Margaret-Speak—we select a floppy head of lettuce. We purchase a half-baguette at the bakery with the red-and-white-striped awning, where the counter girl does not appear to remember that two days ago I did not know that the French word for "sandwich" is *sandwich*, and we detour three blocks out of our way to a tiny *pâtisserie* to buy a half dozen miniature pastel-colored *macarons* for our dessert.

Our last stop is a four-foot-wide, nine-foot-deep, extremely odoriferous cheese shop. The proprietor nods gravely as Margaret describes our luncheon menu and then picks out three cheeses, wraps them in thick white paper, and intones, "*Bon appétit*," as he hands her the packages, bowing from the waist. He doesn't put them in a plastic bag. Margaret is stuffing everything into an expandable cotton net tote she produced from her Louis Vuitton purse.

"You can't live in Paris if you don't have a good cheesemonger," Margaret says as we leave the shop.

Cheesemonger. Snort.

Margaret steers us into a narrow side street where, mid-block, we enter a broad stone building the color of heavy cream. "Sorry there's no lift," she says as we clomp side by side up three flights of wide wooden stairs. Doubtless one of the ways Parisians stay thin. On the third landing Margaret pulls an enormous brass key out of her purse, the kind of key that in movies unlocks the entrance to the haunted house.

"Voilà," she says, pushing open a heavy carved wooden door. "*Bienvenue chez moi.*"

I follow her into a light-filled room with honey-gold parquet floors and butter-pat yellow silk wallpaper. Heavy clove-dark beams stripe the high white ceiling. French vanilla lace curtains border the three tall windows facing the street. "Whoa. I mean, what a beautiful place."

"Thank you," Margaret says, placing her purse on a marble half-moon table next to the door. "My late husband was the only son of an only son of an only son of a very old French family. We were bequeathed this apartment. Along with its many treasures."

I lean my tote bag against a brass umbrella stand. On the wall above the half-moon table hangs a crackled oil painting of a girl wearing a long white satin dress. She is lounging on a brocade settee, one dimpled hand holding a small brown book, the other lazily twirling a lock of chestnut hair. A sleeping black and tan beagle is curled on her lap. The girl's world, dress and settee and beagle, is complete. Nothing will ever be asked of her, no demands will ever be put on her, that beagle will never leave her, that book will never end. Lounging and twirling and reading are all she will ever have to do.

Margaret doesn't even glance at the painting. She ushers me into a kitchen a fourth the size of William's and my bedroom closet back home. I wash the lettuce and whisk together a low-fat vinaigrette. Margaret stuffs the trout with slices of lemon and sprigs of thyme and grape-sized knobs of butter. "There. That won't take a tick," she says, sliding the trout into a tiny oven.

Twenty minutes later we are seated across from one another at a gleaming cherry wood table set with gold-rimmed china plates and crystal goblets and ivory-handled forks and knives.

"It's all so elegant." I run my hand over the creamy jacquard napkin spread across my knees. "Just for lunch."

"Presentation is everything, the French say," says Margaret. "Mind you, they're not far wrong. After all, we eat with our eyes first."

Totally. You can't, you just can't, gobble down food served as beautifully as this. It would be a sin. Observe Margaret's presentation-is-everything rule and you would never be even remotely tempted to overeat. Your only desire would be to savor each bite, to make the pleasure last as long as possible.

"*Bon appétit, ma chère nouvelle amie.*" Margaret lifts a glistening oyster, toasts me with it, puts the shell to her lips, tips her head back, and lets the oyster slide into her mouth. "Aah," she says.

My stomach issues a warning urp. In the kitchen she spritzed the oysters with lemon juice and sprinkled them with minced shallots but that was it. They are 100 percent raw.

I pick up one of the shells on my plate and sniff. It smells like lemon, like shallots, like the sea. Margaret downs a second oyster and then a third. What is she, an otter?

Sorry, old faithful stomach. I bring the rough briny shell to my lips, tip my head back, just as Margaret did, and let the cool meat slip into my mouth. I swallow, fast, before I can change my mind.

Margaret is smiling at me. "Is it nice?" she asks, sipping her wine. Wine. At lunch. Again.

"It was, um, not bad," I say.

Okay, it was more than not bad. It was fabulous. It was thrilling. It was sexy. I eat a second oyster. A third. Rule number twenty-eight of the perpetual diet (corollary to rule number twenty-two): Ninety percent of the pleasure from any food is in the first three bites.

So make 'em count.

Kat never tried raw oysters but she would have loved them, would have laughed out loud at them. They are so brazenly sophisticated, so impeccably French. I slurp down a fourth oyster, and then a fifth. Each one brings with it a small spoonful of seawater and a large jolt of energy and a vivid image of Kat spread out across our dormitory bed.

I eat my sixth, and final, oyster. My stomach maintains a stunned silence.

"I find that oysters are the ideal starter to any meal," Margaret says as she places her platter of empty shells to one side. "Especially when your trusted fishmonger shucks them for you! They don't fill you up. They merely tease one's appetite."

In my case it's usually the appetite that does the teasing. But this is one meal where guilt is not going to be an ingredient so I start on my trout, copying Margaret's technique of slicing along the spine and lifting away the flesh in a single boneless fillet. If Kat, or William, or my mother, could only see me now.

"At home I don't usually drink at lunch," confesses Margaret as she tops off our wine glasses. The label on the bottle says it's Montrachet. "But you are here with me! This is an occasion worthy of celebration!"

We eat as if we have all the time in the world, Margaret dwelling on the subject of the daughter, who has not returned for a single visit since flitting off to Berlin two years ago with the new man. "Ah, young love," she says, shaking her head. "Shall we remove to the sitting room, linger over our excellent wine? We can have our pudding later."

Meaning those darling *macarons* of course. Dessert, after the wine and oysters and trout and salad and bread and cheese. Kat would not bat an eyelash. She would be all for it. Loosen up, she'd say. Live a little. You're in frigging France. I can't admit to her, even in my head, that I came to France to get away from food. It's too embarrassing.

Margaret sinks into a nut-brown leather armchair. "I've always preferred the French lunch to the French dinner," she says. "You have the entire afternoon to recover!"

You need it. I sit across from Margaret in the other armchair. Unlike after lunch yesterday, I am relaxed. I remind myself of rule number twenty-nine of the perpetual diet: Allow yourself the occasional lavish meal. It spikes the metabolism.

"My mother used to say you should eat like a king in the morning, a queen at noon, and a pauper at night," I say. She had a ton of sayings like that. The older I get, the more often they pop into my head.

"Your mother was a wise lady," Margaret says.

Was she? I never had the chance to find out, to know her as a human being, to discover if she was wise or crazy or bad or just sad. Who knows? We might have one day become friends, shopped together, cooked together, shared confidences together, slurped raw oysters together. We might have dieted together. Instead the last words I said to my mother were "I hate you."

"What brings you to Paris, Amy?"

I set my wine glass on a hammered-copper side table and glance at the massive front door that Margaret so carefully locked behind us. If only I could just get up and go. Walk away from questions, from people, from responsibility, from the future. But that would be rude, and what about the *macarons*? And the Godiva chocolate? And, more important, the phone? Margaret has not repeated her offer to let me call the States. Maybe she's forgotten.

"I'm here on behalf of a friend," I finally say.

"A friend? How so?" Margaret asks.

"My best friend died not long ago." As if on cue, tears fill my eyes. I grab my wine, gulp down a few swallows, and glare at a marble carriage clock on the mantelpiece. It has lovely mother-of-pearl Roman numerals, but no hands.

Margaret takes a white lace-rimmed handkerchief out of the pocket of her jacket and offers it to me. "I am so sorry."

I sniff and lay the handkerchief on my knee. "We always planned to come to Paris together. But it never happened. So here I am, for the both of us. It was sort of a last-minute decision—I just got on a plane. Although I would have come to Paris anyway," I add. "Eventually. I've always wanted to. It's been my dream since I was a little girl." A single stupid tear spills out of my stupid eye and slips down my stupid cheek. I do not mention that I came without telling a single soul. I do not use the lacy handkerchief. It is too beautiful.

"Do you have an itinerary? Sites you intend to see?"

"Uh-huh," I say, nodding and wiping my cheek with the back of my hand. "Yes. We made a detailed schedule, my friend and me. Exactly what we would do and see each day. Not that I've been following it. Actually, I haven't even taken it out of my suitcase. Actually, nothing is going the way I thought it would."

"Ah. But that is the way of life, is it not?" Margaret says, the corners of her mouth turning down. Sometimes Margaret looks sad. And old, like maybe sixty. Of course she probably is sixty. And she probably doesn't think of herself as old. You probably never do.

"And, if I may ask, where does your husband fit into all of this?" Margaret continues. "Why did he not come to Paris with you?"

William. Just when I think I've pushed him to the very back of my heart and brain he takes his lawful wedded spot at the very front. Margaret is right. If I were here with William I wouldn't have got my purse stolen. I wouldn't have barfed up my breakfast in the street in front of the Café de la Poste. I wouldn't have been stalked by the Sacré-Coeur biker jacket guy.

But I wouldn't have met Margaret either. I wouldn't be sitting here, inside a real French apartment, the guest of a real Parisian resident, digesting oysters and slugging back Montrachet in the middle of the day. I look around the room, a warm cozy cinnamon-toast kind of room, a room that has always been here and always will be, orderly and clean and elegant and self-assured. I could be happy here, safe here, I could curl up with a good book here, forever.

Margaret smiles at me. "Shall we take our coffee now?" she asks. "Or would you rather have a tisane?"

Oh no. More booze? "Tee—zahn?"

"Tea. Herbal infusion, to describe it correctly. You rather look like you could use a tisane. I'll make us a nice pot of *verveine*."

No more alcohol, thank God, and, apparently, no more questions about William. However, Margaret's obviously forgotten her offer of the phone. If she has a phone. Seriously, nothing in this room is remotely reminiscent of the twenty-first century. Or even the twentieth. No phone, no computer, no television, no radio. Not even a working clock. Only a diamond-encrusted wristwatch that occasionally peeks out from under Margaret's silken sleeve. How long have I been here?

The pear-yellow sun that was pouring through the tall French windows when we arrived is gone, yet the room still glows.

If I did reach William, all this would end. Poof, over, gone, just when it began. So unfair. Besides, is William really worried? He's such a pragmatist. He's no doubt assuming I lost my cell phone, or broke it, or let the charge run out. If the thief happened to answer, William would conclude the phone got stolen. Which, ha, it was. He would never suspect it got stolen in Paris. Would William recognize French when he hears it? Would he mistake it for, say, Spanish? How unpolitically correct, or politically incorrect, whatever. But damn it, I need this trip, this time apart, this break. I deserve it, I've earned it, it's mine.

When the doorbell rings I jump to my feet, the empty wine glass slipping from my fingers.

Margaret hurries from the kitchen to the door. "*Eh bien!*" she cries and ushers forth a slender man, maybe twenty, maybe thirty. When he spots me he raises his eyebrows and looks, for an instant, as if he's about to say something, but then he shrugs and shakes his head.

"Amy," Margaret says, "let me introduce you to my young friend, Emmanuel. Manu, as his friends call him."

Manu reaches forward to shake my hand. He is short, a full inch shorter than me, and has an unruly mass of dark frizzy hair that makes his head look too big for his body. "*Bonjour.*" He smiles, showing crooked teeth.

"Manu is a dab hand at electronics," Margaret explains. "He comes round to solve my computer woes, when I have them, which is often."

Okay, so the woman owns a computer. She must have a phone. Manu makes an awkward half bow and disappears into an adjoining room.

"*Merci infiniment,*" Margaret calls after him.

"I should be going," I say, retrieving the fallen wine glass—unbroken, thank God—from where it landed on the thick chocolate and robin's egg blue Aubusson carpet. The moment to mention the phone call has passed.

"But the tisane is just ready," Margaret protests.

Trapped by the tisane. But, twenty minutes later, it has un-tipsied me and steadied my rattling jalopy of a heart.

"Manu used to court my daughter," Margaret says, refilling my cup.

Seriously? Someone went out with Manu?

"He seems very nice," I say.

"But that doesn't interest you." Margaret smiles. "What interests you is that you have only a short time in Paris and you must select your activities with care. What are your passions? Art? Fashion? Food?"

"Not food. I like history a lot. Museums. I've done a ton of reading about the history of France. But I don't want to do the normal touristy things."

"Ah. You seek the road less traveled by, do you?"

"I do." I cradle the fragile gold-rimmed teacup in my hands. Everything Margaret owns is a feast for the eye and the hand. "But in a way it's enough just to be here. And I don't like hanging out with masses of tourists. Although I realize I am one."

"I entirely understand. You want to have your own unique experience."

"I know a most unique experience to have in Paris," Manu says.

I slosh a little tea across my wrist. Manu is standing behind me, winding a length of computer cable into a lasso.

"You would do," Margaret laughs. "Come and join us. Would you take a tisane? Oh no, of course not." She jumps up and fetches a bottle of dark beer from the kitchen.

"*Merci bien*," Manu says, sitting on a brocade *fauteuil*. "To speak of Paris. I know a place where few tourists go. A very special place." His accent sounds the way French accents do in movies.

"Do tell," Margaret says, curling once again into her armchair.

"It is the catacombs." He has watery blue eyes, probably weak from staring at computer screens. "But not the touristic catacombs. The secret ones. The forbidden."

"I believe I have read about them, as a matter of fact," says Margaret. "Hundreds of miles of tunnels and caves—a veritable city beneath the city. Quarries, not sewers, mind you, where the stones to build Paris were excavated. But my understanding is that, except for the official museum, one is not permitted to go down there."

"But of course it is not permitted." Manu nods, his eyes twinkling. "Nevertheless it is done."

I return my teacup to its saucer on the hammered copper side table and dry my wrist on my jeans. "Catacombs. You mean like graves? And people go down into them? For fun?"

"*Oui. Tout à fait.* I go often," says Manu. "With friends. It is a world apart. *Un monde magnifique.*"

"Did I not recently read that the police came across an entire nightclub down there?" asks Margaret.

"*Oui.* Indeed. Also a cinema."

Margaret's eyes widen. "Fancy that."

Manu grins and swigs his beer. "When the police returned to investigate they found everything removed. Only a note was left there. It said, *tout simplement,* 'Do Not Try to Find Us.'"

"Ooh," giggles Margaret. "It sends shivers up one's spine, does it not?"

Manu winks at me. Margaret frowns.

"Surely, Manu, you do not propose to take Amy down into the catacombs?"

"But no. *Pas du tout,*" Manu says. He looks about to add something when a computer chimes. "*Merde,*" he mutters, jumps to his feet, and hurries out of the room.

I also stand. "This has been so very nice," I say, allowing myself one more long look at the carved marble fireplace and the mahogany bookcases with etched glass doors and the crystal wall sconces. It is time to sober up, grow up, step up. Time, at the very least, to find a phone store. "So lovely. Thank you, Margaret. Wonderful lunch and tea and everything. But I'm afraid I'm taking up your whole afternoon. I should go."

twenty-three

I AM HALFWAY DOWN the stairs when Manu catches up to me. "*Bonjour!* Again."

He finished with Margaret's computer awfully fast.

We descend side by side, pivoting in unison at the landings. Despite the tisane I am still a little drunk, and need to focus on Manu's tomato-red running shoes to keep my balance. "Margaret's a wonderful person, don't you think?" I say after a moment.

"*Oui.* Margaret is *formidable*," he says. For-mee-dah-bluh. "She suggests, perhaps, that I accompany you. To your hotel."

"Accompany me? Oh no, I'm fine really." We have reached the last flight of stairs, which is wider and grander than the rest and opens into a courtyard. "It's not far. I can walk. No problem."

"Indeed it is not a problem," he says, pulling open the heavy door that leads to the street. "*Voilà.* My car, she waits for you."

It's a van, not a car, parked half on the sidewalk and half on the pavement. The windows are pitted, the doors dented, the upholstery ripped, and the cargo area in the back calf-deep in coats, books, computer cables, rubber boots, backpacks, flashlights, headlamps, and comic books. I get into the van because Margaret sent Manu and because my head is hammering like a Gila woodpecker. Maybe I'll take a nap before going out to the phone store. It's not late. In New Jersey, where William is, it's still morning. There's plenty of time to call him.

"I am staying at the Hôtel du Cheval Blanc," I say as Manu hops in beside me and revs the engine.

"*Bon.* I know it. I live in this *quartier*."

We lurch off the curb with a nauseating plop and rattle down the narrow street, missing a clump of parked motorcycles and shooting right through a stop sign on the corner. We brake only when a large white delivery truck wheezes to a halt in front of us, completely blocking the street.

"*Mais non,*" Manu groans as the driver of the truck, cigarette clamped between thin lips, leaps out and starts unloading plastic crates filled with heads of lettuce. "*Ce n'est pas possible.*" He's grinding the van into reverse when two grinning male faces appear in his window.

"*Manu, Manu! Arrête!*" the two men shout, pounding on the glass. "*Balzac! Il est arrivé!*"

Manu cranks the window down. "*Mais c'est pas vrai!*" he cries.

"*Si! Si. Balzac, il est là!*" they answer and all three begin chattering in high-speed French. I listen with every brain cell I have in my head. But it's no use. Four years of advanced placement French in high school. Four years of French composition and French conversation and French civilization in college. And every moment of it, apparently, a total and complete waste of time.

"*Une amie de Margaret, elle s'appelle Amy,*" Manu says, more slowly, when the two newcomers have scrambled into the back of the van. "Amy, these are my friends," he says to me. But does not tell me their names.

"*Bonjour, madame,*" the older one murmurs. He's wearing a thin moustache and a black beret. An actual French person wearing an actual French beret—Kat would go nuts over this. The other man, painfully skinny and much younger, a boy really, just nods, a slight smile on his full, almost girlish, lips.

"Hello," I say. "*Bonjour.*"

"My friends bring fantastic news," says Manu. "A very important *personnage* has arrived. A specialist. He is known as Balzac. He carries the maps to *les catacombes* that I tell you about."

"*Elle vient aussi?*" interrupts Beret Guy.

Manu glances at him, shrugs. "It is essential that we go immediately to meet this Balzac," he says to me. "My friend asks if you will accompany us."

"What?" I say. "I mean, no, I have things I am supposed to be doing. Thank you, but no." Catacombs. Underground, underneath Paris. Are these people insane? Beret Guy's mouth curls into a sneer. He's probably thinking, Good, the last thing we need is a stupid American girl tagging along. I grasp the door handle—I'll just walk home from here.

"*Mais, Amy, c'est vrai?*" says Manu. "I thought you were in search of something—something different. Something special. Not the Paris of the typical tourist. Did you not say this?"

I remove my hand from the door handle. I did say that.

Beret Guy pokes Manu's shoulder. "*Dépêche-toi,*" he hisses.

"If we are to meet this Balzac," Manu continues, ignoring him, "we must go rapidly to the place where he awaits. You can accompany us. If you wish."

Manu smiles at me. Beret Guy glowers. The boy, absorbed in his phone, ignores all three of us. Without a phone, or a computer, I have so much free time now. Time to do things instead of just watching things. "Is that so?"

"Yes. It is so," Manu says.

I watch as the delivery truck driver stacks the last of the lettuce crates on the sidewalk, stretches, rubs the small of his back, takes out a fresh cigarette, and lights up. No one intends to be a lettuce delivery guy. When this man was a little boy, he probably dreamed of becoming a fireman or an astronaut or a doctor. Or, since this is France, a chef. He never could have thought he'd end up delivering salad greens for a living, that one day the most exciting thing that could happen to him would be a tower of blue plastic crates tipping over.

"Amy?" Manu says.

The lettuce delivery guy props himself against the rusting fender of his truck and puffs on his cigarette. He's not old. He's younger than me. Younger than William, than Kat. But his rounded shoulders are old, his pasty skin is old. "That's it," they say. "There is no more than this."

I clear my throat, wrap my arms around my stomach, more protuberant than usual after that humongous lunch. "Okay," I say. Just like that. It pops out of my mouth just like that. "Okay," I say again. "Let's do it."

"Bravo!" Manu cries. He shifts into reverse, roars backwards halfway down the block, and turns left into another narrow street and then right at a traffic light. Soon we are speeding down the same wide boulevard of myriad tiny shops I explored my first day in Paris, which now feels like a month ago. Beret Guy leans forward and speaks rapidly into Manu's ear, from time to time glancing over at me. I pick out a few words. "Catacomb." "Balzac." They are arguing and I'm pretty sure

Manu is taking my side. Weird. Maybe Margaret told him to show a brotherly interest in me, maybe she said to him, "This girl needs help." But Margaret couldn't have meant this. She couldn't think that taking someone down into forbidden catacombs qualifies as "help."

But what does it matter? Kat is gone, William is a million miles away, and I don't have a clue about what will come next, what should come next. Even if I did, I don't want to figure out how to buy a phone in French. I don't want to spend another night alone in my hotel room with a bar of Valrhona chocolate I should not have bought in the first place. I don't want to call William and sit there with the stupid phone clamped to my stupid ear, speechless, no words to explain what I have done, am doing, will do.

Finally Beret Guy shrugs, sits back, and shakes his head. We roll along in silence, Manu surfing the traffic and whistling through his teeth, the boy fiddling with the equipment in the back of the van, and Beret Guy sending regular plumes of acrid cigarette smoke in my direction. When Manu downshifts and enters a narrow street, Beret Guy again leans forward, the smoldering tip of his cigarette a quarter-inch from my earlobe. "*A droite,*" he says in his magnificent voice, a voice like pouring chocolate. We turn right.

For the next couple of minutes Manu follows Beret Guy's commands of "*à droite*" and "*à gauche,*" at length parking in front of a long low cement block building. Maybe we are behind the building because I see neither windows nor doors. "*Superbe,*" the boy says. We all spill out into the silent street.

The air is fresh, especially after Beret Guy's smokefest in the van, and a light rain is falling. In these few days in Paris I have seen more rain than I do in a year in Phoenix. I pull my trench coat out of my tote bag, put it on, and go to stand near a graffiti-scrawled wall. I would bring out Kat's umbrella, too, but it is pink and polka dotted and the guys would no doubt deem it inappropriate to the seriousness of our endeavor. They unload the van, working efficiently, filling two large black plastic garbage bags with hip boots and flashlights and headlamps and lining them up in a neat row next to four fully loaded hiking backpacks.

"*Salut.*"

I step sideways into a puddle that smells like pee. A short man with caterpillar eyebrows and a spade-shaped beard is standing beside the van. He couldn't have emerged from one of the entrance-less and exit-less buildings. We would have heard him if he had arrived by car, or seen him approach if he had come on foot. Nevertheless, there he is, wearing a Chicago Cubs baseball cap, dusty coveralls, and a sardonic grin.

He exchanges swift, sharp handshakes with Manu, Beret Guy, and the boy, looking each of them in the eye for several measuring seconds before nodding. Then he gets to me.

"*Je vous présente Amy*," Manu says. He takes my elbow and draws me forward, out of the pee. "*Elle est américaine*. Amy, this is Balzac."

"*Bonjour*," I say. Though it's late afternoon by now. Shouldn't it be *bon après-midi*?

Balzac's bushy eyebrows bob up and down. "*Bonjour, madame*," he says after a pause. He doesn't shake my hand. He doesn't look me in the eye. He just stands there, arms folded across his sunken chest, taking in my shiny black boots, crisp white blouse, stylish trench coat, and long loose hair. Okay, so I'm not dressed for cave exploring. Spelunking, whatever. But this Balzac person can't make them just abandon me, here, all alone in this creepy deserted warehouse district, can he? The lunchtime oysters do a raucous cha-cha-cha in my stomach.

"I won't be any trouble," I say, hoping no one will realize that claiming you'll be no trouble usually just means you will in fact be trouble. Manu squeezes my elbow. Balzac looks me up and down one more time and then shakes his head, shrugs, and turns to the backpacks.

"*Ça y est*," Manu says, winking at me.

Thank God. They're going to let me come with.

Balzac only glances at the backpacks but makes them empty both garbage bags so he can check out each headlamp, each flashlight, each hip boot. The boy watches his every move, jouncing on the balls of his feet, fists jammed into jeans pockets. Beret Guy sniggers, lights a fresh cigarette, and lounges against the graffiti wall, not seeming to care that he's standing in pee. Manu trots up and down the empty street, whistling a tune that sounds like Yankee Doodle Dandy. I dig in my tote bag as unobtrusively as possible for an elastic band to fasten my hair into a businesslike bun at the base of my neck. Finally, Balzac straightens. "Okay, *on y va*," he mutters.

Va? But where? There are no doors in any of the buildings. The only vehicle present is the van, which they just emptied. I look up, half expecting to see a helicopter swoop up and drop down a ladder for us. We stand there like idiots for several moments until the boy exclaims, "Aha!" and points across the street to a manhole, its iron lid rolled to one side, the round open mouth black as a puddle of molasses. No one noticed it before.

In seconds we are standing in a ring around the manhole—four men, four backpacks, two garbage bags, and me. I lean forward a little and peer down. Beyond the first five rungs of a metal ladder, I see nothing. Only blackness.

It has stopped raining. In fact, the clouds have dissolved to wisps, and the sun, now low over the rooftops, is warming our faces. The glassy wet pavement, the gauzy pale sky, the graffiti-covered buildings— everything around us seems suddenly sad, beautiful, seductive, nostalgic. Even Manu glances wistfully toward the empty van.

"*Alors, mes enfants*," Balzac says. "*Allons-y*." Let's go.

The boy moves first, donning the largest backpack and flashing a thumbs-up as he scampers down the ladder. As soon as a faint "*Allo*" wafts from the opening, Beret Guy ties one of the bulging garbage bags to a nylon rope and lowers it into the hole. A minute later he pulls up the rope, now empty, and ties it to the other bag. After a second "*Allo*," he allows the entire rope to drop into the hole, shrugs into a backpack, the smallest one, and clambers down the ladder, a cigarette dangling from his lips. Manu, who is already strapped into a backpack, the second-largest one, quickly follows. The sun slips behind the rooftops and the blackness of the hole turns, if possible, blacker. I am starting to get a bad feeling.

"*Madame. Je vous en prie*," Balzac says, jerking his head toward the manhole and tapping the remaining backpack, medium sized, with the toe of his hiking boot.

I don't know what that means but I stuff my tote bag into an outside pocket of the backpack and struggle to put it on. I peer again into the manhole. You know, I don't have to go. No one is going to make me. In fact, they would probably rather I didn't.

"*Madame*," Balzac repeats, sighing.

I consider my options. Or rather, lack thereof. Walking back to the hotel is impossible, because we are miles out somewhere in the suburbs. Calling a cab is impossible, because I don't have a frigging phone. Waiting here alone for them to come back is impossible, too, because this street is creepy and deserted.

I said I wanted to come. I said I wanted to do something different, out of the ordinary. And the new Amy, Amy 2.0, would go on just such a lunatic expedition as this.

So all righty then. I flash Balzac a toothy American grin, just to be annoying. Then I turn, kneel, locate the first rung of the ladder with the pointy toe of my Barbie boot, and start down. On the fifth rung, my eyes even with the level of the street, I pause to glance down. Nothing. I can't see even my feet. The molasses blackness is swallowing me—calves, knees, thighs—like a ravening beast. This is truly insane.

"*Dépêche-toi,*" Balzac barks, his mud-caked boots inches from my face. Hurry up. That's what that means—hurry up. Huh. If I stayed in France long enough I might finally become fluent in French.

I hurry down a dozen rungs, and then cannot help pausing to again look up. A perfect circle of ultramarine sky looks back down at me. It's not too late. All I have to do is climb up instead of down, up into the open air, up into the still beautiful world. Not even Kat, much less the new and improved Amy, would do such a crazy thing, venture into catacombs, illegal ones at that, with a ragtag collection of bozos she's known for five minutes. I rapidly move up seven rungs. This is better, go toward the light, not away from it—but just at that moment the smooth ultramarine circle of sky is obliterated by the wrinkled brown lump of Balzac, who leaps into the hole like a mountain goat and slides the lid shut with an eardrum-piercing clang. Darkness rushes in on me from all sides.

"Ow! Hey!"

Balzac has stepped on my thumb.

"*Mais qu'est-ce qu'il y a?*" His voice is rough.

I strain to see, but the only light is an asparagus-thin spear of sun falling from an opening in the center of the manhole cover. "Nothing, it's nothing," I mutter and start again climbing downwards, counting the rungs because that's what William would do. Ten, eleven. The air is soft, heavy, damp, thick—the polar opposite of the hard thin crisp desert air of Phoenix, which I have always hated but which now in my memory seems fragrant and life-giving. Fifteen, sixteen.

On rung thirty-four, I allow myself another brief pause to look down. For the first time I see, far below, a light fluttering in the blackness. Wait. Now it's gone. Better not to look again. Better not to know what's in store for you.

How deep are we going? Apparently, deep. I am on rung number fifty-five, my eyes squeezed as tightly shut as possible, when Manu speaks into my ear. "Two more steps, Amy," he says, his warm hands grasping my wrists. I open my eyes and reel back, blinded by the light from his headlamp. "*Pardon*," he murmurs and points the headlamp away. Like a Boy Scout assisting an old lady, he helps me off the ladder and guides me through a narrow corridor and into a large room. Not a cave, a regular room with smooth block walls and a soaring cross-vaulted ceiling. Beret Guy and the boy are standing in the middle of the space, strobing their flashlights around and yipping like coyotes.

I blink and rub my eyes. Idiots. I am on an idiotic adventure with idiots. Smiling, Manu fits a headlamp over my hair and switches it on. Balzac could have done that. He could have given me some light.

"Thank you, Manu. *Merci*," I say.

That was weird. The sound of my voice was snuffed out almost before it left my mouth.

"*Merci*," I repeat, and it happens again. My words flare like a flame and then disappear.

Balzac strides past us. In addition to not wearing a backpack, he's not wearing a headlamp, is not even carrying a flashlight. He must love darkness, thrive in it, like a mole, like a roach. He scans the area, nods, pulls a battered silver flask out of his hip pocket, takes a swig, and passes it to Manu, who wipes the lip of the flask on his sleeve and offers it to me first. It smells like whiskey. Maybe brandy.

But by this time I am stone cold sober and want to stay that way. "No thanks, I'm not thirsty," I say, and the "ee" of "thirsty" is chopped off as if by a blade. Something is eating my words. Manu was right, this is an alien universe. A foreign, sound-devouring universe light-years away from boring old Planet Earth, from people and relationships and worry and guilt and love and the future.

The boy declines the flask also, and instead starts to gather up the litter. Empty water bottles, crumpled sandwich wrappers, used plastic food containers—the room, otherwise quite beautiful, is strewn with it.

"I'll help you," I say, and the boy winks at me. He has mile-long thick black eyelashes. "Why are beautiful lashes always wasted on the male of the species?" Kat used to wonder.

As we work the boy glances over at me from time to time and smiles, and for that moment we are comrades. It feels good to toil alongside someone, to share a common purpose, even if we can't carry on a conversation. Since the layoff my labor has been pretty much solo. But when all the litter is stuffed into one of the black garbage bags the boy goes to join the others, standing next to Beret Guy and accepting a cigarette. He doesn't look at me. No one looks at me. They just stand there and smoke, taking turns with the flask, silently contemplating the five pairs of rubber hip boots lined up in the center of this well-constructed and almost cathedral-like space. Bet they wouldn't be so stiff and formal if I weren't here. Bet I'm cramping their style.

Well, too bad.

Balzac takes a last swig of whatever-it-is, Beret Guy flicks his cigarette to the floor, the floor we just tidied, and without any discussion the men begin to pull on the rubber hip boots. Manu selects a pair, helps me into them, and hands me a flashlight.

"Thank you," I whisper. Manu is the perfect gentleman. The others probably think I'm sleeping with him. As if. No one who saw William could possibly think I would settle for Manu.

When the boots are donned and the backpacks adjusted we stand in a line facing Balzac, like recruits ready to receive their orders. We are all pathetic to be putting ourselves in the hands of this grubby little man. I glance at the passageway leading back to the ladder. Even now it's not too late to back out. I could just stay here in this elegant and now orderly space, and wait for them to return. I could snack on the *macarons* that Margaret insisted I take with me and just sit, just think about things.

But before I can open my mouth to say, "Listen, I've changed my mind," Balzac plucks a long thin silver flashlight out of an inner pocket of his coveralls and glides through the arched mouth of one of several tunnels leading from the room. Manu scurries after him, gesturing to me to follow. I have to jog to catch up, almost stumbling in the cumbersome hip boots. Beret Guy takes the place behind me and the boy brings up the rear.

At first the passageway is as wide and flat as a supermarket aisle. The white stone walls are solid and smooth, and a white stone ceiling arches fifteen feet above our heads. The hip boots seem like overkill. You could trot along here in flip flops. For what feels like a very long time we keep to this main tunnel, bypassing numerous smaller side tunnels and openings. Some of the doorways reveal caverns strewn with antique-looking machinery. William, who loves anything mechanical and anything old, would want to relish, inspect, marvel, but Balzac sets a brisk pace. One time he does allow us to stop and peer into a narrow passageway that is hip deep in loose bones. Femurs, pelvises, ribs, skulls. Human bones, their deaths uncounted, uncatalogued, uncategorized. After that no one talks for a while.

Several hundred yards after the bones Balzac takes the first turn. A right, then a left, then a right. A right again. Occasionally Manu gestures to numbers stenciled in black on the white stone walls. Eighteen ninety-one. Seventeen seventy-five.

"They are dates of construction," he explains when Balzac halts the party at a star-shaped intersection of five passageways.

"And do you see?" Manu continues, the "ee" of "see" cut short by the hungry rock. "Here?" He trains his headlamp on the words "rue Sainte-Agnès" stenciled in black gothic letters on the keystone of an archway. "We are indeed beneath the rue Sainte-Agnès," he says. "Many of these tunnels mirror the streets above. Rather, the streets as they were at the time the catacombs have been built. It is a living map of history."

Living? But nothing down here is living. Or if it is, it keeps to the shadows. No flutterings of bats or scuttlings of rats. It seems clean down here, actually. The smells are mineral smells, chalk and limestone and plaster. Balzac draws a sheaf of papers out of his coveralls and trains his flashlight on it. "The map," Manu whispers reverently. No one moves or speaks as Balzac squints at the rumpled pages. At this point none of us would have the faintest hope of finding the way out without him. We know it. He knows it. In real life Balzac is probably a mailroom clerk, or a dishwasher, or a janitor. Assuming he has a job and is not just unemployed and living in his mother's basement. But down here, that doesn't matter. Down here, he's the man.

Balzac nods, restuffs the map into his coveralls, and leads us into a three-foot-wide passageway that after a dozen yards narrows to two feet and then starts to slope steeply downward. I am not cold anymore. I am sweating. I unbutton the trench coat and my white cotton blouse shines like a beacon in the flittering beams of the flashlights and headlamps. Ha. Spelunkers do not wear white—they wear dirty, potato-colored clothing, like Balzac. I quicken my pace to keep up with Manu, round a hairpin turn, and step into a puddle.

"*Attention*," Balzac calls over his shoulder.

Soon we are knee-deep in cold clear water. The hip boots no longer feel like overkill. Worse, the stone floor beneath the water is littered with rocks and pebbles and God knows what else, and the walls, giving off a slight mist, are slippery with condensation. I clutch my flashlight with my left hand, palm the slick wall with my right, and slide my rubber-booted feet along the treacherous floor with care. Whatever happens, I must not fall. My passport, my airplane confirmation, my cash—all are fragile paper products and all are in my money belt under my jeans. Ruin those and I'd be screwed.

After what feels like hours of sloshing, Manu slows. "*Enfin*," he murmurs. He turns to me. "*Tu vois?*" he says.

I crane my neck to peer over his shoulder. I do see. Hallelujah. Just ahead, a white stone stairway leads up out of the water. Balzac is already on the fifth step. One by one, we squish after him and emerge, dripping, into a dry cavern. Black as espresso, of course, but dry.

"*On fait une pause ici,*" Balzac announces and seats himself on a footstool-sized white stone. He leans back against a wall, crosses his legs, lights a cigarette. He's not fit-looking, not athletic-seeming in the least, but then again he's not out of breath and wheezing like the rest of us either.

I'm looking for my own stone footstool to sit on when Manu calls out what sounds like a "Wah-ooo!"

"*Venez voir!*" he shouts. Come look. "*C'est si* cool!"

I locate him with my flashlight. Beret Guy and the boy have already rushed to join him and all three men are tracking their beams over a far wall. As I reach Manu's side one of the circles of light picks out a bare ass. Not an actual bare ass. A depiction of one. We join our beams to see what's connected to the ass and more body parts appear. Arms.

Legs. Hair. A swinging penis. More bare asses. Bellies, buttocks, breasts. It's a picture—or rather, a mural. A twelve-foot-high, twenty-foot-wide mural of an orgy.

Wait. Not an orgy. It's hell.

Someone has painted a full-color mural of hell, or his idea of it, on the rough rock wall here deep inside the somber and silent earth. Not so far, when you think about it, from actual hell. Naked, wild-eyed, wild-haired men and women writhe and weep, scream and supplicate. Some wrestle with horned fork-tailed demons. Some tumble with out-flung limbs into seething fiery pits. One, a cartoonishly voluptuous female, huge boobs, tiny waist, wide hips, reaches upward with claw-like fingers, her pointed nails painted blood red, almost but not quite catching the plump pink hand of a smiling cherub reaching down from his plump pink cloud.

"Sheet," Beret Guy says, taking a phone from his shirt pocket and starting to snap pictures. His flash illuminates our inky surroundings like summer heat lightning.

It's not an adept painting, as my college art history professor would have said. The foreshortening is off. The use of negative space is naive. The depiction is hackneyed. But the work is large, ambitious, epic even, and must have taken the artist many months and much dedication to complete. Just transporting the supplies down here would have been a huge effort.

"*Tiens. Regardez le joli chien,*" the boy exclaims. He is training his flashlight on the lower right hand corner of the mural. And there it is, a very *joli chien* indeed, another beagle, black and tan and white, sporting a red leather collar, sitting up on its hind legs, and waving its forepaws as if in joyous expectation of a treat. It's the best part of the painting because it's not just any beagle, but a real, true, individual beagle. The naked men and women are anonymous, generic. You don't care if they are saved or damned, but this hound loves and is loved. William has always wanted to get a dog. He suggested it again the day after Kat's funeral. But while I love dogs, they are just another responsibility really, another chain to tie you down to a life you are not sure you want to lead.

A leaden drop of icy water lands on the top of my head. Balzac waves his flashlight at us from the far side of the room. "*Alors, mes enfants, on y va,*" he calls, indicating the wide mouth of a new tunnel, this one marked with a large red arrow painted on the wall.

When Balzac says *"va,"* you *"va."* We turn and trot after him like beagles, Beret Guy cursing as he pockets his phone. The new tunnel narrows after a few yards but thankfully it stays dry. How far have we come? I should have been somehow keeping track, counting my steps, keeping track of the lefts and rights, marking our trail with crumbs of *macarons*. William would. Assuming, of course, that William would have joined this little expedition, which he would not. Not in a million trillion years. William would have asked pertinent questions, weighed pros and cons, spun likely scenarios, and then chuckled and said, "Count me out, guys."

A couple hundred yards later the ceiling starts to lower. Or the floor gets higher. Soon we are duckwalking, elbows jabbing into the no-longer smooth walls. This tunnel was roughly cut into the raw rock, the way you expect tunnels to be, and has bundles of electrical cables running along the ceiling. Something pointy in my pack shifts and pokes me in the nape of my neck. This pack is too heavy for me. It was probably meant for Balzac, or Beret Guy. I am trying to shift the pack's weight when we round a corner and ahead of me Manu stumbles over a watermelon-sized rock, falling forward onto his hands and knees.

"Merde!"

"Manu! Are you okay?" I squat beside him. "Are you hurt?"

"Je suis—" He is pressing his palm to his temple.

"Qu'est-ce qu'il y a?" Beret Guy demands.

What is the what? But he's not addressing me or Manu. He is scowling at Balzac, who is crouched a dozen feet ahead of us and methodically sweeping his flashlight beam back and forth over the three walls. Three. We've reached a dead end. Thank God. Now we'll have no choice but to turn around, retrace our steps, and duckwalk the holy hell out of here. Not a moment too soon. Manu is bleeding and I am trembling with fatigue, from headlamp to hip boot.

"Ah," Balzac murmurs with satisfaction.

"Merde," Manu says again, this time louder because Balzac is shining his flashlight on a small rectangular hole hacked into the base of one of the walls. He looks around to make sure we all see it, and then throws himself onto his belly and wriggles head first into the opening.

"C'est pas possible," Beret Guy moans as Balzac's boots flip-flop out of view.

But it is possible. Manu squints at me. A black trickle of blood is jagging across his cheek and his face is ashen. He needs bandaging, and a break. We all need a break, and a drink of water. But Balzac, and the maps, and any chance we have of ever getting out of here dead or alive are moving farther away with every passing second.

"Go," I say to him. "Follow." The easiest choice is always when you have no choice.

"*Merde,*" Manu says a third time. Then he casts me a swift look of apology, struggles out of his backpack, shoves it into the hole, and belly-crawls after it. In seconds he is gone.

Our Father who art in heaven. I sit back on my heels and slowly unbuckle the belt of my pack, slowly unhook the straps from my shoulders. It's a hole the size of a placemat and I am supposed to crawl into it. Without thinking about scorpions, or black widows, or tarantulas. Without thinking at all. Don't pause, don't plan, don't hope, don't pray. Just move and do. I am slowly swinging the pack around in front of me when I feel a tap on my leg.

I jump, smacking the top of my head on the low ceiling of the tunnel, but the wildly swinging beam of my headlamp reveals only the pale oval face of the boy. He is gesturing to my coat. My lovely brand new fingertip-length black trench coat. Of course. Belly-crawling into this filthy wormhole will destroy the poor thing for sure. The boy holds out a thick gray hoodie. Beret Guy snorts and huffs, like an impatient dray animal.

"Thank you," I say, my words snuffed out, as usual, the instant they leave my mouth. "*Merci.*" I remove my coat and pass it to the boy, who crams it into a top pocket of his backpack. He also takes my flashlight and stows it into my pack for me while I tug his hoodie over my no-longer-clean-white blouse. The hoodie, still warm from the boy's body, smells like cigarettes and sweat and male adolescent hormones. Not like vanilla.

"*Allez-y, madame,*" the boy says. "*N'ayez pas peur.*"

Go forward, madam, do not fear. My French is getting better by the minute. I crawl on all fours to the crude opening and peer in. No choice. I can't go back to what was. I can't stay here with what is. I have to go forward, into the what-nobody-knows.

"*Bouge-toi!*" Move. Beret Guy pushes me aside and throws himself forward into the opening. One of his flailing rubber-booted feet whaps me on the knee just as it disappears.

The boy and I exchange a look. "*Allez-y, madame,*" he repeats, smiling at me. I try to smile back but the muscles of my face refuse to cooperate. Actually, none of my muscles want any part in what's happening here, but I answer—because I have to answer—"*Oui.*" I have to slide my pack into the opening, I have to push the pack inside as far as I can, I have to lie down flat on my almost flat stomach. And I have to crawl inside. Balzac, Manu, and Beret Guy are already out of sight. Whatever sound they are making is being devoured by the insatiable rock. Thy kingdom come, thy will be done. I come on to all fours, and hesitate.

"*Madame,*" the boy repeats behind me, his voice barely audible, and then he pats me on the bottom. A shiver flitters up my spine. No one but William has patted me on the bottom, patted me anywhere, for a long time. Kat loved my bottom. "You've got the most irresistible heart-shaped ass," she used to tell me, "you've got an ass shaped like a valentine."

If we get lost down here and starve, if the wormhole collapses on us and buries us alive, if we fall into a subterranean lake and drown, if we are slain and eaten by carnivorous cave creatures, the last friendly human touch I will have experienced will be this shy boy's hand on my valentine butt. I drop down and wriggle forward into the sphincter-like hole.

It's a snug fit even for skinny French people. The only way to advance is to drag yourself by your elbows in a side-to-side shimmying motion. With each shimmy one of your hips smashes against a rock wall. Shimmy right, smash. Shimmy left, smash. After only a dozen yards my hipbones are numb and my forearms are sore, despite the boy's thick hoodie. Worse, this passageway is not straight. It meanders, it zigs and zags like a snake.

Snakes. God. I increase my pace, shimmying as fast as I can, which is why at the next sharp bend I don't see the protruding rock in time. It shatters my headlamp and I am again plunged into blackness. Blackness as absolute and indelible as India ink. Blackness with no top, no bottom, no right, no left.

Is Beret Guy still somewhere up ahead? Is the boy somewhere still behind? I listen but all I can hear is the staccato thudding of my own heart. My legs, heavy, remote, encased like sausages in the hip boots, stiffen as the chill of the stone seeps through the rubber and into my flesh. I bury my face in the sleeve of the boy's hoodie.

My breathing slows to a stop. This is what it feels like to be dead. This is what it feels like to be Kat. And it's not so bad, not really. It's restful, peaceful—it's even, crazily, a way to stay in Paris permanently. I could just disappear into this mighty silence. No one would miss me.

Except for William.

Because maybe he would come looking for me. Maybe he would check my Internet history, track me to Paris, go to the Hôtel du Cheval Blanc. But there he would quickly reach a dead end. He doesn't know I met Margaret. He could never imagine that I would dare to penetrate the forbidden underworld of Paris. No sane person would ever attempt such a thing, and William thinks I am sane. He thinks he married a sensible woman with a paid-for house, a college degree, money in the bank, and a not-bad job. People with all that, people with their heads on their shoulders, don't volunteer to go on preposterous adventures with strange men.

William, who thinks he knows me, would never find out what happened to me. "It's the not-knowing that's the hardest to bear," Kat remarked while we were awaiting the results of her first biopsy. "It's always better to know a thing, even if that thing turns out to be really bad."

William would lose me the way I lost Kat. Forever and for no good reason.

"Amy?"

I suck in a long deep breath. It sounds like my name.

"Amy?"

It is my name. I shudder from the soles of my feet to the crown of my head, panting, burying my face deeper into the sleeve of the boy's hoodie, trying to be one with the rock, invisible, immovable. But when something touches my forearm I scream and rear up, scraping my chin on the rough floor of the wormhole.

"Amy! *C'est Manu!*"

For the second time I am blinded by Manu's headlamp. It's Manu, only Manu, rescuing me once again.

"Amy," he says in a lower voice. "*Encore un tout petit peu.*" Just a little more.

He is surprisingly strong for a little guy. He drags me forward until I start to crawl on my own, and then he stays with me, shimmying backward and murmuring encouragement, until my head emerges into a room, where he pulls me to my feet. I sway, nauseated and light-headed, and someone rushes to my side to support me. Beret Guy, it's Beret Guy who helps me. Go figure. Both men lead me to a wooden stool, where I sit and blink until I am used to the light.

I am seated in an airy space roughly the size and shape of the bedroom at home William calls a nursery. Unlike the nursery, though, this room is furnished. The stool I am on is one of eight, made of the same blond wood as the long rectangular table that dominates the room. An ornate silver candelabrum glitters at each end of the table. Above our heads an equally ornate chandelier flutters with multiple tiers of tea lights.

All this would be amazing enough but there's more: The walls are covered with flowers. Painted flowers, hundreds of them, thousands, wall to wall, floor to ceiling. Roses, tulips. Daisies, peonies, geraniums. Lilacs, lilies. Carnations. Forget-me-nots. Hydrangeas. Jubilant, exuberant, joyful flowers that some artist, I would bet not the hell-mural artist, painted with love and care onto the silent and uncomplaining dry white rock.

"Do not cry, Amy," Manu says, unbuckling my smashed headlamp and lifting it off.

"I'm not crying." But when I wipe my face with my hand it comes away wet.

"*Bienvenue au paradis, chère madame,*" intones Balzac from across the room. He is standing at a camp stove, stirring something in a large blue-and-white-speckled kettle. Rule number thirty of the perpetual diet: Only eat when you're hungry. And I am not hungry. I'm still full from Margaret's lunch of oysters and trout. But the room, I now realize, is filled with a heavenly aroma of Thanksgiving, of family, of home. Beret Guy nods at me as if to say, "You see?" and starts to set places at the table with white plastic knives and forks and white paper napkins. Manu extracts three bottles of wine from my backpack and waves them over his head like a prizefighter. The boy—where had he been all this time?—emerges from the wormhole.

"*Enfin!*" says Manu. Someone has bandaged the wound on his forehead with white gauze. "*Et les verres?*" he adds.

The boy opens his backpack, digs around in it, and shakes his head. Manu turns to Beret Guy, who shrugs. He raises his eyebrows at Balzac, who doesn't notice.

Les verres. Our intrepid band of brothers remembered to bring food and wine and candles and plates and knives and forks and napkins on our adventure. However, apparently they forgot to bring glasses.

But Balzac just grins, grabs one of the bottles, and in a single neat motion twists out the cork with his Swiss army knife. He passes the bottle to me.

I shake my head. My throat is as dry as the Salt River and I am dying for a drink. Of water, not wine. But Manu is nodding encouragingly, his white bandage luminescent in the candlelight, and Beret Guy is pantomiming drinking. They are all smiling and nodding and licking their lips. And the fragrance of the wine—plum, cloves, black pepper, raisin—makes my stomach growl so loudly that everyone laughs.

I take a sip. "Bravo!" Manu says. His voice, all our voices, are more normal in this small space.

When we've all had a taste of the wine, which is smooth and strong and (Margaret would agree) strengthening, Beret Guy takes a stack of apple-red metal plates over to Balzac, who fills them with lentils and places a large chicken leg on the top. The boy sets the plates around the table, and everyone takes a place at the table. Balzac is the first to pick up his plastic knife in his right hand and his fork in his left, but he does not start eating. He smiles a lopsided yellow smile, and nods to me.

Normally I need to know exactly what's in the food I consume. Normally I calculate the fat, the fiber, the protein. Normally I consider what I had for my last meal, what I am planning to eat for my next, and ask myself, about any food, any drink, Is this going to make me fat? But Manu, Beret Guy, the boy, and Balzac are waiting for me to begin. They sit obediently, expectantly, as if I am the lady of the house and they are my guests, as if I am the mother and they are my children.

So I say, "*Bon appétit,*" and attempt a forkful of lentils.

Which are garlicky and bacony and creamy. Who knew lentils, bland old flying-saucer-shaped lentils, could be so awesome?

To keep myself from gobbling them all down at once I saw off a morsel of the chicken and pop it into my mouth. Lord. Balzac's chicken is even better than the chicken at the mahogany restaurant. Darker, juicier, richer, more succulent, more luscious, more nuanced. It's the most amazing chicken I have ever tasted.

"*Le confit de canard*," Manu remarks with approval, "*est excellent.*"

It's duck. Not chicken. Duck. Unbelievable. I am drinking wine and eating duck in a candlelit flowered stone subterranean dining room with a crew of filthy, literally, Frenchmen. Not your usual tourist bullshit. I accept the bottle Manu is offering me and take a hearty swig of wine.

"Does it please you?" Balzac asks.

He speaks English?

"Oh yes. It's very good. Wonderful," I stammer. "*Très bien. Magnifique,*" I add, taking another bite of warm lentils.

Naturally, there is bread, too, mangled yet still delicious, that the men use to sop up every last morsel of food. My mother raised me to believe that wiping your plate with your bread is bad manners but everyone is doing it and so I do too. Bread, lentils, meat. So much for the don't-combine-carbs-and-protein rule. Not to mention rule number thirty-one of the perpetual diet: Two-thirds of your dinner should be green vegetables.

But diets, deprivation, discipline, denial, none of that crap means a thing now. Not down here, not to daring catacomb explorers, not to Amy 2.0, not to the Amy who says yes. We eat mindfully, savoring our meal, which now seems like the point of the whole expedition. Balzac asks, in pretty good English, where I am from and if Paris pleases me so far. I answer, in pretty good French, that Paris is amazing and all three men brighten. Beret Guy compliments my pronunciation. The boy passes me the bottle. Manu beams like a proud uncle.

At length, when the kettle is empty and the wine gone, the boy repacks the gear and Balzac begins to blow out the candles in the candelabra and the tea lights in the chandelier. One by one, the flames gutter and die. Maybe now is the time to feel afraid but I don't feel afraid. Not at all.

We watch in silence as the final dancing flame is extinguished and the blackness settles around us like a soft feather quilt.

No one stirs, or sniffs, or shifts, or shuffles his feet. I lace my hands together in my lap and let my breathing slow and deepen. A draft is coming from somewhere and has cleared the room of cooking odors but the tang of lentils and duck and wine is still on my tongue. And Kat, God forgive me, is on my mind. Because if Kat were anywhere, it would be here, in this magical underground bower. It stands to reason. This is the kind of place Kat would choose to hang out in.

So come on then, girl. Send me a word. A touch. A breath. A thought. Something. Anything.

I stare into the blackness until my eyes burn. I listen until my ears pound. Nothing. Of course nothing. Kat is gone forever. The only thing here is pure darkness, a darkness so tangible, so palpable, so alive, so friendly, that it holds me upright in place.

We sit for a long, long while. It's why we have come. For the blackness, the silence, the absence so absent that it is present.

Finally someone, maybe Manu, sighs a deep, satisfied sigh. Balzac murmurs, *"Eh bien,"* and strikes a match. It blazes, and everyone blinks. He lets the match burn almost to his fingertips and then blows it out and clicks on his flashlight, aiming it at the floor so as not to dazzle anybody. The boy, sitting across the table from me, grins, his teeth flashing whitely.

"It washes your head, no?" he says.

"It does, yes," I say.

"It makes one feel new. Like a *bébé*," he adds, blushing.

"Yes," I say again. So. Not a tomb. A womb. I feel myself grinning at him. What a nice kid he is.

We are suddenly on the move, stowing flashlights, strapping on headlamps (Manu supplies me with a spare), picking up backpacks and shoving them back into the wormhole. I take the spot between Balzac and Manu this time, and this time we stay within sight of each other. My poor sore hipbones again smash into the craggy rock walls with every shimmy but my backpack, now that the wine bottles are empty, is a lot lighter. The total distance is probably only around fifty yards. Still, think of all the shimmies it took to transport the components of the table and chairs, the chandelier and the candelabra and the camp stove. Not to mention the supplies for painting the flowers.

All in all, the belly crawl is less horrible the second time around but it is still a thing of joy to emerge, caked with quarry dirt, into the low-ceilinged passageway. Manu and Beret Guy shake hands. The boy kisses me on both cheeks. Balzac smiles beneficently at each one of us in turn. We struggle once more into our backpacks and resume our old order, Balzac, Manu, me, Beret Guy, and the boy. Even duckwalking, we move briskly, fluidly. Maybe it's the *confit de canard* but it's probably the wine. When we reach the hell mural room Balzac lets us stop so Beret Guy can take all the time he needs to snap pictures.

We are clustered in front of the mural when the boy holds up his hand. "*Attention*," he whispers, indicating the doorway behind us. We turn to see a thin shaft of light penetrate the room, followed by a young blond man and an even younger dark-haired girl.

"*Hallo*," the blond man says. He is panting. "The police. Have you seen the police?" He is wearing jeans and a black T-shirt, no boots, no headlamp, no backpack, and the girl is wearing elaborate zombie make-up, a red mini-dress and, yes, flip flops. They are both soaked to the waist and carry a single flashlight between them. The zombie girl, who looks fourteen but could be twenty, is clutching a label-less bottle of wine.

"Police?" says Manu. His voice is skeptical. "Where?"

"Behind. We heard feets, we saw lights." He is not French. German maybe. "We came away, very fast." He glances over his shoulder. The zombie girl covers her mouth with her hand and giggles, like a girl in a cartoon, like Betty Boop.

"You ran?" I ask.

"*Ja*," says the blond man, nodding. "We ran like—like rats."

"Tee-hee," the zombie girl giggles, and gazes up at him adoringly.

"*Les touristes*," Balzac snorts, shaking his head.

The two grin at each other and turn toward the tunnel marked with the red arrow. Are they headed for the secret flower room?

"It's a dead end down there," I call after them. "You won't be able to go any farther." They pause and look back, hesitating.

"Come along with us," I say. These stupid people are not worthy of the flower room. What do they know about the absolution of silence? What do they know about the elegance of the void? The zombie girl takes a step toward us but the blond man grabs her arm and whispers in her ear.

She giggles again. Manu glances at me and shrugs. The flower room is not a secret. Of course it isn't. "Ciao, you guys," the zombie girl calls over her shoulder as she trots after the man. She thinks she knows what she wants.

Balzac is already moving toward the exit. We have to hustle to catch up but again the return trip seems shorter, easier, faster, as return trips always seem to do, though when we get to the knee-deep water it is not any less hazardous than before.

I am concentrating on maintaining my footing when I hear voices. Not the young German man. Not the zombie girl. Men. Many men.

"Police!" someone yells.

I stop and clutch at the slick wet wall.

"*Police! Arrêtez!*" Beams ten times brighter than our puny headlamps bleach the tunnel an excruciating white.

Behind me Beret Guy mutters, "*Merde!*" Ahead, Balzac wheels around, his shoulder striking Manu, who tips backwards into me. I try to stay on my feet and turn to run because that is what everyone else is doing, that is what Manu, who has righted himself and is sloshing past me, is doing. But my heel hits a bed of loose gravel, I lose my tenuous grip on the wall, my left foot shoots forward, my right foot shoots backward, I twist, flail, and go down. Face first.

Icy water gushes down my neck. Fills my rubber hip boots. Soaks through the boy's thick hoodie and into my blouse and my jeans and the money belt under my jeans. The water weighs me down, pulls me down. I struggle to the surface, cough, gasp for air, and reach for Manu, for Beret Guy, for the boy, for the wall, for anything. But my hair has come out of its bun and long sodden strands are covering my face and the stone floor is slippery and the diamond-brilliant lights are strobing and the police officers are shouting. Everywhere there is water and light and sound.

And I am heavy. So heavy. As if I have gained a hundred pounds in five seconds. My feet skid across the gravel again and I go down again, this time swallowing an enormous mineral-y mouthful of frigid, frothing water.

twenty-four

"GOOD MORNING, sleepyhead!" Margaret looks up beaming from her crossword puzzle.

It is good. Sunshine pours through the lace curtains and bathes the room in crisp lemony light. I am dry and warm. And hungry.

"I'm glad you're still able to smile," Margaret says, putting her puzzle aside. "Despite that rather nasty bruise on your forehead."

I touch my temple. However bad it might look, it's nothing compared to the saucer-sized black and blue marks on my hips. "I'm fine. Really. Is it late? What time is it?" I pad barefoot across the plushy chocolate and robin's egg blue Aubusson carpet and curl up in the leather armchair next to the hearth, where Margaret has a small fire going. "Actually, what day is it?"

"Saturday. Half ten. Good for you. You needed a lovely long lie-in." Margaret springs to her feet. "I'll put the kettle on straightaway. And what may I offer you for *petit déjeuner*? I have porridge," she calls from the kitchen. "And bread. Also, fresh croissants." She appears in the doorway brandishing an oil-stained white paper sack.

Saturday? How did it get to be Saturday? "I think, a croissant," I say, my pulse quickening. "Of course. Please."

Margaret's smile crinkles her face like a raisin. "Bravo."

I hug my knees to my chest. Yesterday a law-breaking trespasser held by the French police. Today a pampered guest in a French home. I stroke the silken hem of the blue-and-white-striped robe I'm wearing, the robe that, with its matching tea-length nightgown, was laid out on the bed in the guestroom, waiting for me, when Margaret brought me home last night. "This is beautiful."

"The dressing gown? It suits you. Keep it," Margaret says. She places a mustard yellow teapot on the table and looks at me. "It complements your beautiful baby blue eyes."

Keep it? I'd like to keep it all. The silk robe and nightgown, the cherry wood dining table with fluted legs and matching chairs, the marble fireplace, the hammered copper side table, the tole lampshades, the needlepoint footstool. This room, this apartment, this building, this street, this city. I yawn, hugely, and stretch.

Margaret sits down at the table and gestures to me to join her. "So, darling," she says, pouring out the tea, "how is it that you ever came to go down into the catacombs with that wretched band of blackguards?"

I add milk and sugar to my cup. It's automatic now, it's the only way I will ever drink tea ever again. "I'm not sure exactly. I ran into Manu on your stairs. He offered to drive me to my hotel and on the way we met his friends and one thing led to another."

"Tell me all about it. Tell me everything. I am agog."

By the time I finish describing Beret Guy and Balzac and the boy, the labyrinth of underground passages, the hellfire and damnation mural, the terrifying wormhole shimmy, the enchanted flowered room, the mouthwatering repast of lentils and *confit de canard*, the young German man and his zombie girlfriend, the appearance of the police and the ensuing panic, we are on our second pot of tea and settled in front of the flickering fire.

"Were there rats?" Margaret shudders. "I cannot bear rats."

"No, no rats. No bats. No bugs, no slugs. It was pretty clean really." Impossible to convey the awesomeness of the catacombs. The total blackness. The total silence. The total peace.

"Bones? Did you see bones?"

"We did. Some."

"And the boys abandoned you when the police arrived? Even Manu?" Margaret's cheeks are hot pink and her eyes are sparkling.

"It was a big huge mess. Bright lights flashing, lots of shouting and splashing. I lost my balance and fell. It's no one's fault. Maybe they thought I got away, somehow." I cradle my mug of tea in both hands and study the fire. No way can I pin the blame on Manu, or on anyone. It was my choice to go. I'm an adult, free to make life choices. Or not.

"The police were actually very nice," I add.

They were. They didn't file charges against me. They didn't even fine me. After a brief questioning, in English, they wrapped me in a warm blanket and gave me a camembert sandwich and a cup of thick black coffee while they verified I was who I said I was. Which, incredibly, took hours and hours, the entire day, during which time I drifted in and out of sleep on a hard chair in an empty office, tired and sore and disoriented and wishing I had something to knit, or to read. Finally, around six p.m., Margaret swept in, gave whoever was in charge a talking-to, brought me home in a taxi, and put me to bed, where I slept straight through to this morning. Which is how it got to be Saturday. But that's okay. For the first time in a very long time, I feel truly rested.

Before I can prevent it, rule number thirty-two of the perpetual diet pops into my head: Sleep a lot. People who sleep a lot are thin. Possibly because when you're sleeping you're not eating.

But, you know, maybe it's about time I'm no longer ruled by the rules. I place my cup on the hammered copper side table. "Margaret. I'm wondering. The police, how did they know to call y—?"

"The police," Margaret interrupts, "are not interested in imprisoning nice young American girls like you. They would like to get their hands, however, on this Balzac person. Balzac. Quite the *nom de guerre!* An over-educated and under-employed young man, I daresay, with not enough to keep him occupied. In any event, all's well that ends well." She chuckles. "Good job I gave you my *carte de visite* yesterday."

"Your what?"

"My *carte de visite.* A visiting card, with my name and phone number. All French people have them. Or at least they used to. I tucked it into the box of *macarons* and it somehow survived the soaking. The police said they found it when they went through your bag." Margaret nods toward the kitchen. "Everything is in there now, drying."

I hurry to the kitchen, where my jeans are tented over a portable drying rack, my no-longer-white blouse is hanging on a plastic coat hanger, and my formerly new boots are cleaned and stuffed with paper. Most awesome of all, my tote bag, passport, flight confirmation, credit card, and cash are spread out on a towel. Wrinkled, yet dry and intact. While I slept, Margaret did this, took care of my stuff, of me. I pick up the cash and flip through it. All there.

Margaret appears in the doorway. "I say. It's nearly one. I've an appointment with my *coiffeuse* at two-fifteen. Let me find you something to wear and you can get ready while I do the washing up." She is of course fully dressed. Pearls, pumps, another one of her skirt suits—pale rose this time—and a lettuce-green blouse.

I return my wrinkled valuables to the money belt. "But I need to phone William. I really should, Margaret." If it's Saturday that means I have, incredibly, missed three Daily Phone Calls. My stomach tightens. Not talking to William has been a lot easier than talking to him—or rather than lying to him—but this is a task I have let slide for far too long.

Margaret shakes her head. "Think, child. Paris is hours ahead of the States. Better to wait a bit, wouldn't you agree?" Before I can answer she leads me to her bathroom, which looks like it belongs in the pages of an architectural magazine—creamy white claw-footed porcelain tub, gold-plated fixtures, matching toilet and bidet, and a crystal chandelier dappling light across the painted tile walls. I am just finishing with my bath when the door cracks open. "I think these will fit," Margaret calls, sliding in a hanger holding a black wool pencil skirt and cobalt blue silk tee.

They do fit, perfectly. They must belong to the absent daughter, these yummy clothes that probably cost more than my entire wardrobe back home. Or maybe to Margaret's idea of who the daughter is, or could be, because when I emerge from the bathroom, bathed and dressed, my damp hair gathered up and pinned, more or less, in a French twist, Margaret claps her hands to her cheeks and cries, *"Magnifique!"*

At the hair salon I sit in a sunny window and flip through *Elle* and *Marie Claire*. I am not wearing any underwear. Margaret provided me some, a black lace thong and matching bra, but putting them on felt too weird. I carefully cross my legs, glad I shaved them with the disposable razor thoughtfully tucked into a basket of French-milled soaps, and glance down at the beaded kitten-heeled sandals that Margaret insisted I wear. And that also fit perfectly. Manolo Blahniks. Even in Phoenix people have heard of Manolo Blahniks. Incredible. To Margaret's truant daughter, this luxury must have been old hat, ordinary, disposable, easy to throw aside in favor of Berlin and a new boyfriend.

It's just warm enough in the sunny window for me to feel comfortable and well and whole, the way I have felt ever since waking up in Margaret's cheerful blue and white guest room. No nausea today. No headache. The silk tee rests lightly, coolly, on my breasts. I flip a page of the magazine, stop, and stare. A model, her blue-black hair cut in a sassy bob, gazes back out at me.

"That style would be perfect on you," says Margaret, placing a light hand on my shoulder. She smells like coconut and her shining silver hair is freshly coiffed. "With your bone structure."

It should not have been so easy for Margaret to convince me to let the *coiffeuse* cut off all my long hair. But it is another thing, this time an easy thing, to say yes to. As we step out of the salon I rake my fingers through the razored chin-length ends. My head feels so light. All that hair must have weighed five frigging pounds. We head for the Café de la Poste, located on the sunny side of the street, aboveground, like everything else in Margaret's world, and sit at the same table as the morning we accidentally met at breakfast. Which was the day before yesterday, I calculate with some effort. Feels like eons ago.

"Penny for your thoughts," Margaret says after we order.

I laugh. Dad used to say that. "Oh, just that when I was a little girl I always wanted to have my hair cut this way. In a bob. My friend Kat used to nag and nag me to do it."

"Kat. Is that the friend who died?"

"Yes." I tug on my naked earlobes. Kat's silver horseshoe earrings are lying on the nightstand in Margaret's guestroom.

"I am so sorry," Margaret says. "She was the friend of your heart, was she not?"

Friend of my heart. What a perfect way to put it. "Yes." She was exactly that, and more, for all four years in college and ever since. She was everything to me, I was everything to her, until I met and married William.

Margaret takes a sip of her wine. "It is a great good fortune to have had such a friend."

"Yes, it is. Was." I fiddle with my newly shorn hair.

"I still think of my husband every day. I'll be scrambling eggs and I'll hear his voice. 'Oh, Maggie, you must not let the egg set, you must stir gently all the while.' He reminded me a thousand times and yet my eggs always turned out hard and rubbery!" Margaret laughs a silvery tinkling laugh, like a film star from the forties. "Georges was a marvelous cook."

"How did you meet?" If I encourage Margaret's ramblings I won't have to deal with her prying questions.

"A commonplace story, I'm afraid. He came to London to study English. I was at Berlitz and was assigned to be his tutor. A dashing young Frenchman. Terribly handsome. What could I do but fall in love? I assure you, my family were not best pleased when I married a dishy foreigner and flitted off to Paris! But the heart wants what the heart wants, *n'est-ce pas*?"

Our salads arrive. "We had nearly forty blissful years together," she adds, lifting her glass in a toast.

"You must miss him."

That was lame. But I've sat in the front row at three funerals so far in my life, and the one thing I've learned is that there are no really good words for talking about loss.

Margaret spreads a paper napkin over her lap. "Yes, I miss him very much, of course. Nevertheless, as we know, every relationship ends in pain."

I put down my glass. "Excuse me?"

She looks up, wrinkling her nose. "Yes, it's true, my dear Amy. Every relationship, no matter how long or short, how good or bad, must come to an end. Sooner or later. And then there is pain." Margaret laughs. "Look at the two of us! Whingeing on about what cannot be mended," she says, picking up her knife and fork. "What about you? How did you meet your husband?"

My husband. My husband, William, fully functioning, still very much alive, and aboveground William. I look around the café and see a woman in a mirrored column across the room looking back at me, a woman with a sassy black bob, a grown-up-looking woman wearing Manolo Blahniks and lunching in a Parisian café with her older, chic friend. What would my husband think if he saw me here, like this? What would my mother think?

"We met at work," I say to my reflection. "Not a glamorous story, like yours."

"But there was romance, was there not?"

"Romance?" I take another sip of wine. This time it's light, grapefruity, tart. Practically diet wine. "We met at the company Christmas party and were married by March. Love at first sight, I guess." I do not mention the accidental pregnancy and subsequent miscarriage. Margaret seems not only easily shocked, but susceptible to sadness of any kind.

"Indeed." Margaret studies me. "Why, then, did you travel to Paris without him, Amy?"

Obviously, Margaret is going to keep asking this question until she gets an answer.

I tuck my hair behind my ears and it springs right back. "I'm not sure," I say. "It was something I had to do."

"As you said. For your friend Kat."

"Yeah. Yes. But for me, too. I've always wanted to go—somewhere. Paris specifically. And I guess I needed to get away a little."

Kat's death, William's wanting to start a family, the siren song of food—I traveled ten thousand miles, all the way to France, to get away from those things. But they came right along with me.

"*Bonjour, mesdames.*" Manu, grinning like a politician, a fresh bandage stuck cockeyed to his forehead, is striding up to our table, my black fingertip-length trench coat, now dirty and rumpled, tucked under one arm.

"Manu! *Enfin!*" Margaret jumps up and aims two solid minutes of machine-gun French at him. The only words I recognize are "catacomb," "police," "danger," and "idiot." Manu listens, the corners of his mouth twitching.

"Now, young man, you will apologize," Margaret concludes in English, retaking her chair.

He sits down next to Margaret and hangs his head like a naughty schoolboy. "Amy," he begins, "I am sorry. To leave you—it is *impardonable.*" Am-par-doh-nah-bleh.

I smooth the black pencil skirt over my bare thighs. I feel like an actress in a play, wearing a costume she will have to give back at the end of the last act. "No problem. Don't worry about it."

Manu holds up his hand and shakes his head. "*Quand même,*" he insists, "I must ask for your forgiveness. I have not acted—" He glances at Margaret, who hisses, "like a gentleman."

"I have not acted like a gentleman," he says.

True. William, for example, would never have left me floundering in three feet of icy water to be fished out by armed officers of the law. Not in a million billion years. William would not be quick to forgive Manu.

"You have changed your head," he adds.

"My head?"

"He means," Margaret explains, "that he approves of your new hair style."

"And also 'le look,' no?" he says.

I feel myself blush as I caress the blue and white Hermès scarf Margaret arranged just so around my neck after the session at the salon. Manu noticed the new me right away. Would William notice?

Enough. I push away from the table and stand, tugging at the skirt. "Excuse me," I say, picking up the leather biker-style jacket Margaret also gave me to wear. It's Saturday. My sixth day in Paris. I've missed three Daily Phone Calls and am in danger of missing a fourth. How is this possible? I must be insane. William must be insane, with worry. "I must telephone my husband right away," I say, louder than I intended. "Please."

Margaret grabs her wine glass and takes several deep gulps.

"*Mais oui*," says Manu, rising. "*Naturellement*. Your husband. *Pourquoi pas?*"

Margaret stands up, too, smiling brightly. "Of course you must. Immediately."

The apartment is no longer lit by lemony sunshine because leaden mashed-potato-looking clouds have coated the sky. Margaret ushers me through her bedroom and into a small study. Aha. Here is where the twenty-first century dwells chez Margaret—computer, printer, phone, radio, stereo, television, DVD player. The DVD player clock displays the time as sixteen hundred. Four p.m. Making it nine a.m. in New Jersey. Certainly not too early for a phone call.

Margaret hands me the phone. "Dial one-six-five-six, then oh-oh," she instructs, "then a one, and then your husband's number." She turns and closes the door with a crisp click, leaving me alone.

I dial fast before I forget the digits Margaret rattled off so rapidly. First nothing happens. Then a series of clicks is followed by a long pause, another click, another pause, and, finally, a ring tone. Sounding exactly the way ring tones in Phoenix sound. I sink into the tufted leather desk chair, slip out of the Manolo Blahniks, bring my knees up to my chin, remember I'm not wearing underwear, and put my feet back down on the floor.

Five rings. Six. Maybe he's in a meeting and can't pick up. I clear my throat and prepare to leave a voice mail. William, I'll say, I am happy to finally get in touch with you, there is so much I need to tell you.

Seven rings. Eight. Then the call flips to voice mail. "You've reached Will Brodie." William's voice, the same as always, deep and delicious. I feel a reliable stab of desire.

"Leave a message. I'll call you ASAP," he says. There's a short pause. "If this is Amy," he continues, "Amy, I'm taking a red-eye to France. Will meet you, your hotel, Saturday noon, Paris time." Click.

The DVD player says sixteen hundred and one. William got to the Hôtel du Cheval Blanc four hours ago. William is in Paris.

twenty-five

MANOLO BLAHNIK BEADED SANDALS with kitten heels are god-awful to run in. I stuff the sandals into my still-damp tote bag and take off running for real.

I notice people frowning at my bare feet as I sprint across the wide boulevard of myriad tiny shops, race past the bakery with the red-and-white-striped awning, dodge around an old man carrying a wire basket of leeks, and burst into the tiny smoky lobby of the Hôtel du Cheval Blanc. The deskman, same one as my first day in Paris, looks up.

"Hello! I mean, *bonjour.* Is my husband here? A man—*un homme*—tall, like this?" I hold my left hand three inches above my head. "*Un grand homme*? With brown eyes?" I persist though it's obvious William isn't here. Except for the grinning deskman, and me, the lobby is empty. Of course William gave up on waiting for me and left long ago.

"*Ça va, madame, ça va,*" the deskman says, holding out a business card.

I grab it. It's William's card. His neat block printing covers both sides. "Amy," it says, "if you get this, come to the Hilton. I have a room there. Your hotel people won't let me into yours. W."

"Your lover," the deskman calls to me as I dash up the stairs, "your lover, he wait all the afternoon."

Thirty seconds later I am wearing Kat's pink ballet flats and dashing down the stairs. William is in France, in Paris, at the Hilton Hotel. Hilarious. I know where that is. I've already been there, with Bob and Roseanne, my first day in Paris, so very long ago.

But a dozen yards down the street I stutter to a halt. The Hilton is too far to walk to, or run to, even in ballet flats. The Métro? No way, the Métro is underground and I am not going back down there anytime soon. Besides, I'd be sure to get lost, to end up somewhere completely different from where I intended to be. I should've accepted Manu's offer of help—as I raced out of Margaret's apartment, yelling goodbye and forgetting to thank her for the clothes and the lunch and the use of the phone, Manu slipped me a card with his phone number printed on it. "Call me if ever you need me," he whispered. After the whole catacomb imbroglio, Manu is eager to make things up to me. He would totally have driven me to the Hilton.

But what if William sees me get out of a strange man's vehicle? Nope, things are going to be tricky enough to explain as it is.

I return to the hotel lobby and the smirking deskman. "Taxi? Could you call me a taxi, please, *monsieur*? To take me to the Hilton Hotel? Taxi? Please?"

"*Mais oui, chère madame,*" he chuckles, picking up the phone. "But of course."

He even tells the driver where I want to go and that I am in a hurry. In record time I am dashing across the marble lobby floor of the Hilton, where the deskman is wearing a navy blazer instead of a wrinkled T-shirt but is not nearly so helpful. First, he declares no one by William's name is staying at the hotel. "*Non, madame. Non,*" he says, shrugging. When I show him the name on the business card he shrugs again, consults his computer, and allows as how William is staying there after all. But he won't divulge the room number, no way. All he will do is point to a red service phone.

Seventeen rings later I hang up. William is obviously not in his room. I prowl the spacious lobby. Deserted. Peek into the restaurant. Empty. Peer into the bar. A half dozen drinkers, none of them William, nurse their drinks.

But take a look at that. There, in a dimly lit corner booth, chowing down on very American-looking burgers and fries, are Roseanne and Bob. They don't notice me because they're too busy stuffing their faces.

The last thing I want to do right now is make conversation with Mr. and Mrs. Middle America. So I back out of the bar and locate the elevators, stationing myself behind a newspaper stand. This is a perfect place to wait. William flew all the way to Paris to find me. There's no way I'll miss him now. I should never have made this trip without telling him. What was I thinking? He's going to be confused, of course he will be, but maybe—now that William is actually in Paris—maybe we can stay on together for a few days. That'd be awesome. I've seen hardly any sights yet and this is William's first visit to Paris, too. We could stroll the Champs-Elysées, explore the Latin Quarter, ride to the top of the Eiffel Tower, picnic in the place des Vosges. He's here. Really here. Everything is going to be all right.

"Amy? Is that you?"

William has rounded a corner and is standing in front of me, not smiling.

"Will! You're here! You came! Oh my God, I'm so glad!" I launch myself into his arms. Huh. He smells like cigarettes. Despite his one-smoke-a-day habit, William never smells like cigarettes. William always smells like vanilla.

I automatically raise my face for his kiss, but he does not kiss me, and returns my embrace only because I have grabbed his arms and am forcibly wrapping them around my waist. "Come on," he mutters into a spot behind my ear. "Let's get out of here."

In the elevator I can't help myself. I am so frigging glad to see him I twine around his arm and bury my face into the shoulder of his white shirt. No, don't cry, I look so bad when I cry.

Too late. I am sobbing, big, ugly, hiccupping sobs. William doesn't say a word, doesn't even seem to register my presence, much less the hideous blubbering that I fail to get under control all the way to the fourth floor and all the way down the long dim corridor. When the heavy black door to his room sighs to a close behind us I again throw my arms around his neck. I shouldn't because William's jaw is rigid and he is standing at parade rest, a sign that he is pissed. "You're here," I say, my voice cracking. "I can't believe it!"

"I can't believe *you're* here," says William, removing my arms and crossing the room to seat himself in the desk chair. The room's one window is behind him and his backlit face is unreadable.

"What's going on, Ames?" he asks, his voice adobe dry.

My heart thumps in my ears. When William comes home from trips the first thing we do is make love. It's always new again, fresh again, sweet again, like the first time. That is obviously not going to happen now. Of course not. Of course he would be furious. And I am an idiot to hope otherwise. I wipe my face with the backs of my hands and kneel on the tan nubbly carpet next to his feet. If he knew I was going commando, would it make a difference?

He scowls down at me through narrowed eyes. Probably not. "Well. It's a pretty long story," I say.

"I've got nothing else on the agenda," he says, leaning back and tenting his hands under his jaw. His shirt is, unusual for him, not crisp and spotlessly white. It's creased and has a stain on the front. "Shoot," he says.

Though I know he doesn't really want me to, I circle my arms around his legs and rest my chin on his knee. His hard, unyielding, cigarette-y knee. "It was The Plan," I begin. Two scalding tears spill out of my eyes.

"What plan?"

How is it is possible to explain The Plan without sounding like an insane person?

I sniff and look around for Kleenex. "Ours. Kat's and mine. While she was sick we made a plan, a sort of secret plan I guess, to come to Paris when she got better. We bought clothes, sent for passports. Stuff like that."

Those were good days, fun days, despite the cancer treatments. "And then she never did get better," I continue, peering up at his stony face, "and then you said you were going to New Jersey for ten whole days, which is how we were going to do it, you know, while you were away on a business tri—"

"Wait one minute." William holds up a palm. A muscle in his jaw twitches. "You planned to take a trip to France without telling me?"

I lift my chin from his knee. "Yes. No. I don't know. I guess so, sort of. I have always wanted to come here and Kat wanted us to do it together. It started out as just a crazy fantasy. Something to talk about, to pass the time during chemo, and then it got bigger and bigger, and realer and realer. And I never would have actually done it, I don't think, I really resisted doing it, in fact, but—" I stop talking. I am sounding like an idiot. If I tell him about Kat's video, about the airline gift cards, he's going to get even madder.

He leans forward, props his elbows on his knees, and laces his hands together, making a cage I cannot get into. "Why, Amy?" he asks.

He's right here, right in the same room with me. But he may as well be in a different galaxy, light years away.

"Why would you do all this?" he asks again, his face eggshell white. "Plan a secret trip. Sneak off. Why wouldn't you just tell me you wanted to come to goddamn Paris?" He stares at me as if I have just dropped down from the moon. "When you stopped answering your phone, I thought at first something was wrong with the service. Then I thought maybe you lost your purse or something. But when I got a call from the bank about weird charges on your credit card, I checked the accounts online." The two vertical creases between his eyebrows, one a sixteenth of an inch longer than the other, are deep, deeper than I've ever seen them. "That's when I saw payments for that little hotel you're staying at. Which at first I assumed was a mistake but then more charges came in—one from Super Shuttle, another from a restaurant called Café de la Poste. I got a bad feeling and called the neighbor. He said they saw you getting on an airport shuttle Sunday afternoon." He stops and rubs his eyes with his knuckles. "So yesterday I took off work early and flew straight here. On a hunch."

"I was going to explain," I say, though I know this is a lie. I reach up to twist my hair into a bun but the short razored ends slip through my fingers. William was worried about me. Worried enough to get on a plane. To Paris. Maybe he knows me better than I thought. "I'm so sorry, Will. I never meant to freak you out. Truly. I wasn't thinking. I wasn't thinking at all." That, at least, is the honest truth.

He grimaces. "What I can't understand is how you could keep so much from me. I thought I knew you, Amy. But now I'm not so sure."

I get up and go to sit on the foot of the bed, my knees clamped together because the state of my underwear, or lack thereof, is no longer a subject I wish to have introduced. "It was—just a thing with Kat, you know what I mean?" I doubt he will know but he could cut me some slack. Kat has been dead less than a month. "It was a girl thing," I add in a whisper, two hot heavy tears plopping into my lap.

"A girl thing?" William leaps up, knocking over the desk chair. "A girl thing?" he repeats, shouting. "You are not a girl! You are a woman. You are my wife. And I'm your husband, Amy!" His face is now radish red, and he is clenching and unclenching his fists.

I stay sitting, gripping my icy kneecaps. We glare at each other
for five, six, seven seconds and then William pivots on one heel and
stalks to the window. He stands with his back to me, hands jammed
into his pockets, looking out at Paris but not seeing Paris. Somewhere a
ventilation fan starts to roar. Somewhere the singsong notes of a French
police siren swell and fade.

"Amy." His voice is almost too low to hear.

I don't answer.

He clears his throat. "Amy. Is Kat more important to you than I am?"

I slowly rise to my feet. "No. I mean—" I stand there trying to figure
out what I do mean. "I mean, it's just that—in a big way—I owed her."

William whirls around to face me. "You owed her? What could
you owe her?"

I don't answer.

He takes two rapid steps forward and for a moment I think he might
actually punch me. "We have a life together, Amy. We have a marriage.
We could have a family, if only you'd stop whining about Kat."

I lift my chin. I don't like the way he says Kat's name—Kaah-aat.
Whiney sounding. Is that what he thinks I'm doing? Whining? How
could he, after everything that has happened, after all I've been through?
"You don't—you don't understand. I always—you don't know—what
it's like to have a friend of the heart."

But the words, so apt and elegant when Margaret used them,
sound ridiculous coming out of my mouth.

"*Friend of the heart?*" William's upper lip curls in disgust. "Well, let
me tell you what your friend of the heart did." He spits out each word
like a curse. "Four years ago when you and I started dating? Your
friend showed up on my doorstep one night." He pauses, and folds
his arms across his chest. "She showed up. Looking to get laid."

A tsunami of nausea rushes through me and I have to sit down
on the bed again. "What? What do you mean?"

He snorts. "Just what I said. She came on to me. Just to see if anything
would happen. Your precious wonderful Kat. Your 'boo hoo—she's
gone.' She tried to play me, to stab you in the back."

"No, Will, you're wrong." I jump up and start to pace around in
tight circles. "You must have misunderstood. Kat would never do that,
she would never—Kat doesn't, didn't." I stop and turn to face him.
"I should tell you something. Kat was gay."

His expression doesn't alter. "No shit," he says.

"Yes. She tried not to make a big deal out of it."

"And you?" he asks, one eyebrow lifting. "Are you gay?"

"What? No. No, I'm not." Which is true. Which is how I hurt Kat.

"Are you bi?" William is sneering. I've never seen anyone actually sneer. I've only read about it in books.

"I don't like labels," I finally mutter.

"What the hell is that supposed to mean?"

"It means no. No, I'm not."

Neither of us speaks for a moment. Then he says, "Is that a lie, too?"

I groan. "We had—we had a thing when we were roommates at ASU. Not that it's any of your business. I was lonely. Freaked. I didn't date much in high school and I didn't know how to deal with people." Until Kat swooped into my life and became my first friend. My first lover. I don't want them to but more tears fill my eyes and travel down my cheeks. "It wasn't a big deal. A lot of people experiment in college. It's normal. My point is, that what you say she did? Propositioned you? For sex? Kat would just never have done such a thing."

William is shaking his head. "I flew all the way to Paris," he says in a soft voice.

"Will. Look at me. You're asking me to believe that my best friend would totally betray me."

He looks up, his eyes like onyx, and nods. That's all. He just nods.

My heart stops for a moment.

William rights the desk chair and sits down heavily. "I thought I knew you, Amy," he says again. "I questioned your choice of best friend but I thought I knew who you basically were." He pauses, peering up at me. "Are there any more secrets? Things you haven't told me?"

The cash-back savings, the food storage locker, the home pregnancy test—William would probably count those as secrets. But no way am I going to reveal every little humiliating shred of my chicken-shit soul. He already thinks I'm crazy, or stupid, or both.

I move toward the door. "Listen. I can't do this," I say. "I can't be here right now."

"You're running away? Again?"

"Just give me some time. To get my brain together." Or something. I reach for the doorknob. "Will, I would like to know one thing," I add, pausing to look back at him. "Why didn't you tell me? About the thing with Kat? What you said she did?"

He stands up. "You know why."

"No. No, I don't. Why?"

"I didn't want to ask you," he says, his lips barely moving, "to have to choose between us."

twenty-six

I MAKE IT as far as the hotel lobby, where I drop into a low, too-soft armchair facing a lush tree-filled inner courtyard.

Kat. Did you really do what William said? I wrap my arms around my persistently poochy stomach and fold over, focusing on my feet. When Kat bought these shoes, the pink ballet flats I am wearing right now, we were so happy. Kat had finished her first round of chemo and we were sure it would be her last. And she was glad, very glad, that my attention had slid from William back to her, even if only temporarily.

"Madame. Puis-je vous aider?" A man in a navy blazer is scowling down at me.

I sit up. "Yes. No. I mean, I don't need help. *Merci.*" I flash my biggest American smile. "I am waiting for—I have a *rendezvous.*"

Whatever the man intends to reply is interrupted by the sound of loud, un-French, laughter. We both turn to see Bob and Roseanne, arm in arm, goofy grins on their faces, emerge from an elevator. They head across the lobby toward us, passing close enough to my chair that Bob's mentholated aftershave prickles my nose, but they are oblivious to me and everyone else. In the middle of the spacious room, they pause, giggling, to bend their frizzly gray heads over a folded-out map. Roseanne whispers into Bob's ear, her lollipop-red lips tickling his bristly gray sideburn, her plump hands massaging his forearm. I cannot look away.

Bob's shoulders shake with laughter. "You bet," he says, his deep voice booming across the lobby. He folds up the map, pockets it, takes Roseanne's hand in his, and leads her back to the elevators.

A fresh supply of tears spills down my cheeks, fat jealous futile tears I cannot command or control. Damn Bob. Damn Roseanne. Damn

William. I jump to my feet, push past the man in the navy blazer, sprint across the marble floor, and burst through the revolving door onto the empty sidewalk outside. The uniformed doorman lifts his eyebrows. Crazy person, the eyebrows say. Damn him, too.

I pivot to the right and run as fast as I can for six solid blocks—it feels good to move, to run—not looking back until the ache in my side forces me to stop. But Bob and Roseanne are not behind me, waving their rumpled map and grinning. Neither is William, jogging to catch up, to say, "Ames, wait, let's talk." I am the only person on the street. This *quartier* is hushed and sad compared to Margaret's lively neighborhood. No bakeries, no dry cleaners, no sushi bars or flower shops. No cobblers or cheesemongers.

I continue in the direction I was running, but walking now. Left, right, left, right. All I want to do is move, go, it doesn't matter where to. A dozen blocks later, I emerge from under a canopy of recently leafed-out trees and stop to stare across a diagonal intersection.

It's the Arc de Triomphe. The goddamn Arc de Triomphe, more imposing than I expected from the pictures, tiny tourists strung out along its top like a row of jagged teeth. One of the must-sees, like the Eiffel Tower, or the Louvre. But I turn my back on it, cross the intersection, and keep moving. It begins to rain and I zip up Margaret's daughter's leather jacket, regretting that I left my raincoat, disheveled as it is, at Margaret's.

The new street I am now on is the widest street I have seen so far in Paris. It's frigging immense. The sidewalks are over-sized too, at least thirty feet wide, and thronging with pedestrians. I let the throng catch me up and carry me past grandiose cinemas, glamorous shops, glittering cafés. Everything here is big and hideous. It's true—Paris can be hideous. Ella Fitzgerald must never have noticed. And, oh look, phone booths, the first public phones I've seen all the damn week. But now I don't need them, and they don't matter anymore. I glance back at the gradually receding Arc de Triomphe. From this vantage, it looks like a giant stone prong plugged into the earth.

Fifty yards later I spot a street sign. Well, well. It seems that I am walking down the Champs-Elysées, the most romantic avenue in the world.

But not in real life. In real life, the Champs-Elysées is broad and flat and noisy and about as romantic as an airport concourse. Yet the sidewalks are packed full with people strolling side by side, people seated across from each other at sidewalk cafés, people holding hands and gazing into each other's eyes and laughing and talking.

William used to hold my hand and we used to talk and laugh together like this. One evening early in our marriage he spent a whole dinner explaining how Tesla coils work. "You can boost, say, ten thousand volts to a million," he said, slathering butter over a homemade whole wheat roll. "I remember in college we made one with stuff we found in the garage. A lamp shade, some old cord, a tube from plastic wrap. Those old-timey stovetop grease catchers. The capacitor we had to purchase of course."

I should have tried harder to understand Tesla coils.

"*Excusez-moi.*" A woman wearing a full-length fur coat—in the rain, in April—has bumped into me. You can't slow down here, in Paris, on the hideous Champs-Elysées, you can't take a moment to stop and think. I carve a path through the crowd to the shelter of a doorway, rest my back against a cold stone column, and study the passing multitudes, the blessed humanity. No William among them. No Bob and Roseanne, no Beret Guy or Balzac. Not even the Sacré-Coeur leather biker jacket guy. "Men think with their dicks," Kat always said. William is jealous of what Kat and I had. That's all it is. Jealousy. Kat was jealous of William and William is jealous of Kat, even now. It would be hilarious, if it weren't.

I am starting to shiver so I open my tote bag to look for my umbrella and notice Margaret's map. It takes me quite a while to find the right page and orient myself. But eventually I figure out that if I turn right I will return to William, who pretty much hates my guts right now. If I turn left and continue going straight east I will eventually reach Margaret, who does not.

I drop the map into the tote bag, tighten the blue and white Hermès scarf around my throat, deploy my umbrella, plunge back into the unending throng, and turn left. I pass more cinemas, more shops, more cafés, until the unromantic Champs-Elysées stops, just ends, at an enormous empty paved square. An obelisk juts up out of the middle of the square like the point of a very dull sword. It is also pretty ugly, if you want to know the truth. I circumnavigate the square and enter a series of covered arcades, which eventually morph into a garish shopping district of lingerie, eyeglass, and shoe stores, which, after another twenty minutes, finally settle down into the smaller, cozier, grimier shops of Margaret's neighborhood. Look, there's the we-sell-only-white-dishes china store. There's the mini-market, the rosebud florists, the bakery with the red-and-white-striped awning. There's the Café de la Poste. All so familiar, so dear, already. At Margaret's building a man is exiting just as I arrive. I grab the door before it has a chance to close and step into the cobbled courtyard. My tears have dried to salt on my jaw; my nose is burning and is probably as red as a pomegranate. But this is as good as it's going to get. I stick my new chin-length hair behind my damp ears and trudge up the wide wooden stairs.

"Amy!" Margaret swings the door wide, her face lighting up. "What an unexpected pleasure!"

"Hi. Can I come in?"

"Of course, my dear."

Someone is smiling at me. Someone is glad to see me. I head for the fireplace and hold my hands over the flames.

"You look knackered," Margaret says, following me. She indicates a silver tray laden with a hunk of pâté, a round of camembert, a platter of sliced apple and bread, and a small golden bowl of Godiva chocolates. Like everything Margaret puts her hand to, it looks gorgeous. "I was about to indulge in a light supper. Would you care to join me?"

I accept a small plate and sit down. "Thanks. Thank you, Margaret." If William is eating anything at all, he is probably having room service, or sitting in the hotel bar in one of those dark booths, alone. And here I am being fed and cared for and smiled at.

Margaret fills two crystal goblets with red wine and takes her seat in the other armchair. She doesn't ask, "What happened?" She doesn't comment, "You should be with your husband right now, should you not?" She sits, she sips. A Chopin prélude tinkles in the background.

"Margaret. I saw my husband."

She says nothing.

I continue. "He got mad. And I got mad. So I left."

A shadow of a smile flickers across Margaret's powdered face. She's wearing make-up and pearls and hose and high heels, all by herself, at home. "Is that what you want?" she says.

I take a big gulp of the wine. It burns all the way down. "What? No," I say, coughing, "I want to be with him, of course."

Margaret tops off my glass. "Indeed. Have you told him so?"

"Of course I have."

Just not recently.

Margaret leans forward, her pink cheeks pinker than usual. "I am new to your story, Amy. But to me you don't seem entirely certain about what you do want. Your husband may be sensing this. He may feel that your affections are," she pauses to lick her lips, "split."

A log shifts in the fireplace. Hisses.

Split. I get up and drift to the window. Margaret's apartment building is not on a bus route. No day-oh guy would dare to stand outside Margaret's window and strum and sing all the night long. But he doesn't have to. His anthem is burned into my brain.

Margaret clears her throat. "All roads lead to your friend, Kat. Do they not?"

Kat.

That time she showed up drunk at my old central Phoenix bungalow in the middle of the night, ranting about William, repeating, "What you see is what you get." That was when she must have done what William said she did. It's so obvious now. "What you see is what you get," she muttered over and over, like it was a bad thing. The argument we had the next morning makes sense now, too.

"I tell you this because I care!" Kat shouted. She'd phoned first thing. "You could do better than this here Will-yum person."

"Oh?" I replied. "How so? I don't get you. You nagged and nagged me to meet a man and settle down and now I have and you still aren't happy."

"He's, I dunno. Too straight arrow."

"Maybe I like straight arrow."

"Seriously?" Kat said. "You don't think it's boring as shit?"

"Boring? Not at all. You're just jealous."

At that Kat screamed, "I do not do jealous!" and hung up. We didn't speak for three solid weeks. Then on a Friday night Kat texted and asked me to help her sew curtains for her kitchen on Saturday morning. By Sunday, everything was back to normal. I was so relieved I never tried to revisit our earlier discussion. Life went on as if nothing had happened. Except that William avoided Kat when he could, and tended to say little when she was around. How ridiculously obvious a red flag that seems now.

I straighten the creamy lace curtains hanging on each side of Margaret's window and turn to face her. The room is as impossibly beautiful as a movie set. But like the day-oh guy, I don't belong here. Like the day-oh guy, I am a stranger in a strange land.

"Margaret. I need to go. Back to the Hilton, to William."

"Amy." Margaret rises, smoothing her skirt. "My child. You're cold. You're tired. You need rest. Why don't you get ready for bed? I'll bring you a nice tisane."

From my spot at the window I can see into the guest room, where the blue and white silk negligée is laid across the foot of the bed, ready and waiting, as if Margaret were expecting me. But that's impossible.

"I'll bring a cup to you in bed if you wish," Margaret calls from the kitchen.

What? No.

"Margaret, I can't stay. Thanks, but I need to go to William. Now."

Margaret stands in the kitchen doorway, cradling the mustard-yellow teapot. It looks, in her arms, like a leprechaun's pot of gold.

"Now," I repeat, heading for the door. "Can we, can you, call me a taxi?"

"Are you sure?"

"Yes, of course. I am. I am sure."

Margaret rubs the belly of the teapot, shaking her head. "You don't want to sleep on it? Or just, say, telephone William?"

"No. I don't. I need to see him. Face to face."

"Really, Amy, I'm beginning to think you are being entirely unreasonable."

"No. I think I'm being entirely reasonable. For the first time in a long time. And I'm sorry to be such a pain but could you call a taxi for me? Please?"

Margaret insists on walking down the three flights of stairs to wait with me for the cab. The sky is now a midnight blue and a pale portly moon hangs low over the mansard roofs.

"What will you do when you get there?" Margaret asks. "What is your plan?"

Plan? What good do plans ever do? Plans are the cause of all this unholy mess.

RULES FOR THE PERPETUAL DIET

As the cab pulls up Margaret clutches my shoulder. Her bony fingers feel like claws, and she looks shrunken, old, standing there alone on the sidewalk in the dark. I pull away, toss my tote bag into the backseat, and face her to say goodbye.

"Margaret, I—" But I have no idea what to say. The woman has fed me, clothed me, lodged me, listened to me, even rescued me from the police. She's been amazing. Too-good-to-be-true amazing.

Margaret kisses me first on the right cheek, then on the left. She smells, as always, like Shalimar. But underneath the perfume is another odor. The aluminum odor of tears. I know that aroma well.

"Come with me?" I say. Just like that. It pops out of my mouth just like that.

Margaret's face bursts into a wavering smile. "But of course," she cries, rapidly climbing into the backseat next to me. She rattles off instructions to the driver and we speed down the silent street.

Another cab ride to the Hilton. Less scary with Margaret by my side but this time it takes ages. We cross the Seine, which I did not expect, crawl through a maze of narrow congested streets, loop around the Eiffel Tower—my first close-up view of the Eiffel Tower—and then recross the Seine. I am about to ask if we are lost when I spot the Arc de Triomphe. Two minutes later, we pull up in front of the Hilton. At last. Everything is going to be all right.

But William is no longer at the Hilton.

In ragged, rapid French I do not remotely begin to follow, Margaret learns that he checked out of his room an hour ago.

I cover my face with my hands. While I was wandering along the Champs-Elysées like a stray cat, while I was sucking down red wine at Margaret's, while the goddamned cabdriver was taking the goddamned scenic route, William packed his bags, checked out of his room, and left. At least that is what Margaret says the desk clerk said.

"Are you sure?" I mumble through my fingers.

"Quite sure."

"Isn't there anyone else we can check with?" I persist, dropping my hands. It's hard to believe that he could have left so quickly, not after coming so far. He would have tried to get a night's sleep first. Plus William would have wanted to get his money's worth out of his room at the Hilton. He is careful about things like that.

Sighing, Margaret interrogates a bellhop, who nods. "*Mais l'aéroport, madame*," he says.

That I understand. The airport. William is on his way to the airport. Leaving Paris. Leaving me. My heart thumps like a kettledrum in my chest.

"Right then," Margaret says, linking her arm into mine and steering me in the direction of the hotel bar. "Let's have a nightcap, shall we?"

I pull away. "Margaret, no! I'm going to the airport."

"The airport? At this hour?"

"Yes. Right away. Thanks so much for everything. I'm sorry I've been such a pain. You've been so great—I'll write you when I get back home." I dart for the revolving door. There is not a moment to lose. "Thank you. I'm sorry. Goodbye."

But Margaret insists on coming with me in the cab to the airport as well. A lucky thing, too, because Margaret knows everything about managing in France, everything about making things happen the way you want them, need them, to happen. I lean back in my seat. My Paris trip is almost over. I am scheduled to return to Phoenix tomorrow, Sunday. Unless I catch up with William? Snag a seat on the plane with him tonight? I feel for my money belt. It's all there, my cash, my credit card, my passport, my return ticket info. I could leave everything else, my clothes and my suitcase, behind in Paris. Those things aren't important now. What's important is getting back to real life. To normal.

As the cab pulls up at the airport curb Margaret says, "We'll go directly to international departures and inquire there. Surely he has not managed to secure a flight back to the States so quickly."

"Surely," I echo. But my stomach is twirling.

We begin with Air France. *Non, non, mesdames*, no flights to LA that evening. Ditto for Continental, United, American.

"He has to be somewhere." I scan the crowds for William's lean face.

"We'll try Delta," says Margaret.

Oui, oui, mesdames, Delta indeed has an evening flight from Paris to Phoenix, stopping in Houston. But, *malheureusement*, it departed fifteen minutes ago.

"That's that then," says Margaret. "Let's go home."

twenty-seven

MARGARET INSERTS the shining brass key into the door of her apartment. "My word," she says, "I could murder a cup of tea."

But I brush past her, stomp to the kitchen, grab a water glass, and fill it with red wine.

Margaret follows. "Wouldn't you like to nibble on something with that, my dear?"

"I'm not hungry."

"Perhaps. But perhaps you should not be drinking so much wine."

I drain the glass, pour myself another, and take it to the living room, where a few glowing embers from the fireplace still throw off some heat. I am again chilled to the bone. A person born and raised in Phoenix, Arizona, a person with desert-thin blood, has no business running around Paris on a cool April night in a light jacket and a barely legal miniskirt.

Margaret watches me for a moment before returning to the kitchen. "I'll put the kettle on," she murmurs. I listen to her fussing with water and crockery and humming a tune that sounds like "Hello Dolly." It is so easy for her. She had it all, a husband, a child, a home, a life, a future, and now she is old and doesn't need or want those things anymore. Now, her existence is smooth, simple, settled. When she gets up tomorrow morning her biggest decision will be whether to have a plain croissant or a *pain au chocolat* for breakfast. She'll probably have both.

Damn Margaret.

"What time is it?" I call, gulping down a few more glugs of wine.

Margaret appears in the doorway, consulting her diamond-encrusted watch. "I think, yes, past midnight. Are you sure you aren't hungry, darling girl?"

"I'm sure." I'm being rude, but what does it matter? Nothing matters. I set my glass on the mantle and kick off the now disintegrating ballet flats. My toes are beet red and blistering, but sore feet are the least of my worries right now. I flop down on the Aubusson carpet, lie on my back, suck in my stomach, and pull the money belt out from under my skirt. All day long I worried about it coming loose and slipping down around my ankles like a baggy pair of fat-girl underwear. But it stayed put. It even offered some warmth around my middle.

"My plane is at 1:30 tomorrow afternoon," I say in a politer tone, smoothing out the puckered flight confirmation.

"Is it?" Margaret is arranging bone china cups and tiny silver spoons on a silver tea tray. In Margaret-Land, tea is the answer to every question.

"My suitcase and stuff are still in my room at the hotel," I add.

"I imagine they are."

Tonight would have been my final night at the Hôtel du Cheval Blanc. I should go there now, pack my bag, and prepare to leave Paris forever. But I am exhausted, stiff, bruised, and fairly inebriated, and it is warm and comfortable and safe here at Margaret's. Nothing about this trip has turned out the way I thought it would. It was supposed to be a glorious voyage of discovery, of consummation, of doing a thing just for me. Just this once. That couldn't have been so bad, could it? But it was bad. It was a big fat fiasco from start to finish.

"I'll have to show up at the airport around eleven." Still lying flat on my back on the floor, I count on my fingers. "And before that, I have to go over to my hotel and pack my stuff."

Margaret carries the tea tray over to the hammered copper side table. "Have you considered, Amy, staying on here for a bit?"

I sit upright, my legs stretched out in front of me. "What do you mean?"

"I am referring to you staying here in Paris! Why ever not? You need time to gather your wits about you, in my opinion. You have much to consider, *n'est-ce pas*?"

I smooth the mini-skirt over my black-and-blue goose-pimply thighs. I've gone the whole day with no underwear on. My mother would have been appalled. Kat would have been amused. But the truth is, it doesn't matter what either of them would think anymore. I chew on my lip. "Consider what?" I ask, swinging my legs to one side and struggling to rise from the floor without exposing myself.

"Well, for instance, that your husband has given up on you rather speedily. You had a row, and off he went without so much as a by-your-leave." Margaret pours out the tea. "I daresay he has made his position crystal clear," she says, sniffing.

Outside, on the street below, a car door slams. A dog yelps. A woman laughs. Inside, in Margaret's apartment, it is quiet and snug. Timeless. You would not know what year it is. Margaret's husband's French forebears gaze down from the butter-yellow silk walls. The fluted-leg cherry dining table glows in the firelight. Margaret's ever-present Shalimar graces the air with notes of bergamot. Come to think of it, William did beat it out of Paris pretty fast. He was hasty and unconsidered, not like him really.

"Well, he was awfully mad," I say, holding my still-frozen fingers to the fire. "You don't know him, but he hardly ever does get mad." And, this time, he had a point. He was sort of entitled, this time.

"Ah." Margaret drops a heart-shaped lump of sugar into her cup. I have never seen sugar cubes like the ones Margaret uses. They are in the shapes of card suits—hearts, diamonds, clubs, and spades. They are, like everything in Margaret's world, exquisite. "Even now you defend him."

"Defend him? Why wouldn't I?"

"Why would you?"

"Because—because I love him."

"Love him? I wonder if you even know him."

"Of course I know him!" I go broiler hot from my toes to my ears. This is crazy. William is the one solid thing in my whole pathetic messed-up life. I dart from the fireplace to the window, stumbling over the ballet flats, and glare down into the deserted street.

"Yet I can't help but speculate," Margaret says behind me. "If you loved your husband, would you have made this trip without his knowledge? It's not the kind of thing one normally does, does one? You weren't thinking of him very much at all, were you, when you set out on your Parisian adventure?"

I puff a scrim of hot breath onto the cold windowpane. "No," I say. "I guess not."

"All roads lead to Kat, it seems. Do they not?" Margaret asks.

I close my eyes. In college, that was true. "Lesbian until graduation," we used to joke. But even after college, when Kat and I were "just friends," we were best friends. We were all each other ever needed. Until William and my unplanned pregnancy, when everything changed. Kat was hurt by this, abandoned. Devastated even. Which is why when she got sick I dropped everything and stood by her. Because I owed her at least that much.

"And now she is gone," Margaret persists, like a dog worrying a bone. "No longer a reality. And I even wonder a little about this William. Is he a reality? Your image of him, I mean. I only mention this because I care about you, Amy—but think. Is this steadfast love of his real? Or is it something you have invented for yourself?"

I open my eyes and spin slowly around. Of course William's love is real. William is true blue. If he didn't love me, he wouldn't want to have a baby with me. If he didn't love me, he wouldn't have come all the way to Paris to find me. He has held up his end of the bargain, which is more than I can say for myself. For a moment, I pity him.

Margaret smiles. "I'm only saying, my dear, that he strikes me as a trifle too good to be true. As if butter wouldn't melt—that's the impression I'm getting." She brings her teacup to her mouth and then lowers it again without drinking. "In any event, you needn't act in haste. You have the option to take your time, think things through. Meanwhile, you are ever so welcome to stay here, until you get your feet back under you."

I pad over to the leather armchair, my leather armchair, the one closest to the fireplace, and sit down. "Margaret. That's very kind, but I don't want to cause you any more trouble."

Margaret titters. "Oh, Amy! You are not causing me trouble, as you say. Not at all! It is my great pleasure to have you in my home. You are wonderful company for me."

"That is so kind," I say again, spreading a beautifully ironed jacquard napkin across my bare knees. "Thank you so much. But I need to get going. I do. I need to go back to my real life. Right away. Tomorrow." I accept a brimming teacup from Margaret's trembling hands. "So I know it's late and all but could you wake me up around seven? It's early for Sunday morning, I realize. But I don't have a clock, or a phone."

The tea is another tisane. Not *verveine*. A new kind.

"Of course, dear heart. Whatever you wish. You must do what you believe is right." Margaret smiles but her cheeks are no longer their usual pale dusky rose, they are white, white as the inside of the fragile teacups, and the corner of her left eye is twitching.

Actually, the whole room is twitching. This morning I felt wholly rested but now I have not been this worn out since my senior year in high school, when Dad was dying in the hospital and it was during final exams and I didn't tell anybody, not even my favorite English teacher. I just slogged through the exams and the dying and the funeral and attended my graduation without a gown because I forgot to order one in time. I sip my tea, slump back, sigh. It's been a long day, a hard day, a big fat hairy mess of a day from croissant to coiffeur to confrontation.

Tomorrow I'll make it right.

Tomorrow, through the miracle of time zones, I will arrive in Phoenix the same day I leave Paris.

Tomorrow William and I will be together again.

twenty-eight

"MARGARET! What time is it?"

"Ah. There you are. Good morning." She is seated next to the fireplace, completely dressed. Another Chanel-style suit, another impeccable pair of spectator pumps.

"The time!" I shout. "What *time* is it?"

"Just past two," says Margaret, folding up her crossword puzzle. "I confess, I've already had a bite of lunch." She shrugs. "I was famished!"

"Two? Two o'clock in the afternoon?" The room is dipping and spinning. I grab a bookcase for support. "Are you kidding me?"

Last night Margaret promised me she would wake me up at seven a.m., in plenty of time to go back to my hotel room, pack my stuff, get to the airport, and catch my flight back to Phoenix. But the sun pouring through the creamy lace curtains is not pear-tender morning sun. No. No. It's hard-as-peanut-brittle afternoon sun. I stumble forward a few steps, clutching the blue and white silk robe around my shoulders. "My flight was at one-thirty! I missed my flight!" I grab Margaret's newspaper and fling it into the fireplace, where it quivers for a moment before bursting into flames.

She does not so much as flinch. "Come, come, you needn't worry about that," she says, chuckling. "You can schedule a flight anytime. You were up so very late and had such a difficult day that I reckoned you needed a jolly good lie-in. After everything you've been through." She rises, smoothing her skirt. "And now you must be peckish. Come and sit down. I've put together a little something."

But I am not sitting down. I'm racing into the bathroom, both hands clamped over my mouth. I make it just in time to throw up some bile and that odd-tasting tea. What was up with the tea? Was it drugged?

Would Margaret actually do such a thing? I kneel before the toilet, embracing the cool smooth sides of the porcelain bowl, clean and beautiful and well made like everything in Margaret's apartment, and retch again. Nothing comes up but another tablespoonful of bile.

"Poor dear." Margaret is crouching beside me, stroking damp strands of hair away from my sticky face.

I tremble. No one but Kat has ever stroked my face like this, the way a mother would stroke her child.

"There now," Margaret croons, "it's going to be all right." She dampens a velvety washcloth and uses it to sponge my forehead.

"No, it's not." I yank the washcloth out of Margaret's hand and hurl it into the sink. "Leave it!"

I have barfed more in the past three days than in the last ten years— neutralizing all the French cuisine I've been gorging on, thank God— but even when I was pregnant, four years ago, I didn't throw up like this. Come to think of it, I didn't throw up at all. But I do not have time for this. I need to think. William left Paris last night, Saturday night. He might not have landed in Phoenix yet. He might still be in the air. Meaning I have a chance to make sure a message is waiting on his cell when the plane touches down. And one on the land line when he gets back to the house. That feels like a thing I should be doing, showing him I'm trying to contact him. I struggle to my feet.

"Margaret," I say, as kindly and calmly as I can. "I need to use your phone, please. Now. To call the States. Right now."

Margaret retrieves the washcloth, gives it a housewifely shake, and hangs it over the side of the sink. "The telephone?" she says, arching her thin eyebrows. "But of course, my dear. Wait here just a tick."

She exits the bathroom with surprising speed for a woman her age. I follow but make it only halfway across the living room before needing to sit down.

"Ow." I had aimed for the brocade *fauteuil* but missed it and plopped on my butt on the carpet, barking my shin on another bookcase. I rub my leg with one hand and clutch my head with the other, looking around. None of Margaret's fancy glass-doored bookcases hold books. They are filled to bursting with porcelain figurines, framed photos, glassware, knickknacks, china teacups, and vases. Who can live without books? I never could. I peer into Margaret's bedroom, which is orderly and unoccupied. Margaret must be in the room beyond the bedroom, the study, where the telephone lives.

"Now then." Margaret has materialized in front of me. "Come along," she says. "If you still insist on using the phone."

"I do," I say, allowing her to help me to my feet.

I am unable to remember and punch in the long series of numbers Margaret again rattles off, the ones to make an overseas call, so she does it for me, jabbing at the buttons and then handing over the phone, her lipsticked lips pinched together. I sit in the tufted leather desk chair and press the cool plastic handset to my ear. "William," I'll say, "William, I'm coming home. To try and start over. Give me a chance. Please."

But this time there are no clicks, no whirrs. No ringing. No dial tone even.

"I can't hear anything," I say, handing the phone back to Margaret.

She punches in the numbers again. Jiggles the cord. "Oh dear," she says, the corners of her mouth twitching, "I'm afraid the phone is out of service."

"Out of service?"

"Yes. So sorry." She chuckles and shrugs and hangs up the phone with a sharp clack. "It happens from time to time. The phone, computer, television—they are all part of the same system—just mysteriously stop working. But not to worry. Everything will sort itself out in a couple of days."

"A couple of *days*?" I grab the phone and mash buttons at random. The stupid thing doesn't even light up.

Margaret chuckles again. "It will be fine, Amy. Don't worry. Meanwhile, what I think you are most in need of is something to settle that poor upset tummy of yours. Come now," she says, wrapping her smooth hard fingers around my wrist, "up with you, my girl!"

But instead of getting up I lay my burning forehead on the cool surface of the leather writing pad. Walking. Eating. Not doable.

Margaret grasps my shoulder and gives me a shake. "If you eat a little something, you'll be surprised how much better you feel," she coaxes. "I promise."

I lift my face a millimeter. The DVD clock, the only clock in the whole damn apartment, flashes from fourteen-hundred thirty to fourteen-hundred thirty-one. Past two-thirty in the afternoon already. I let my head drop back down onto the writing pad and moan. "I can't move."

"Don't be a goose. Of course you can move! Come on."

The whole room seems to tip and shift. "Margaret. I think I could be really sick."

"What's that?" Margaret says.

"Sick. Unwell. I think there's something really wrong with me."

"Unwell? Rubbish!" Margaret's face relaxes into a lopsided smile that reveals a chipped incisor. "Not at all, my dear. You are not poorly. Quite the opposite." She tugs at my arm. "Come, come. You need to give yourself and that lovely baby something to eat."

I sit up.

"What did you say?"

Margaret giggles and gives me a quick tight hug. "My dear girl. Did you think I did not know that you are carrying an itty bitty baby in that teensy tiny tummy of yours? It's as plain as day to anyone with eyes in their head to see!"

I rub my eyes. Margaret's crooked smile is blurring into and out of focus.

"Heavens," she says. "You can't be implying, my dear, that you do not know. Or suspect." She laughs her silvery laugh. "Surely the morning nausea must have been an indication to you. Of course, you are in strange surroundings and have had a good deal of other issues on your mind. And, of course, I could be mistaken. But I don't think I am. You have a luminousness about you, darling Amy. Have you taken a good look in the mirror lately? Your skin, your eyes. You're radiant. Everything about you fairly screams fecundity."

I lick my dry salty lips. "You don't understand. Margaret. There is no—" My voice cracks. "Itty bitty baby."

Margaret steps back and places her hands on her trim Chanel-clad hips. "I beg to differ! Forgive me for asking such a frightfully personal question, Amy. But isn't it true that you haven't menstruated for quite some time?"

This is ridiculous. My periods are none of Margaret's business. And I know I'm not pregnant, I just took a test last week. I push myself to my feet. It's time to go. Now. I'll get back to my hotel, somehow, pack up my stuff, find my way out to the airport, somehow, jump on a plane, and get back, somehow, to Phoenix. To my normal life.

Margaret trails me out of the study and to the living room. "Amy, my dear, I know right now this all seems like nonsense to you but I urge you to consider what I'm saying."

At the door to the guest room, I turn. "What have you done with my clothes? My own clothes?"

Margaret pouts her lips into a little moue. "Why, I sent them to the *blanchisserie!* They needed special attention after your mad adventure in the catacombs. Besides, you don't need them, dear, there are plenty of other things here. Lovely things."

"I do appreciate that. Thanks. But I need something to wear now, Margaret. I need to get dressed now." And then get the hell out of here. I'll mail the daughter's clothes back to Margaret later.

"Of course. But, first, do one small thing for me, Amy. Just one thing. In the bath, you will find a blue box on a shelf in the cabinet under the sink. It's marked '*test de grossesse.*' That's a pregnancy test. Just try it. Just take the test."

Margaret possesses a pregnancy test? I grab the doorframe for support. If only the room would stop twirling around. All this is craziness. Craziness piled on top of craziness. You can't tell people are pregnant just by looking at them. At least not right away. Anyway, I'm not. Granted, I have barfed three times in the last six days but there are plenty of other reasons for that. Jetlag. Stress. Grief.

Guilt.

"Amy, please," Margaret says, taking my arm and tugging me in the direction of the bathroom. "I am not trying to frighten you. I am trying to help you!"

The concern in her voice, the sincerity in her eyes, is genuine. Not psycho. But that's the thing with psycho—you can never really tell.

"If you take the test and it's negative, then there's no harm done, right?" Margaret persists. "If it's positive, as I believe it is, then you simply must know. I'll leave you to it." She gives me a gentle shove in the direction of the bathroom. "If you need me I'll be in the sitting room."

It is now the middle of the afternoon but I have not yet peed today. And I need to. Bad. But when have I had the chance, what with the barfing and the broken phone and the dealing with batty Margaret?

Thinking about peeing makes me need to pee even more. I hurry into the bathroom and lock the door behind me. But instead of sitting on the toilet I open the cabinet under the sink. I can't help myself. There, on the top shelf, is a blue box labeled "*test de grossesse*." Seriously, could the French think of a more disgusting word for pregnancy? The box has been opened and there is just one wand rattling around inside. The printing on the packaging is in French, but it's the same kind of deal as at home. You wouldn't need to know a word of French.

I can't resist. I plop down on the toilet, tear the plastic off the wand, and wave it through the rapid stream of urine. Just like the test at home, it has a plus sign and a minus sign. But since it is a French pregnancy test it says "*Enceinte*" next to the plus and "*Pas Enceinte*" next to the minus.

In less than thirty seconds a red dot appears.

Pas Enceinte. The red dot is next to the *Pas Enceinte*. Negative.

twenty-nine

I SHAKE THE WAND, just to be sure.

Still negative.

"Amy!" Margaret is on the other side of the bathroom door. "Amy! I can hear that you are—" She pauses and clears her throat. "I do apologize. I simply cannot contain myself. Have you tried it? Have you taken the test?"

I let the wand clatter to the tile floor. Well, okay then. I wanted to know, for sure, and now I do.

"Amy? Are you quite all right?" Margaret calls, jiggling the doorknob. There's a pause, and then a key is turning in the lock. I only have time to leap to my feet and flush before Margaret bursts through the door.

"Do forgive me," she says, ignoring the look of horror that I'm sure is on my face, "but I just could not bear to stand out there another moment. It is positive, isn't it? Oh, yes, I can see by your face it is!" She spots the wand under the footed tub and springs to snatch it up. For an older woman, a woman with silver hair, Margaret is extremely agile.

"Just as I thought. Marvelous news, just marvelous," she says, glancing at the wand. "Amy my dear. It's too thrilling!" She flings her arms around me. "Oh, you are ice cold. We must warm you up."

"What are you talking about?" I squirm out of Margaret's cloying embrace and pull the wand out of her hand.

Now the red dot is next to the plus. The *Enceinte*.

I rap the wand against the edge of the sink, and rub at the red dot with my thumb. "I—It—Margaret—"

But Margaret is not listening, she's steering me out to the living room. I let her swaddle a pink cashmere shawl around my shoulders and seat me next to the fire. "I can see you are in a state," she says, taking the wand out of my hand. "I've put the kettle on. Let me get you something for your feet." She disappears and reappears holding a pair of embroidered Moroccan-looking leather bedroom slippers.

"You must not fret, dear Amy, that you never suspected your condition," she croons, kneeling in front of me and fitting the slippers over my feet. "You would not be the first to do so, I can assure you. My mother had a distant cousin who didn't have the faintest clue that she was expecting until she went into labor." She hops up and stirs the fire. "Truly! According to my mother this cousin woke up in the small hours with contractions, which she took to be indigestion from the fish and chips she'd had for supper the night before. Mind you, she always was a stout woman. But in the end she had a perfectly lovely baby girl called Charlotte." Margaret leans against the mantle and smiles a wistful half smile. "In the end, everything turned out just beautifully. Just as it will for you."

The tea kettle wails. Minutes later, Margaret places a tray on the hammered copper side table. I throw off the cashmere shawl because now I am sweating. Too cold, too hot, positive, negative, it's enough to make a person want to barf.

Meanwhile Margaret continues to natter on. "Of course, we must get you seen to. The proper vitamins and whatnot. But we have time, all the time in the world." She splashes milk into a pink and white flowered china cup, drops in a lump of sugar the shape of a diamond, and pours in the tea. "A baby," she sighs, passing me the cup. "How wonderful. How delightful." She proffers a plate of shortbread cookies. "Biscuit?"

I take a sip of tea, the normal English black kind this time, and accept a cookie. If I drink something, eat something, I will be able to think. And I need to think.

"I am wondering," I begin, and choke on the dry cookie. "Margaret," I start again, "why did you have a pregnancy test in your bathroom?

Margaret chortles. "Oh that. Two years ago my daughter was pregnant. Or believed she was pregnant." The smile fades from her face. "A false alarm, I regret to say. But she at least was relieved. It was right after that she scarpered. She never even told me whom she thought the father was." She shakes her head. She looks old and sad, the way she does when she doesn't think anyone is looking.

I shudder and put down my teacup. If I focus on the perpendicular lines of the bookless bookcases on the opposite wall, the room steadies a little. There's something else I'm supposed to be asking about. Right, the results from the pregnancy wand.

"Margaret, the first time I looked at that wand, it showed negative."

"Surely not, dear!"

"No, really, it did."

"Tut tut. Enough of this nonsense," Margaret says, adding a sugar heart to her tea. "Now you need not look so tragic, Amy. Health care in France is excellent, and not ruinously expensive like in America." She leans forward and enfolds my icy hands in her warm ones. "I know this is a lot to take in, dear child. But give it time. I predict that you will soon find it all quite wonderful. I promise. And I will be here, to help you, every step of the way."

"But Margaret, that's craz—I mean, I can't stay here." Even if I were pregnant. Rather, especially if I were.

"Why ever not?"

"Well, I don't live here for starters. I don't belong here. I'm not French." More than that, there's William. If there were a baby, he would want me back. He would make up his mind to forget about Kat, overlook my little escapade to France, and concentrate on our future as a family. William is good at stuff like that.

Margaret again laughs her silvery laugh. "Well, I'm not French either! And haven't you always wished to live a cosmopolitan life in Paris? Now you can have it. It can all come true. All your dreams can come true."

All my dreams. Paris in the springtime. Paris in the fall. Paris when it sizzles, when it drizzles. Is this what Ella Fitzgerald was trying to tell me? I stroke the creamy silk of my gown and robe. Of Margaret's daughter's gown and robe.

"There is plenty of room for you to stay here with me," Margaret is saying, her eyes sparkling, her cheeks pink as punch. "Eventually I can help you gain residency papers in France. Perhaps you may even become a citizen one day. You wouldn't even have to give up your American nationality. You would have two passports. You would be a citizen of the world!"

Amy, lately of Phoenix, Arizona. Now, citizen of the world.

"Are you thinking of that husband of yours?" Margaret asks. "I, too, would like to have a word with that young man. To just go off and leave you like that. Unconscionable!"

True, William did leave me. Margaret is right. He is disgusted with me. He has given up on me. That could be the only explanation for why he left Paris so precipitously.

"But never you mind." Margaret is still talking. "There will always be the two of us. Soon to be three!" She beams. "Besides, nowadays, people create their own families, do they not? In any case, my dear child, nothing needs to be decided immediately. You are not risking a thing by staying here a while and reflecting a bit. You really do have all the time in the world."

All the time in the world. No. No one has that. I stand up, teetering.

"Sit, child," Margaret commands. "Your tea is growing cold. Or— oh my goodness—are you hungry? I'd be willing to wager you are! When was the last time you had a proper meal? Let me throw together an early supper."

The room swishes around like the inside of a Maytag. I sink back down into my armchair. Food. That will help. I tighten the pink cashmere shawl around my shoulders, because now I am freezing again, and lean back in my chair with my eyes closed while Margaret rattles around in the kitchen. Twenty minutes later a quiche—*tarte aux poireaux*, Margaret calls it—appears on the polished cherry dining table.

"Wait a minute," I say as Margaret glugs white wine into my glass. "If I am preg—" I clear my throat. "If you think I am really—pregnant, I shouldn't be drinking wine."

Margaret bursts out laughing. "Goodness gracious, child, a little *vin blanc* isn't going to hurt you! Pregnant women have been drinking wine for thousands of years. But, if you insist, I can offer you sparkling water. Only half as fortifying but twice as refreshing." She pops up, hurries to the kitchen, and returns with a bottle of Badoit. "Now tuck in. But leave room for dessert!" she says. "I am proud to be able to offer you my very own *poire belle-Hélène*."

I eat two slices of the quiche. Drink two glasses of the sparkling water, not because I am pregnant but because at the moment wine just doesn't appeal to me. *Poire belle-Hélène* turns out to be vanilla ice cream and poached pears topped with warm chocolate sauce and whipped cream. I eat that too. I eat it all.

thirty

THE APARTMENT IS STILL and silent when I wake the next morning. Last night, after the quiche and the *poire belle-Hélène*, Margaret made a pot of tisane—the familiar *verveine* this time. I wanted to ask about that other tea, the tea that made me sleep so long and so hard the night before, but Margaret brought out an enormous trunk of baby clothes, saved from the daughter's designer babyhood, and spent the rest of the evening exclaiming with delight over each tiny cap, each wee bootie.

I roll onto my side and come nose to nose with a plate of saltines on the nightstand. The woman doesn't give up. Of course that tea the other night was only tea. Or at most an herbal sleepytime-type tea. Margaret, who believes I am pregnant, who is over the moon at the prospect of an insta-daughter and an insta-grandbaby all rolled up into one handy package, would never drug me. At least not with anything dangerous. Sure, the woman's a little nutty. But not certifiable, not insane.

I stretch, sit up, swing my legs out of bed, and eat two of the crackers, for the salt and the crunch, not because I am pregnant. This morning my head is clear, my stomach calm. I cross the room and examine my face in the armoire mirror. The cookie-sized bruise on my forehead is turning from grisly purple to lurid yellow and my chin is still sore from where I scraped it in the catacombs, but other than that I look pretty good. Yesterday, the day I was supposed to fly back to Phoenix, is the past. Today, a brand new day, a clean crisp clear day, is the future.

And I am not alone, not stranded, not desperate. Margaret is offering me wiggle room, is offering me time and space—in Paris!—to decide my next move. Okay, she is a little bit of a loon, but also she's lovely. As a matter of fact, Margaret, even loony, would make the most adorable and adoring grandmother. The exact opposite, it needs to be pointed out, of my own mother, who disapproved in some molecular way of children and childhood, who had a gift of making me feel as if my very existence was a huge inconvenience.

But forget all that. Because I am not pregnant. After all, I have taken two tests. Plus I was pregnant once before, and it didn't feel anything like this.

A pink cashmere sweater and a pair of black wool crepe trousers are hanging on the armoire door. I can tell by looking at them that they will fit perfectly, and they do. I tiptoe into the living room—what Margaret calls her sitting room, so cultivated, so chic—and cross the Aubusson carpet to the three tall thin windows overlooking the street. Below, a trim middle-aged woman in a cream-colored raincoat is walking an overweight chihuahua. A sinewy man in a jalapeño-green jumpsuit is using a matching jalapeño-green plastic broom to scour the gutters. A schoolgirl skips across the narrow street, her backpack the same toasty gold as her ponytail and as the croissant she's munching.

Now there's an idea. I'll slip out to the *boulangerie* and buy fresh croissants for breakfast. Margaret has done so many things like this for me, so many kind, generous, thoughtful things. Now it's my turn. I cup my hands around my stomach and laugh without making any noise. One thing for sure, this is not a baby pooch. It's a croissants pooch, purely and simply. Buttery, carbie croissants, which strictly speaking are on the do-not-eat list but which Margaret, now snoring lightly in the next room, consumes every single morning of her life. And Margaret is slim and elegant, even past menopause.

If I stay in Paris for a little while longer I'll learn Margaret's slenderness secret, and then I'll be ready to face food, to face the rest of my life. Maybe even, in the fullness of time, to face William.

A wave of nausea sweeps over me with such force that I have to stand still and clap both hands over my mouth until it passes. Nothing. It's nothing. Or at least nothing a bakery-fresh croissant won't cure. I grab my tote bag and, because it looks like rain, pluck my crumpled fingertip length black trench coat from where it hangs next to Margaret's impeccable tan Burberry. I glance over my shoulder at the room as I gently pull back the bolt on the massive front door. The honey-gold parquet floors, the butter-pat yellow walls, the nut-brown leather armchairs—all so familiar already. The only imperfections are the handless clock on the mantelpiece and the fact that the bookcases contain no books. Maybe in addition to croissants I'll get some *pains au chocolat.* And some fresh raspberries from the greengrocer. A "punnet" of raspberries, Margaret would say.

"Punnet." "Greengrocer." "Cobbler." "Cheesemonger." These are words I would use every day, if I stayed in Paris, with Margaret.

The door squeals as I pull it open and Margaret's soft snoring skips a beat, but I slip out quickly, sprint silently down the stairs, scoot through the courtyard, and step out onto the sidewalk. The green-clad street cleaner nods at me as I cross the street. Like Margaret's apartment, Margaret's neighborhood also already feels familiar, more familiar than Phoenix ever has. I know the exact route to take to get to the bakery with the red-and-white-striped awning, which is at the top of the rue des Mauvaises Filles, the street where my hotel is. I pause to imagine a second, subterranean rue des Mauvaises Filles deep in the silent earth beneath my feet. One thing is for sure. My Paris has not been anyone else's Paris.

As I near the hotel I pause again. What I should really do is retrieve my suitcase and settle my bill. It's the adult thing. Wrap up loose ends, finish one thing before starting another—that's what Dad would say. What William would do.

"*Bonjour, madame,*" the deskman says as I enter the tiny smoky lobby. Same guy as always—he must work here twenty-four seven. A knowing smile forms around the corners of his mouth. Of course, he thinks I'm a slut. The kind of woman who reserves a hotel room and then disappears, showing up days later with a new haircut and new clothes.

Or not. Most likely he doesn't even remember me or my hair or my clothes. "*Bonjour, monsieur,*" I say. "*Je m'appelle Amy Brodie. Je cherche ma valise. S'il vous plaît.*"

The deskman stares at me as if I'm speaking Mandarin. But it's right there, my valise, standing behind the reception desk, the Manolo Blahnik sandals with the kitten heels perched on top, as if whoever packed up the bag somehow knew they did not belong with the rest of my things.

"*Ma valise,*" I repeat, pointing to the suitcase.

"Ah. But of course," he replies.

That's right, he speaks English. He just doesn't like to.

"Your bag, she is here," he says, and rolls it out from behind the desk.

"Yes, thank—"

"*Mais, madame!*" The deskman holds up his hand like a traffic cop. "*Attendez!* Your lover, I regret to say to you, your lover, he is not here." He rummages through his desk drawer, brings out a white envelope, and waves it in my face.

My mouth goes dry. Yes, I know, my lover, William, is not here. He has gone, left me. And the whole damn world seems to know all about it.

The deskman leans forward, tapping the envelope on the desk. "Your lover, he tell me, 'I have to go now.' But I know he is sorry."

I turn toward the door. Because I really don't need to hear this.

"He come," the deskman continues, raising his voice. "He come three times. He wait. For you. He is very sad."

Three times? I look back. "What do you mean? He didn't come three times."

"*Mais oui, madame.*" The deskman nods vigorously, as if relieved that I am not turning out to be as simple minded as I look. "He return here. Three times. *Trois fois.*"

I step back into the lobby, letting the door click shut behind me. "When exactly?" I ask, my scalp prickling. "Can you tell me when he was here? What day?"

The deskman grins in triumph and holds up a thumb. "First time, day before yesterday." Adds the index finger. "Second time, yesterday morning." Adds the middle finger. "Third time, yesterday evening. *Hier soir.*"

Hier soir was Sunday night. But that's impossible. William left Paris on Saturday. That's what Margaret said.

I stagger over to an orange plastic chair and sit down.

"*Ça va, madame?*" the deskman says, hurrying over and stooping to peer into my face.

"He was here just last night? Sunday night? *Dimanche soir?* Are you sure?"

"Most sure." He holds out the envelope he has been waving around. "He give me this. For you."

I tear it open. Inside is a folded piece of yellow legal paper, the paper William likes to use at work. The message starts halfway down the page. "Amy," it says, "I can't believe I'm leaving you another note at this stupid little hotel. I thought you were coming back. To the Hilton. Now I don't understand what you're doing. I hope you do. Meanwhile, I need to get back home. Major stuff is going on at work. You got yourself to Paris, so I guess you can get your way back. W."

I let the yellow paper waft to the floor. William waited for me, here, in this very spot. While I was only three blocks away, arguing with crazy-daisy Margaret, taking ridiculous pregnancy tests, chowing down on yet more food, William was here in this same tiny smoky hotel lobby, sitting in this same orange plastic chair, expecting me to come back to him.

Margaret lied.

Saturday night when Margaret and I took that slowpoke cab to the Hilton and Margaret said William had checked out, that was a lie. When we supposedly followed William to the airport, to catch up to him, to stop him from leaving—that was a lie, too. And the pregnancy test? The you-can-be-a-citizen-of-the-world business? Lies, all lies. Even the out-of-order phone—that was probably a lie as well.

That tea. It did have something in it. A fresh wave of nausea sweeps through me. I clench my fists and rock back and forth in the hard chair.

Two college-aged girls, blonde and tall and hearty, burst into the lobby, bringing with them a pair of bulging backpacks and a blast of cool air. The deskman busies himself with passports and keys and dispatches them upstairs, which gives me time to furtively check my tote bag. Which stupidly I did not do before I left the apartment.

But it's still all there. My money belt, my passport, my flight confirmation, my credit card, twenty-four hundred dollars, and three hundred euros. Margaret may be a liar and a kidnapper but she's not a thief. That's something.

When the girls leave I stand up, but before I can tell the deskman what I want he dashes for the door. "*Un instant*," he says, winking.

I call, "Wait!" but by the time I reach the door he is already across the street. Now what? He can't be going off to get Margaret. That would be impossible, he doesn't even know Margaret.

But it's becoming harder and harder to know what's impossible anymore. I may have no time to lose. I locate the card with Manu's phone number in my tote bag, stumble to the reception desk, grab the phone, and punch the buttons with a trembling hand. He answers on the fifth ring.

"*Allo*?"

"Manu? It's Amy. I'm sorry to call you so early in the morning."

"Amy," he says. "Talk to me." He doesn't sound in the least bit surprised to hear from me.

"I—I need your help."

"Yes. Of course."

"I'm sorry to ask, but could you, would you, take me to the airport? And help me buy a ticket to go home?"

I could get out to Charles de Gaulle on my own but negotiating a one-way, last-minute ticket? I would probably get arrested as a terrorist. And Manu did once offer to help me.

"Ah. Yes. Of course. Tell to me your location."

The lobby door whooshes open. "My hotel! The Hôtel du Cheval Blanc. I think you know where it is." I slam down the phone and whirl around.

The deskman is back. Not with Margaret, but with a red plastic tray holding two cups of steaming milky coffee and a basket of golden croissants.

"*Et voilà*," he says, placing the tray on the reception desk. He drags the orange chair over to the desk, and gestures to it. Sets a croissant on a thin paper napkin, and offers it to me with a courtly bow. "*Madame. Je vous en prie.*"

Buttery. Flaky. Crunchy.

"*Bon appétit*," he says, nodding.

I sink down into the chair. Accept the croissant. Accept the coffee.

thirty-one

I LOOSEN MY SEATBELT and admire the fat fluffy clouds floating beneath my window. So far so good. Better than good. The hotel deskman fed me breakfast, Manu drove me out to Charles de Gaulle, and—after Manu's skillful persuasion—the airport ticket agent sold me a reasonably priced ticket to Phoenix.

And they say the French are standoffish.

On the way to the airport, Manu also explained about Margaret.

"Amy," he said as we rounded a corner. "Can you relate to me what has occurred?" He was wearing the same black jeans and T-shirt as in the catacombs, only cleaner.

"Margaret," I said, and snorted. I was still really mad about the lies, the deception, the craziness. "She wanted to—sort of—keep me."

Manu laughed. "It is not shocking."

"It isn't?"

"Margaret is delightful. Formidable," he chuckled, braking for a woman in a green and yellow headdress pushing an enormous black baby stroller. "But she is not well. She has suffered a great loss. She had a daughter." He shook his head. "She had a daughter, who disappeared."

Great. The daughter again.

"I got that. She moved to Berlin with a guy, right?"

Manu glanced at me. "No, not to Berlin. *Pas du tout.* One morning two years ago, Margaret's daughter left the apartment to go to her *cours* at the university. And that was all."

"She ran away?"

"We do not know."

"She was kidnapped?"

"We do not know."

"So what happened?"

Manu paused. "We do not know."

"Oh," I muttered. Manu was telling me the story of a tragedy. Not a routine tragedy, the kind you can anticipate, brace yourself for, like bankruptcy or your grandmother dying or a divorce, but an enormous random tragedy that comes out of nowhere and flattens you. On an ordinary morning, a morning like any other, Margaret said goodbye to her daughter. Maybe it was a casual offhand goodbye, the kind where you barely look up, barely smile, barely register the person's leave-taking. Then she never saw or heard from her again. She doesn't know if her daughter is dead or alive. All she knows is that she's gone and that she, Margaret, is alone, and for no good reason.

"I'm so sorry, Manu."

He nodded. "After the police investigation, which found nothing, Margaret became terribly *malade*. She was obliged to stay in hospital many months."

"I didn't know," I said. "I feel bad. This morning I just left without telling her. I sort of snuck out actually." He must think I'm a great big fat jerk. Because, while Margaret's daughter may have abandoned her unwillingly, I surely did so on purpose.

"Of course. You are not the first. Margaret is amiable. *Conviviale*. And when she meets someone like you, someone who resembles her daughter—*eh bien*, some are kind, like you. Some are not."

Manu showing up to fix Margaret's computer that day—that was no accident. He probably stops by all the time, to keep an eye on her. "Does she have no other family? Like in England?"

"*Malheureusement non*." He goosed the gas to make a light. "She has no brothers or sisters. Her parents are of course deceased."

"She is lucky to have you."

"Ah. Well."

I was no longer mad at Margaret. Like me, she lost the person she loved the most. The one person who is irreplaceable. "Manu, will you thank her for me? For everything? She was really kind, for the most part."

"But certainly," he said.

We rode along in silence for a while. I did not ask if Manu had really been the daughter's boyfriend, or if he had figured in the possible pregnancy. It doesn't matter anymore. What matters is that Margaret has someone who cares about her. Weird to think I'll never see her again. Weird to think how distant and remote everything we shared already feels—the secret garden, the Garde Républicaine horsemen, the chocolate-milk Seine, the cheesemonger, the delicious meals at the cherry dining table and at the Café de la Poste, the endless tea and conversation beside the flickering fireplace.

In fact, when I get back to Phoenix and tell William the whole crazy story, he's going to have a hard time believing it. I don't even have proof that any of it happened. Only a new haircut and a strange outfit. I glanced down at my slacks and sweater.

"Manu," I said as we sped down the freeway. We were out in the country again, trees, meadows, fields. "These clothes I'm wearing, they belong to Margaret. To her daughter."

"*Oui*. I know it."

"Well. I should return them." Along with the Manolo Blahnik sandals riding in my tote bag.

Manu shrugged, waved his hand. "*Bof*. It does not matter."

"Still. Margaret might like to have them," I insisted. "I'll change at the airport." Amy 2.0 doesn't steal clothes.

"As you wish," said Manu.

The rest of the drive I kept an eye out for the giant green bottle by the side of the road but I either missed it, or we took a different route, or I hallucinated it the first time. I did not ask Manu, because if it was all in my head I really don't want to know. Even though it's no weirder than eighteenth-century horsemen clip-clopping down twenty-first century city streets, or a fire-and-brimstone mural of hell painted on a rock wall hundreds of feet below those same city streets. Or a pregnancy test that shows negative and then positive.

At the airport, it all goes as easy as pie—ticketing, passport control, security, boarding—and now the plane that is going to carry me back to real life, to the future, is hurtling five hundred miles per hour through the air.

I cannot sleep. I watch three movies, read five magazines, and am sitting with my eyes closed when we begin our descent into LA, where I have a tight connection. Which I make, again easy as pie, and, only twelve hours after leaving Paris, sooner than feels possible, I am pulling my trusty carry-on through Phoenix Sky Harbor's drab Terminal 2. Near the exit, I slow at the single payphone still remaining in service.

No. Face to face is best. I hurry past the phone and in less than an hour the shuttle van is gliding down my butter-smooth East Valley street.

"Right here. Here's where I live," I tell the ponytailed driver. I scan the façade of the house. Nothing has changed. Everything has changed.

I tip the driver even though he addressed me, twice, as ma'am, grab my tote bag and carry-on, fluff my new hair, smooth the skirt of my little black dress—it seemed like a smart idea to put on something I look and feel good in—and start toward the house. It's odd to walk up your own front walk, into your own courtyard, and knock on your own front door, like a mailman or a Mormon missionary. Especially at night.

"William?" I call, rapping on the door with the shiny brass-plated knocker. My voice is loud in the empty night. "Hey. Will? It's me."

He must be in bed. Of course. It's late and he has to be at work tomorrow morning. And he is not exactly expecting me. I wield the knocker again, this time with more force. I press the bell. Press it again.

But the living room light does not flicker on, the front door does not swing open, William does not burst out of the house, arms opened wide, to embrace me, to welcome me back, forgiven and restored to my so-called life.

Well, he always has been a dead sound sleeper and, now, with jetlag added to the mix, he must really be sawing logs. I unzip the carry-on and fish my house keys out of the same secret compartment I stashed the bar of Valrhona chocolate in. Maybe it's for the best. I can quietly hop in the downstairs shower, brush my teeth, slap on some of the jasmine-scented cologne he gave me last Christmas. When I sneak upstairs and crawl beside him into our king-sized bed, I will be clean and fragrant and irresistible. Sounds like a plan.

I use the key that four years ago William labeled "FD" for "front door" and give the door a soft shove, but it opens only three inches before stopping. The chain is hooked. Weird. We never bother with that chain.

"William?" I call, wedging my face into the opening. The air-conditioned air is crispy on my skin. "Hello! William! I'm home. Let me in!"

A car turns down our street, its headlamps sweeping the courtyard like prison camp searchlights, and without thinking I leap away from the door and crouch in the shadow of a rubber tree. Which is crazy— I'm not a burglar, I'm a homeowner trying to gain entrance into her very own home. I stand up and give the brass knocker four more good loud clacks. Try to see in through the living room picture window but the blinds are pulled shut. Odd. We never pull these blinds shut.

My forehead throbbing, I leave the carry-on by the front door and circle around the east side of the house to a wooden gate that leads to the backyard. We always keep this gate locked and it is so now, the key labeled "EG" for east gate hanging not on our key chains but on a hook next to the kitchen door in the garage. I rattle the gate anyway. It's a strong lock and a strong gate and a strong fence.

"William?" I shout. "Babe. Are you there? It's me." But, just as at the front of the house, the side of the house is stolid and silent. This is not how I imagined my homecoming.

I return to the courtyard and sit on my carry-on. The courtyard is the new front porch, the real estate lady told us during our hasty house-hunting four years ago. Ours boasts a waist-high adobe wall, handmade octagonal Mexican clay tiles, and a thirty-foot queen palm. Now a desiccating wind rustles the queen palm's knife-like fronds. I shiver, though the breeze is warm. No one knows I am here, between worlds, between possibilities, between lives. I could do anything right now. I could even pee in the lantana bushes and no one would know, or care.

The lantana, notoriously impossible to kill, would certainly not care. And I really have to pee. I should have gone at the airport but I was in such a huge hurry to get on a shuttle bus and get home. I calculate on my fingers. My flight landed at ten-oh-five. It took probably twenty minutes to disembark, and forty-five minutes for the shuttle ride out here. Making it eleven-thirty at the very earliest. I kick at the lantana. Maybe William took something to help him sleep. It's not like him to resort to artificial means but if he couldn't doze off he might have chugged some Nyquil, or even located some of the Ambiens left over from Kat.

Meanwhile there is still the matter of my bladder. I study the neighboring houses. All are dark—no night owls on this prim suburban street. Tomorrow morning everyone has places to go and things to do. Anyway, unlike William, I apparently don't know any of the neighbors well enough to call on them for assistance. Not even the people across the street with a ceramic plaque nailed to their door saying *Mi Casa es Su Casa*.

The lantana crackles. Rather, something deep within the lantana crackles. Just when peeing all over its sprawling purple and yellow flowers—each plump blossom like a Barbie-sized wedding bouquet—was starting to sound like a good idea. But here, in the desert, crackly sounds tend to mean something poisonous, something predatory. Tarantulas, scorpions, rattlesnakes, Gila monsters, black widow spiders. One morning not long ago we spotted a coyote trotting down the middle of our street, the corpse of a rabbit dangling from its jaws. Desert means danger.

In any case, only eight blocks away, on Gilbert Road, is a twenty-four-hour gas station with a perfectly acceptable toilet. I leave my carry-on in the courtyard, out of sight behind the waist-high adobe wall, and set off down the sidewalk, fast. After I've peed I'll be able to think more clearly.

At the gas station the bearded and turbaned attendant hesitates before handing over the block of wood attached to the key to the ladies' room. It's the same attendant I do business with every time I gas up the Honda, now locked up in the garage and inaccessible, but tonight he doesn't recognize me. Maybe it's the late hour. Maybe it's my new haircut. Or maybe, on foot, without a motor vehicle, I have become unrecognizable, the *other*. In Phoenix, pedestrians are not...pedestrian. They are the suspect, the bizarre, the what-is-wrong-with-this-picture.

In the ladies' room I take an extra minute to wash my face and comb my hair, the idea being to ensure that William is glad, not repelled, to see me. In that respect the little black dress—tight bodice, short skirt—was a good choice, but two minutes later, as I cross Gilbert Road, a tricked-out pickup truck roars by me.

"He-ey, *mamasita!*" A tequila bottle skitters across the pavement, bouncing off one of my heels. I squeal and sprint for the sidewalk. "It's a good safe neighborhood," William noted with satisfaction when we were house hunting. But not in the middle of the night. Not for a lone woman wearing a little black dress.

I cower under the drooping branches of a pepper tree until the rap music and the marijuana smoke fade away, and then take off my shoes and run the rest of the way home, the sidewalk smooth and warm under my bare feet. At the house I again unlock the front door, pushing it open as far as it will go.

"William?" I shout, my nose pressed against the metal chain. Nothing.

I again circle around the east side of the house, this time to lob pebbles at our second-story bedroom window. Hey, it works in the movies. But William's face does not appear in the glass; he does not slide open the window and call down to me like Rapunzel or Juliet. I sort through my keys, but the one that opens the wooden side gate has not magically appeared. Here's another key though. It unlocks Kat's ministorage locker on Gilbert Road.

Ten minutes later I am rolling up the orange accordion door of the storage locker. No all-night security, thank God, is around to see me step inside and pull the door down after me. The muscles of my legs quaking, I flick on the overhead light, sink onto the thin carpet, hug my knees, and look up. Well, one thing has not changed—my ten-foot-high tower of plastic storage bins packed to the lids with ramen noodles, Vienna sausages, freeze-dried soups, canned sardines, caffeinated energy drinks, chemical-y crackers, processed meals-in-a-box, trail mix, and more, is still there. William, if he were in the mood to be amused, which most likely he is not, would laugh to see all this stuff.

William. It would be awful if he weren't even in Phoenix. If he were, somehow, still back in Paris, looking for me.

thirty-two

WHEN THE FIRST harsh ray of yellow morning sun shoots through the crack under the orange door and heats my toes, I get up. It is time to get back to the house.

Because it's impossible that William could still be in Paris. He left Phoenix before I did, and when I left the security chain was not hooked. Therefore, William must have done it. Therefore, he must have returned.

However, before leaving the storage locker I have to move the food boxes. Last night I stacked them in front of the door because— news flash—you can't lock self-storage lockers from the inside. This is probably the first thing that people who try to live in them learn. I experimented with jamming the mechanism with a toothbrush but it didn't seem secure, and neither did a shoe, and neither did a two-pound sack of elbow macaroni, so I ended up moving the entire collection of boxes. Then I sat down and waited for morning, staring at my protective wall of food. I will donate it all to some worthy charity soon. Or, better yet, throw it out. Why should people who need to take charity have to eat crap?

Dinner on the plane was more than twelve hours ago so, also before leaving the storage locker, even though I am not that hungry, I excavate an energy bar from one of the boxes. The industrial-strength sweetness makes my teeth curl. A far cry from real French croissants for breakfast, just as the canned coffee that I use to wash down the energy bar is disgusting compared to a real true French *café-crème*. Still, it's wet and I need the caffeine. I'll have a bowl of cereal when I get home. Oat bran. With cumin.

No one is around, thank God, to question why a woman who obviously slept in her clothes is emerging from a rented mini-storage locker at dawn. I run my fingers through my hair. I'm sure William's going to like my new look, I'm sure he's going to like the new and improved Amy 2.0.

On our street I am the only thing moving, automotive or animal. For the third time since returning to Phoenix I hurry up my own front walk, enter my own courtyard, and unlock my own front door.

For the third time, the security chain is still hooked.

"William? Are you up yet?" I call. "It's me. Amy." I clang the brass knocker, punch the doorbell button. "Will?"

But the house is as silent and still as the Paris catacombs. I circle around to the side gate but it is just as locked, just as impassively impassable, as before. "Will?" I call again.

Nothing. I missed him. No doubt jetlag woke him early and so he went into the office early. Stuff is going on at work, he said in his note.

I feel silly again parking my carry-on behind the adobe wall and again heading for the gas station on Gilbert Road. But I am still phoneless. The attendant, still the same one as last night, is busy with a customer and does not see me beeline across the blacktop to where a pay phone stands housed in a half-booth under a spindly palo verde tree. When I left for Paris, only a little over a week ago, the palo verdes were covered with tiny yellow flowers. Now the pale blossoms have dropped to the ground and are wafting about in golden powdery drifts. In the desert, blink and you'll miss spring, Dad used to say. I lift the dusty phone receiver from its cradle, insert my single-girl credit card into the slot, and enter our home number into the keypad. We must be the last people in North America to still have a land line. I don't expect William to answer, I was just over there, but my plan is to leave a strong, positive message on the voice mail, for him to hear should he decide to check it.

The ringtone is cut short by my own cheerful voice. "Hi, you've reached William and Amy, leave us a message and we'll call you back right away."

I crush the receiver to my ear. When I recorded that jaunty message four years ago Kat was healthy, I had a job, and William was a jigsaw-puzzle-doing, baseball-watching, math-loving husband. My life was normal.

"W-William?" I stammer. "Will? I'm back. I can't get in the house. You hooked the chain. I don't have my phone. I'll be—"

Where? Standing next to a public phone in a gas station parking lot? Sitting on my carry-on in our front courtyard? Sleeping on the floor in the food storage locker?

I don't have a plan. I never really had anything remotely resembling a plan. I drop the receiver, stagger around the palo verde tree, and spew the energy bar and the canned coffee all over a creosote bush. Not again. This is ridiculous.

"Hey. What are you doing?"

The gas station attendant is standing a little off to one side, fists on hips, a scowl crinkling the upside down V of his orange turban.

I slowly straighten, wiping my mouth with the back of my hand. "What the hell do you think I'm doing?" I say. "I'm using the phone."

"Are you sick?" he asks, eyeing with disgust the splats of undigested energy bar coating the spindly branches of the creosote bush.

He still doesn't recognize me as the regular customer with the late-model silver Honda SUV, the thinnish not-bad-looking woman who buys an over-priced bottle of Pellegrino every time she fills up. No, as far as he's concerned I'm a homeless person, a vagrant, a bum, a cast-off of society needing to be hustled off the premises before she scares away his paying clientele, decent God-fearing folk who don't wander Gilbert Road on foot at all hours of the day and night.

"It's a public phone," I say. He wears a hairnet around his beard. Funny I've never noticed that before.

"You can't—" he begins, but just then an RV the size of a city bus wheezes up to the gas pumps.

Saved by the profit motive. As he hustles away, I pick up the dangling receiver and pause. I don't know William's office number. I know his cell number because it's only one digit different from mine, but unless he's traveling William never answers his personal cell during the day. He is probably the last person in the western hemisphere to not take personal calls at work. He will respond to texts, but of course I can't text because I don't have my smart phone.

The only other phone numbers I have memorized are my own, Kat's, and the library's. That's the one disadvantage of smart phones— you don't keep numbers in your head anymore.

I again shove the credit card into the pay phone, and dial the library.

Seven rings later, Rose answers.

"Hello, is Sara there?" I say. Sara is the sweetest of the volunteers, the kind of person who smiles while she speaks.

"No, she doesn't come in till ten." Rose pauses. "Amy?"

I take the receiver from my ear and clasp it to my chest but I can still hear Rose's voice.

"Amy? Is that you?"

It's Rose. Snoopy, interfering old Rose, who has an opinion about everything under the sun and never hesitates to share it with anyone within earshot. But it's someone, someone who knows me, someone who wants to talk to me. I slowly bring the receiver back up to my ear.

"Amy? Are you there? Is something wrong? Where in the world have you been? We've been trying to reach you all week."

"Hello, Rose. I—I'm locked out of my house."

"What? Where are you now? Have you called a locksmith?"

A locksmith. Now that's an idea that had not occurred to me—a locksmith to help me break into my own house. I really must be brain dead. "I lost my phone," I say.

Rose is silent for a few seconds and then says, her voice low and urgent, "Listen, Amy. Is everything all right? You don't sound so good."

At this moment the bus-sized RV rumbles away, farting diesel fumes, and the gas station attendant once again heads toward me. Screw this. Kitty-corner across the intersection is another gas station with another pay phone. I hang up the phone and hurry away, blowing my nose on a cocktail napkin from the airplane.

This time Rose picks up on the first ring.

"Amy?" she says. "Is that you?"

"Yes, I'm sorry. We got disconnected."

"Where are you, honey?"

"I'm at a gas station. On Gilbert Road. The, um, Arco."

"And you're locked out of your house? And your husband can't leave work to let you in, is that it?"

"Listen, is Jenna there?" Another of the volunteers, this one closer to my age.

"No. Stay where you are," Rose says. "I'll come get you."

"What? No, you don't have—"

"Stay where you are. I'm coming."

I wait in the relative cool of the gas station ladies' room, which someone left unlocked and which, like the phone, is handily out of sight of any attendants. The day is already pizza-oven hot. April is nearly gone and soon the bullying summer sun will seal us all indoors, will make prisoners of us all. Why would anyone choose to live in such a god-awful climate? Honestly, you expect to see cow skulls lying by the side of the road.

"Gadzooks. You look like hell," says Rose as I slide into the passenger seat beside her.

"I'm, um, jetlagged," I say. "Thanks so much for coming to get me."

"Where to? I can run you over to your husband's office if you like."

"Oh no," I say. "That's too far. Halfway across the Valley. Maybe we can just use your phone to call a locksmith?"

"You bet." Rose, surprisingly, doesn't pepper me with questions. Instead she produces an actual phone book from her overstuffed book bag and together we locate a locksmith and arrange to meet him at the house.

"So what have you done to yourself?" Rose asks as she pulls her ancient but well-cared-for Toyota into my driveway.

"Done?"

"You look like somebody clobbered you with a baseball bat."

"Oh. Right." I touch my still-bruised temple, and the scab that has formed on my chin. "It's nothing."

"But your hair is—wow," Rose adds.

"My hair? I got it cut."

"It's fab. The perfect length for your face."

"Thanks."

I fiddle with the razored ends. Razored greasy ends. It hasn't been washed since I got it cut, days ago now.

"I'm sorry about not coming into the library last week," I say. "I should have notified you. I went on a—a trip. It was sort of, um, unplanned." How excellent it would be if the locksmith showed up soon. Like this very moment. "You know, you don't have to wait with me, Rose. You must be busy."

But Rose insists on staying until the arrival of the locksmith, who uses bolt cutters to slice through the security chain and who takes credit cards.

"Where did you say your husband was?" Rose says, trailing me through the living room and into the kitchen.

"He's at work." Of course he is. Where else would he be? "He goes in early sometimes. I guess you do, too."

"I like to get a few good hours in before we open. While it's still quiet." Rose places her plump hands palms down on the granite countertop. Her skin is smooth, creamy. She is wearing tomato-red capris and a black-and-white Missoni tunic. Probably Missoni from Target but still.

"Amy," Rose says now, "I'm just going to put this out there. I'm worried about you. For weeks you've been coming in to work with red eyes and a red nose. Then you disappear. Then you show up days later in a gas station parking lot. You obviously slept in that dress. You're beat up. You're locked out of your own house. You don't even know where your husband is, do you? Not really?"

I sit on a barstool and twirl slowly around, looking at my house that is not an apartment in Paris. Still, I sort of missed it. Missed my books, my computer, my shower. Rose rat-a-tats on the countertop with one of her long red fingernails. I've never noticed Rose's nails before. And her rings. Turquoise and silver. At least a half dozen of them. She was super helpful with the locksmith and all and it was great, but now it would be even more super if she would just go.

Fat chance.

"I have to ask," Rose says, "has he done something to you?"

"Who?"

"Your husband. He hasn't beat you up, has he?"

"What? Oh my God. Rose!" I jump off the barstool. "You don't know what you're talking about!"

"Okay," Rose says, holding up her hands like an actor in a bad Western. "I get it. Back off, right?"

Right. Also please go. I remember to smile. "Rose. Thanks for everything. I really mean it. Thanks."

"No prob. What are friends for? I'll check on you later though. Just to see that you're doing okay."

I stand at the living room window to watch Rose's Toyota swerve into the street and squeal away. Funny. I have lived in Phoenix all my life and I know a lot of people, but Rose is the one who came to my rescue, Rose is the one who was there when I needed somebody. I will thank her better later, get to know her better. Later.

When the Toyota's brake lights wink out of sight around the jacaranda tree on the corner, I return to the kitchen. Everything looks as organized and clean as when I left it, just one week and one day ago. There isn't even a dirty coffee cup in the sink. But when I take the orange juice pitcher out of the refrigerator and hold it up to the light, I see the change I'm searching for. The level is a good four inches lower than when I left. Proof positive that William has been here. I pop the lid off the plastic pitcher and stick my nose in. Orange juice doesn't smell like oranges. It isn't even orange.

But my mouth waters because orange juice is frigging delicious. I pour myself a big sunshiny yellow glass—a flagrant violation of rule number nineteen of the perpetual diet—and carry it and the portable phone over to the white leather sofa. What I would like to do is curl up with a pillow and blanket and sleep, sleep, sleep, for days on end. But that is not an option.

William's direct office number is number three on our speed dial. I sit on the arm of the sofa and run my thumb over the smooth plastic nubs of the keypad. I push three.

thirty-three

IT RINGS. And rings.

This is not normal. When I worked there, company policy decreed that you or voice mail had to pick up by the fourth ring.

So I dial his cell, again knowing he will not answer, and again hearing the message he left me before he came to Paris. I wait for the beep and say, my voice all quavery, "Will, it's me again. I'm at home now. I got in the house. Give me a call. When you can." Then I hang up the phone and guzzle down the entire glass of orange juice.

Ah, sugar. There's a reason we're all hooked. Sugar gives me the strength to pull the little black dress, now filthy, over my head as I hurry upstairs to shower. Because I need to be clean, I need to be ready, I need to have my act together. In case, for instance, William happens to come home early, as he might since he went in early.

Thirty minutes later I am fresh and dry and slipping into my own underwear—not a lacy thong but my own soft white cotton undies. I select my turquoise top, William's favorite, and yoga pants, pure comfort after Margaret's daughter's tailored couture. And flip flops. An outfit no one in Margaret's world would be caught dead in.

What will Margaret do when she realizes I have gone for good? Manu must have explained by now. He must have returned the cashmere sweater and wool crepe trousers, probably staying for lunch, which was probably raw oysters and trout with their heads on. At the airport he jotted down Margaret's mailing and email addresses and gave them to me. "Perhaps you will be her friend," he said, kissing me first on the right cheek, then on the left. "I will," I promised, "I will."

Despite the orange juice calories, my stomach is now rumbling urgently so I head down to the kitchen, mix up a big bowl of oat bran, and stick it in the microwave. While breakfast nukes I try William's office number again. This time it does go to voice mail, without ringing even once.

"The number you have reached," a computer voice says, "is no longer in service. If you feel you have reached this number in error, please try dialing again."

That can't be right. I ignore the microwave beeping the status of the oat bran and run up to the den to dig out the hard-copy list William keeps of all our phone contacts. I need to sit down as I dial the extension for Robert, who sits in the cubicle next to Will, because I am suddenly feeling very shaky.

"The number you have reached," the computer voice begins. I do not let it finish. I race downstairs, grab my keys, and head to the garage without even putting on make-up.

There is no reason to panic. The company's phone system is wonky today, that's all. But I feel in my gut that something is wrong.

Traffic is light this time of day so only forty-five minutes later I am squealing into the parking lot of William's office. The lot is half empty— my layoff was only one of many—but as usual the U.S. and Arizona flags are hanging limply from their shiny aluminum poles beside the front door. And as usual Weird Norman's car is parked in the Employee of the Month spot right next to the poles. Norman, who works in quality assurance, is awarded this spot two months out of three. "I think it's rigged," I said once, but William shook his head. "No, it's metrics," he said. "Norman's numbers are always high. It's as simple as that."

I troll up and down each and every row of the parking lot. Seven of the vehicles are Jeeps. Three of the Jeeps are white. Zero are William's.

Numbers. Our friends.

I park the Honda in the visitor's spot and enter the cool black and silver lobby, which I have not set foot in since the day I was escorted out of the building by my confused and apologetic boss. Jackie the receptionist hurries out from around her desk, her usual phony smile planted on her face.

"Amy! You cut your hair! I almost didn't recognize you!"

"Hi, Jackie," I say, accepting her hug. "I'm stopping by to give Will something. Is he around?"

Jackie's smile fades. "Will Brodie? Your Will?"

Of course Will Brodie. Who does she think? I nod.

Jackie's black eyes are as round as olives. "Will left for lunch early with Robert and the rest of his team." She pauses. "You know, to celebrate. His big promotion." She does not add, "You should know this. In fact, you should be with him," but she doesn't have to. Her face says it all.

I stand frozen for five long seconds before fake-slapping my forehead with the heel of my hand.

"Right! I knew that! I must be losing my mind. In fact, I'm on my way over there now," I babble, hastening for the door. "You're looking great, Jackie, by the way. Good to see you. Bye." She's a distant cousin of the CEO. She will keep this job until they have to carry her out feet first.

Outside, I accidentally shift the Honda into drive instead of reverse and bump up onto the sidewalk, hitting the brakes just in time to keep from plowing into the plate glass lobby door. I grind my teeth and my gears, shift into reverse, thump back down off the sidewalk, and lay rubber out of the parking lot, not looking back to see if Jackie is watching. Because of course she is.

I understand now. William got his big promotion, the one he's been gunning for since the whole T-30 thing started. His extension no longer works because he's been moved to the fourth floor, where management lives. And he's out celebrating, with the gang, not checking his phone, not wondering if I got back from Paris in one piece, or at all.

Maybe Margaret was right. Maybe William isn't the person I believed him to be. Maybe I never truly knew William, just as I never truly knew Kat. Or, for that matter, Margaret.

Or, for that matter, myself.

The traffic has thickened and it is ninety minutes before I am guiding the Honda into its usual place on the left side of our garage. The right side, where William's Jeep goes, is still empty. I am still famished and dehydrated but the first thing I do when I get into the house is again dial William's office number. His extension should have been routed to his new office by now. But I get the same this-number-is-out-of-service message as before. I try his cell, just in case, but get the same recording as the last two times, and do not leave a message.

Because I can't think of anything to say. William is living a rich and full life without me. Good things are happening for him and to him, without me. I check the time. One-thirty. If everything were normal he would be back from lunch and returning my call by now.

I pace around the upstairs den in tight circles, clutching the phone to my chest. Everything is not normal.

I wander downstairs and into the guest bathroom, where the Sacré-Coeur still hangs. It did not care at all about me when I was actually there. Still, I have a feeling it isn't done with me yet. Or, rather, that I'm not done with it.

Maybe Granddad knows something. William and his grandfather are tight. He might have called him first thing, with the great news. William's grandfather is Will's biggest fan.

He picks up on the third ring.

"Amy! What a nice surprise! How's my favorite pretty girl?"

He sounds, as always, like a distilled, boiled-down, purified version of William. How William will sound in sixty years.

"I'm good. Fine. How are you?" I can't ask him if he knows where William might be because William's my husband. I'm supposed to already know where he is.

"Darlin', any day you wake up on the right side of the grass is a good day."

William's grandfather still lives on his own at age ninety-three and never lets you forget it.

"Hey, did you hear the one about the Scottish pub owner and the parakeet?"

Before I can answer he launches into a convoluted tale. "And then," he concludes fifteen minutes later, "the old guy says to his wife, he says, 'Shoot low, Mavis, they're riding Shetlands!' Hee hee hee."

"Granddad," I say, laughing in spite of myself, "I have to get going. Just thought I'd check in."

Because it's obvious. William's grandfather is either a master actor or he has no idea anything is going on with William.

thirty-four

I HEAR FOOTSTEPS.

He's home, he's here, finally. "Will?" I shout, dropping the phone. "I've been looking all over for—"

But it's not William, it's Rose, lugging two bulging Whole Foods grocery bags. "Amy! You weren't asleep, were you? Your front door was unlocked so I let myself in."

"The front door was unlocked?"

But Rose is not pausing for explanations, she's heading to the kitchen. When I catch up to her she is plopping the bags on the counter. "Figured you wouldn't have anything in the house to eat," she says, "so I picked up some lunch." She takes a hot, fresh, organic roast chicken out of one of the bags.

Crispy. Meaty. Juicy.

But no. I can't do this right now. "Rose," I say. "I thank you, but I don't have time for lunch. I'm really really busy."

She rolls her eyes at me and takes out the contents of the other bag. Carrots, radishes, scallions, grape tomatoes, a long thin English cucumber, a bag of mesclun greens, and a trio of bell peppers, red, yellow, orange. Ingredients for salad. Not salty fatty mayonnaise-y prepared salad from the deli section, but real true raw fresh salad, straight from the Garden of Eden. I have to grab a wall for support. The armpits of my turquoise top, so clean and cool when I put it on a couple hours ago, are sticky with sweat, yet my arms themselves are covered with goosebumps. I am boiling and freezing at the same time.

I guess that's how much I like salad.

"Amy!" Rose drops the bag of greens. "Cupcake, what's wrong? What is it?" She hurries over to me, wraps her arm around my waist, and guides me to a barstool. "Sit," she commands. I sit. She grabs a brown paper sack, empties out the mushrooms it was holding, and holds it over my mouth.

"Breathe," she says. I breathe.

She locates a bottle of sparkling water in the refrigerator and places it in front of me. "Drink. Take your time," she says, plucking a chef's knife from the rack on the wall and looking around for a cutting board.

I drink.

While Rose slashes the lacy tops off the carrots I rest my elbows on the counter and hold my face between my hands, watching. The sight and scent of so much magnificent food is very nearly unbearable. But food is not going to help me. Food is not going to save me. Nor is it going to condemn me. Food is just—food.

"Bet you're surprised," Rose says as she rinses scallions at the sink. "Bet you thought I'd be more likely to show up with a bucket of Kentucky Fried Chicken. Or a bag of Big Macs." She smirks.

"No, not at all," I lie. "But Rose—" I glance at the clock. It has somehow become two-fifteen. "Rose, I'm sorry, but I don't have time for a big meal right now."

"*Au contraire.* You're going to eat something before you drop."

Rose's knife skills, as William would say, are primo. And maybe she's right, maybe some sustenance will help. After all, I haven't consumed anything since dinner on the plane last night, unless you count that yucky energy bar at dawn, which I didn't keep down long enough to even begin to digest.

"Your salad looks lovely," I say. She finishes coining the carrots, cubing the cucumber, dicing the scallions, and slicing the mushrooms before I find the strength to get up and fetch her a salad bowl.

"Ya think? I knew it would be just the thing for you." She grabs a paring knife and swiftly carves the radishes into roses. "Because I've had my eye on you, Miss Amy. You don't eat anything that's not *moltissimo* healthy. Or calorie-free."

"Not true," I protest, cradling a glossy red bell pepper in my hand. It is achingly beautiful. "I eat plenty of non-healthy-type food."

"At the same time staying so willowy? I don't think so," Rose says, appropriating the bell pepper and reducing it to slivers. "What's your secret?"

"Secret?" The aroma of vegetables, crisp, delectable vegetables, is making my toes tingle. I filch a carrot and nibble on it. I will eat a little something, just enough to get my energy level up, and then get rid of Rose. Kindly.

"Your secret to staying so slender," she says, waggling her ample hips while she whisks together a vinaigrette. "As you can see, I am in pressing need of your wisdom!"

My heart sinks. Wisdom. What a joke.

"Seriously," Rose says. "I'm curious. I really want to know."

I eat two mushrooms and go to get plates. "Well, I have rules," I finally say, setting the table for three. Because what if William walks in? I need to be ready for any and every eventuality.

"Ooh. What kind of rules?"

I sigh. My so-called rules for the perpetual diet. It's been days since I've thought of any of them. They feel now like something from long ago and far away, something not important anymore, something ridiculous and juvenile I no longer have time for. "Different kinds," I say, glancing at the clock. "You might think some of them are a little crazy." I wish she would finish the salad.

"Come on," Rose persists. "Lay a couple of 'em on me."

I align the placemats so they are exactly one-half inch from the edge of the table. Presentation is everything, Margaret would say.

"Talk to me," says Rose.

"Well, for instance," I say, straightening a fork, "two-thirds of your dinner should be vegetables."

"Yeah? Tell me more."

"Drink a lot of water—that's another one."

"Those don't sound crazy. I want to hear something crazy." Rose transfers the chicken to a platter and proceeds to carve. "Just tell me one really weird one," she coaxes.

Table set, I lean my perenially poochy stomach against the cool rounded edge of the granite countertop. I can't tell Rose about the no-fat-friends rule because Rose is, in fact, a friend. And, crazily, she is turning out to be a sort of gift from the universe. All those awful jokes Kat and I made at Rose's expense. My cheeks burn. Kat led me wrong there.

"Okay," I say, tracing my fingers along one of the swirls in the granite. "I have an elbow test."

"Elbow test? Loving it already."

"Every time I sit down I check to see if I can feel the flesh of my waist on the insides of my elbows. Usually I can't." I don't have the courage to look up at Rose, whose eyes I can feel on me. I know she has stopped slicing chicken and is listening with rapt attention. "But if I can, I know I've gained," I continue. "So then I can dial back on the eating before the situation gets out of hand. Ideally."

Rose snorts. "Hmm. Never would have thought of that one. Where do you get these rules? Out of a book?"

"No. I just sort of make them up as I go along."

"Sounds like you have it all figured out."

"Not really. I just don't want to get—um—"

"Get fat? You can say it."

I look up at her then, but she's not mad, she's grinning.

"Listen," she says, placing a platter of chicken in the center of the table next to the salad. It's a beautiful meal, a healthy, delicious, enticing, delightful meal, everything a meal should be. "Listen," she repeats, "everyone has a problem. Everyone overdoes something. I overdo things by overdoing them. You overdo things by—er—underdoing them." She laughs. "What I mean is, gorging on dieting is as bad as gorging on eating." She pulls out a chair and plops down. "Anyhoo, I am the last person to be passing out diet advice. But I'd bet you dollars to doughnuts there's a way to appreciate food without turning into, for example, *moi.*"

Doughnuts. God. I sit down at the table. Rose serves herself a thin slice of chicken breast, no skin, and loads up the rest of her plate with salad. As if she were trying to implement the rules. Or is mocking the rules. It's impossible to tell.

"So what's up? What's going on?" Rose asks after we have eaten in silence for a few minutes.

I swallow a tender mouthful of chicken. Sip some sparkling water. Rose was right. Food helps. Food gives strength. And I'm going to need strength. "I went on a trip," I say.

"Yup. You told me."

"My husband. I saw him there. We had a sort of—fight. And then he came back before me, but now he seems to be gone again." I spear a grape tomato, pop it into my mouth, and let my gaze rest on the phone sitting mutely on the kitchen counter behind Rose. William must be long back from his celebration lunch by now. Jackie must have told him about my visit. Yet he does not call.

"Hold on," Rose says. "Start from the beginning. You said you went on a trip. Where to?"

I put down my fork and swallow hard. "Paris."

Rose's eyes pop. "Paris? Really? And you say you 'saw' your husband there? You mean you didn't go together?"

"It's a long story," I say.

"I love long stories."

Slowly at first, and then in one big data dump, I relate the whole tale. Kat's death, The Plan, meeting Margaret, losing my phone, the catacombs, being arrested, connecting with and then not connecting with William, the sort-of kidnapping. Everything but the pregnancy test. After all, it's a non-issue. I figured out on the plane that the two-year-old test Margaret had was sure to be defective in some way.

"Gadzooks," Rose says. "What a saga!"

I again glance at the clock. Nearly four p.m. now. And still no sign from William.

Rose squints at me for a moment and then slowly gets to her feet. "So, my dear, what's your next move?"

"Find William. Apologize. Get on with my life. Our lives."

"Really. Is that what you want?"

"Of course it is." Why do people keep asking me this?

"I realize it's what you *say* you want. Believe you want." Rose retakes her seat across from me, places her creamy hands on the table between us, laces her fingers together, and leans forward. It must be hard to be Rose. She's smart and well educated and capable, but I know people don't take her seriously, just because of her appearance. "Listen," she says, "you say you want to be with this guy. But what do you do? Five minutes after you get married you start to secretly stash away cash. Then you spend three years planning a secret trip without him. Then you actually go on the trip, keeping up the secret through numerous phone calls. Then you two somehow miraculously connect in Paris, but after an argument you walk out on him." She smiles at me. "Correct me if I'm wrong, but I'm sensing a pattern here."

Before I can open my mouth to deny or contradict Rose goes on.

"I'm not saying you're lying, or a bad person. I think you do care about William because I get the feeling he's a pretty stand-up guy. But when you should move toward him, you always seem to move away from him. And while I can't be sure, I think he's doing the same. He did just leave you stranded there in Paris. I mean, good Lord. And now he's AWOL. You don't even know where he is, do you?"

"Stop!" I finally cry, jumping to my feet.

Rose leans back and shrugs. "I'm sorry, Amy. This is just how things look from where I sit."

I turn my back on her and stride over to the sliding glass door that opens to the patio. "You don't know what you're talking about," I mumble, resting my forehead on the warm glass. In the backyard, not a blessed thing stirs. Not a leaf, not a twig, not a frond. It's weird to say, but in Phoenix it is heat that freezes everything in place.

Rose chuckles. "Well, kiddo, it wouldn't be the first time."

Outside a gang of grackles comes to roost in a carob tree. I didn't want to plant a carob tree because the pods are messy and in the spring the blossoms smell like semen, but William insisted because they are drought tolerant. I shake my head and turn around. "Thanks for listening, Rose, and for the lunch," I say as I hurry to the living room and the front door. "It was delicious. Really, really good. But do you mind going right now?" I call over my shoulder. "I have a lot to do."

A moment later Rose appears, purse in hand, sheepish smile on face. "I'm sorry if I've upset you, Amy. But sometimes we need other people to reflect our stories back to us. If that makes any sense."

I smile back at her, because she really does mean well, and then open the front door as wide as it will go. As she crosses the living room, Rose glances at my carry-on, still standing at the foot of the stairs, and winks. "I see you haven't unpacked yet."

I clench my jaw and do not answer. Please, please just go. Rose pauses at the threshold. "Here are my phone numbers. Home and cell. And my address, just in case," she says, fishing a business card out of her purse. "And another thing. That assistant job at the library? It's yours if you want it. Just say the word."

I accept the card she is holding out. "Thanks. That's great of you. Really."

She snaps her purse shut, hooks it over her shoulder, steps out into the heat, and pauses once again. "I just had a thought," she says. "Your husband located you using credit card records, isn't that right? Maybe you can find out what he's been up to the same way. Ciao. You look fab, by the way. I've been meaning to mention it. This morning you looked like something the cat dragged in but now—wow. You're radiant."

"Thanks," I murmur as for the second time today I watch Rose take her leave. A ton of people have helped me recently. Rose, Manu, Margaret. Even Bob and Roseanne. One of these days I am going to have to start being the helper instead of the helpee.

Meanwhile, the credit card idea has merit. I bound up the stairs to the den and the computer and log onto our Visa account. Bingo. It reveals a charge from only two hours ago at a trendy downtown Phoenix restaurant. Over five hundred dollars. That's one major amount of celebrating. But William should have been back from even a five-hundred-dollar lunch ages ago. Even if Jackie never told him about my visit, which would be just like her, he should have gotten my voice mails and be calling me back.

I scurry around the house and rattle every receiver on every phone to make sure none are off the hook. I check the kitchen bulletin board, where we sometimes leave each other messages. I return to the computer and open up my email, in case he sent an email instead of calling. It is now four-thirty. Normally William gets home from the office around six. But nothing is normal today. Maybe nothing will be normal ever again.

I am still sitting at the computer so I take Kat's go-to-Paris DVD out of the bottom drawer and watch it. "I don't want you to be alone," she said. But I am alone.

I run my finger over the scab on my chin. Somewhere underneath Paris there is a tunnel with tiny drops of my blood in it. What is Manu doing right now? And Margaret? Sleeping, probably. Tomorrow they will wake up, Margaret in her sunlit apartment with the nutmeg-colored floors and the creamy lace curtains and the chocolate and robin's egg blue carpet. Manu wherever he lives, maybe in a tiny studio. I wonder if they miss me. I did not expect to feel this, but I miss them.

I jump to my feet. I know what happened. William forgot that I lost my cell phone and texted. If he wants to contact me from work he always texts, never phones.

I close the computer, drive to the mall, and buy a new smart phone. It feels great because it's hellish to be without a cell. It's like being without arms and legs. Plus, the shopping trip fills up some time. It is six o'clock when I get back home, six-forty-five by the time I've transferred all my contacts and downloaded all my favorite apps to the new phone.

Still no William. No text either.

I mindlessly surf the Internet until ten minutes past seven, when I again open the Visa account. You would not believe how fast charges show up on your account nowadays. Three new ones have popped up since the last time I checked. One is for my new cell phone. Two are for upscale downtown Phoenix bars.

He has to know I'm back in Phoenix. Yet he does not call me. He does happy hour instead.

I slam down the lid of the computer. I am shivering even though the house is warm. My fingertip-length black trench coat, still stiff from its soaking in the catacombs, is lying across the bed in the bedroom and I get it and drape it around my shoulders. It served me well in Paris, faraway Paris. I thump down the stairs to my carry-on, still standing on the bottom step, unzip it, and leaf through the contents. My perfectly chosen travel clothes, mostly unworn. The carry-on itself doesn't even look as if it's been on a trip; it looks as if it's still waiting to go.

I put everything back into the carry-on and zip it up. I don't know where William is but I do know that I don't want to be here waiting, like a fool, like a wifey-poo, whenever he does come rolling in, probably drunk and probably not that glad to see me. Rose has been several steps ahead of me all along. She won't be the least bit surprised if I take her up on her offer, she won't mind if I stay with her tonight, or even several nights. I take the carry-on, my money belt, the tote bag, and the trench coat, and throw it all into the backseat of the Honda.

Just before leaving I run upstairs one more time and retrieve Kat's DVD from the computer's disc drive. As I am backing down the driveway, it occurs to me that a bowl of half-cooked oat bran is congealing in the microwave. That will drive William crazy when he finds it. At the long stoplight on Gilbert Road, I program Rose's address into my GPS app. She lives in Mesa, only eleven minutes away.

I am tooling west on Route 60 when it hits me.

I know exactly what William is doing, and exactly where he will be next. He's making the rounds of the same series of bars he and Robert and the rest of the T-30 gang went to the night Robert found out Jen was pregnant.

I find him at bar number three. He is just coming out of the men's room and doesn't notice me enter the dimly lit lobby. He's not shit faced, not yet, but he's wedged an unlit cigarette behind his ear and has neglected to tuck in the tail of his shirt.

The old Amy would be crying buckets right now. The old Amy would rush across the lobby to William and fling herself into his arms, simultaneously begging forgiveness and demanding an explanation for why he hasn't called. But my eyes are dry. As dry as an arroyo, as dry as my heart. I step into the shadow of an artificial ficus tree and watch as he weaves his way into the bar. Though well on the road to shit faced, he still manages to look hot.

Maybe that was our only thing. Maybe that was all we ever had going for us. If that is so, then he deserves better. So do I.

"Brodie!" someone shouts. "It's your round, bruh!"

The entire T-30 team, all male, all in varying degrees of intoxication, is present, sprawled around a long rectangular table littered with beer glasses and trays of half-eaten nachos. William straddles a chair at the head of the table and grins. He is in his element.

I study his face. It is relaxed and open, an expression I have not seen him wear for a very long time, at least around me. Maybe I should be angry, or jealous. But I don't feel anger or jealousy. Every relationship ends in pain, Margaret says. But I don't feel pain.

The T-30 team bursts into raucous laughter. William's laugh is the loudest, and longest. Just as the noise dies down he turns his head and spots me lurking behind the ficus. His expression hardens, but none of his buddies notice because a waitress is delivering two more pitchers of beer. We stare at each other for a long moment. And then his eyes flicker away from mine, he takes a long swallow of beer, and shifts in his chair so I can no longer see his face.

I lean against the rough wall. He did get my messages. He does know I am back in Phoenix. He just doesn't care. I feel sadness and regret and a little surprise. But no huge pain. Not yet. More laughter erupts from the T-30 team as I straighten up, turn, recross the dim lobby, and head out into the soft night air.

The Honda is waiting in the half-empty parking lot just as if the bottom had not dropped out of everything I thought was true about my life. I get in and again take out my new phone. The GPS app informs me that Rose's place is now forty-two minutes away. I merge onto I-10, notch up the air conditioning, and point the Honda toward the East Valley. Flat featureless Phoenix stretches out on both sides of me.

I have never felt more free. I have never had less to lose.

It's the tail end of rush hour and the traffic is slow so I have plenty of time to take notice of the shamrock-green highway sign with the white airplane on it announcing the upcoming exit for Sky Harbor. As I pass under the sign I smile.

Because I have everything I need—my suitcase, my passport, a credit card, nearly three thousand dollars and euros in cash, an intact bar of Valrhona chocolate, and no earthly reason to stay one more single minute in Phoenix, Arizona.

For this I don't need a map app. I flick on my turn signal and merge lane by lane through the heavy traffic to the airport exit. By the time I get there all I have to do is tip my steering wheel a half inch to the right and roll down the ramp.

So I do.

Rule number thirty-three of the perpetual diet: French people don't get fat.

the rules

1. Fidget as much as possible. Fidgeting burns calories. Fidgeting gives your hands something to do other than to stuff fat piggy food into your fat piggy face. Fidgeters are slender.

2. Nothing tastes as good as feeling skinny feels.

3. Drink a ton of water.

4. If you snack, snack while in motion.

5. Put on something a little tight in the morning, when you are at your thinnest, and you will be less likely to overeat during the day.

6. Eat regular meals. Regular meals are what set us apart from the animals.

7. You should be a little hungry when you go to bed at night and a lot ravenous when you wake up in the morning. If not, you are eating too much.

8. Weigh yourself once a week only. Not every day, whatever you do. Daily weighing is for morons. Daily weighing is the path to madness and despair.

9. At times during your diet your body will decide there's a famine, and in a bid for self-preservation it will start to hoard calories. You still police every morsel of food you put in your mouth but you stop losing pounds. You may even gain a few back. It's only the plateau. You must not freak out.

10. Hang mirrors everywhere.

11. Abstention is easier than moderation.

12. Skinny friends keep you skinny; fat friends make you fat.

13. Never eat processed food.

14. Don't eat in front of the television. Or the computer. Or while reading. Or under any circumstances that encourage the mindless consumption of food.

15. Not eating calories in the first place is better than eating calories and then trying to burn them off.

16. Boldly colored dishes make food taste better, and when food tastes better, you eat less of it.

17. Be a picky eater. Picky eaters eat less. Picky eaters are thin.

18. Do not allow yourself to get so famished that you mindlessly devour whatever's put in front of you.

19. Fruit is good, but fruit juice is not good. Eat whole fruit. Drink plain water. Eschew the juice.

20. When you sit, check to see if you can feel the flesh of your waist on the insides of your elbows. If you can, you weigh too much.

21. If you do let yourself get completely empty, which you should not (see rule number eighteen), don't then turn around and gobble down something sweet.

22. Don't be a gulper. Gulpers are fat.

23. When you are sick, eat what tastes good to you.

24. It's okay to eat protein and vegetables together, or starch and vegetables together, but never protein and starch together.

25. Feast your eyes first.

26. In addition to going to bed a little hungry (rule number seven), you should be a little bit hungry all throughout the day, too.

27. Exercise helps you lose weight only if you don't then use it as permission to pig out later.

28. Ninety percent of the pleasure from any food is in the first three bites.

29. Allow yourself the occasional lavish meal. It spikes the metabolism.

30. Only eat when you're hungry.

31. Two-thirds of your dinner should be green vegetables.

32. Sleep a lot. People who sleep a lot are thin. Possibly because when you're sleeping you're not eating.

33. French people don't get fat.

You can learn more about "The Rules" at www.ksrburns.com.

acknowledgments

Huge thanks to Lynn Wiley Grant (who read the manuscript multiple times), Tere Gidlof (ditto), Mary Casey, Christine Johnson-Duell, Oliver Ciborowski, and Royce Roberts. Your patience and loyalty and good sense have made this book possible. Thank you.

I also want to express my gratitude to Kit Bakke and Cindy Springer, for looking at the big picture; Erika Mitchell, for keeping my dialogue youthful; Francoise Giovannangeli, for correcting my French; Sarah Franklin and Tania Scutt, for correcting my British; Joanne Shellan, Barb Tourtillotte, and Elizabeth Kincaid, for their fabulous artistic eyes; and Marsha Perry, for her website genius and ever-calm temperament.

I am of course indebted to my publisher, Booktrope, and to my amazing Booktrope team: Laurel Busch, you are every writer's dream of the ideal editor. Laura Bastian, you are not only fantastically organized, you make book promotion fun. Tatiana Vila, your cover design is simply smashing.

Finally, I owe more than I can say to my husband, Steve, who willingly listened while I read every word of this book to him out loud. Your suggestions were always astute, and you didn't doze off even one time. Thank you and I love you.

Did you like this book? Please tell your friends! And please consider writing a review on the website of your choice.

reading group guide

1. At the beginning of the book, Amy is trying to lose twenty pounds. But in fact she has been fighting extra weight since she was a teenager, and "rules for the perpetual diet" constantly run through her brain. Are Amy's rules a useful tool for her, or a neurosis? In general, do you think life rules of this sort are helpful or hurtful? Do you have any rules?

2. Amy has an obsessive love/hate relationship with eating. She thinks about it all the time and even describes things in terms of food (pear-yellow sun, meringue-white clouds). Do you think Amy has an actual eating disorder? Or is she just uncommonly passionate about food?

3. Amy, after some resistance, leaves her hometown of Phoenix and takes off for Paris without telling anyone. Have you ever wanted to just chuck it all and "run away from home"? Was running away a smart move for Amy? Can it ever be a smart move for anyone?

4. William, Amy's husband, is a steady decent guy with a good job. Some people might think he is perfect husband material. But do you think William was a good choice of husband for Amy? For that matter, do you think William is less perfect than he seems?

5. Why do you think Kat betrayed Amy by coming on to William? Do you think Kat was a truly good friend to Amy?

6. Did any parts of the book offend you or make you feel uncomfortable? For example, Amy rants quite a lot about fat and fat people, especially

in the early part of the book. Do you feel this is at all justified? Do you think Rose knows about Amy's attitudes?

7.   Did you have a favorite scene? Is there one thing in the story that was new to you, or that sticks with you? Who was your favorite character?

8.   Margaret, Kat, and Rose all told Amy she wasn't a good fit or happy with William, but Amy didn't really "hear it." Why not? Have you ever not listened when multiple people have shared the same bit of wisdom?

9.   Amy is a person who kept much to herself. How did that help her? How did it hurt her?

10. The women in this book are far more influential than the men. Amy's mind is filled with the insistent voices of Kat and of her mother; she is led and advised, in very different ways, by Margaret and Rose. Why do you think the women in this book are so powerful? Are women in general more of a force in an average person's emotional growth than men are?

11. Amy takes a pregnancy test in the beginning of the book (it is negative) and again halfway through the book (the results were inconclusive). In the end Margaret is convinced Amy is pregnant, Rose seems to have suspicions, and Amy is convinced she is not. What do you think?

12. On the last page of the book, Amy impulsively returns to France. Were you surprised/satisfied/irritated? What do you think happens next? If you were going to write a sequel to *Rules for the Perpetual Diet*, what would you make happen?

Publisher's note: A sequel to *Rules for the Perpetual Diet* is in the works! Stay in the loop by signing up for K. S.R. Burns's mailing list at www.ksrburns.com. Feel free to nag her to write faster. (Teaser: The sequel's working title is *Eating it Too*.)

a conversation with k. s. r. burns

Amy is obsessed with dieting and weight control. What about you? Are you a dieter?

In my twenties I was a little pudgy, but did not diet. In my thirties, I got into fitness big time. But around age forty I developed a tendency to put on pounds no matter how much I exercised, or how little I ate. Like many people, I guess! It is a popular theme nowadays but one of the specific reasons I used the idea of "rules for the perpetual diet" is that just before I started writing the novel I had my annual physical and my doctor told me that I "definitely" needed to lose weight. I was so annoyed. It seemed natural to take this struggle and, for Amy, just ramp it up.

Have you ever "run away from home," the way Amy did?

Well, no. But there have been plenty of times I've wanted to. The only thing I have in common with Amy is that, like her, I grew up in Phoenix and, like her, I was not crazy about the place (sorry, good citizens of Phoenix). So it made sense to use Phoenix as the place she wanted to get away from, and Paris—which like Amy I also love and where I was lucky enough to live for several years—as the place she yearned to escape to.

Have you ever gone down into the forbidden Paris catacombs, the way Amy did?

No. You could not pay me to go down there, quite frankly. It sounds terrifying. But the research was not a problem because many people do go, and some of them write detailed accounts of their adventures and post them on the Internet. All of the things Amy sees and does—the murals and the rooms full of bones, the old machinery and the street signs, even the scary belly crawl through the wormhole—do actually exist, in one form or another. By the way, the "forbidden" Paris catacombs are not the same thing as the official tourist destination just off Métro stop Denfert-Rochereau in the 14th arrondissement. That is not scary and I've gone down there several times, just to get a feel for the place.

Who or what was your inspiration for the character of Margaret?

I'm not sure where she came from. You could say that Amy and Kat reflect parts of me—I'm bookish and dithery like Amy and, to be honest, smart-alecky like Kat. But Margaret is her own separate person. I have never really believed authors who claim that "their characters just write themselves," but Margaret did truly come out of nowhere, fully formed, wanting to be a part of things.

Do you feel that this is a story of triumph for Amy?

Oh yes. I hope you do, too. Amy starts out grieving and lost, yearning for she knows not what, annoyed with William, pretty much mad at the whole world. In the end she's in a completely different space. Or at least on her way to a completely different space.

Why did you write *Rules for the Perpetual Diet*?

This is easy. I am a member of two book groups. We love talking about stories and characters, why we liked or didn't like a novel, what books and reading mean to us. I've done a lot of pondering about what makes a satisfying reading experience. Simply put, I wanted to write a novel that my book groups would enjoy reading and talking about.

Finally, Amy is also obsessed with food and cooking. Are you? Do you like to cook?

Actually, I am not that crazy about cooking. But I do prepare meals, mostly from scratch, every day, because I believe that it's the healthiest and cheapest way to eat. In fact, I have even started to share some of the recipes I use; you can find them at www.ksrburns.com.

Writing as Karen Burns, K. S. R. Burns is also the author of *The Amazing Adventures of Working Girl: Real-Life Career Advice You Can Actually Use* (Running Press 2009). She's written for many magazines and newspapers, and currently writes a weekly careers column for The Seattle Times. *Rules for the Perpetual Diet* is her first novel.

MORE GREAT READS FROM BOOKTROPE

Double Album **by Mary Rowen** (Fiction) This genre-defining collection explores the complex–and often maddening– influence of music in the lives of two very different women. Includes the novels *Leaving the Beach* and *Living by Ear*.

Dismantle the Sun **by Jim Snowden** (Fiction) A novel of love and loss, betrayal and second chances. Diagnosed with cancer, Jodie struggles to help her husband Hal learn to live without her. As Hal prepares to say goodbye to his wife, he discovers the possibility of happiness—in the arms of one of his students.

Dove Creek **by Paula Marie Coomer** (Fiction) After a disastrous and abusive marriage, single mother Patricia draws on her Cherokee roots for courage. She finds her place as a Public Health nurse, but she must constantly prove herself—to patients, coworkers, and family members—in her quest to improve the lives of others.

The Long Walk Home **by Will North** (Fiction) Forty-four year-old Fiona Edwards answers her door to a tall, middle-aged man shouldering a hulking backpack—unshaven, sweat-soaked and arrestingly handsome. What neither of them knows is that their lives are about to change forever.

The Paragraph Ranch **by Kay Ellington and Barbara Brannon** (Fiction) A motley group of writers and a cast of small-town Texas characters prove that maybe you can go home again, and find love in the unlikeliest of places.

Swimming Upstream **by Ruth Mancini** (Fiction) A life-affirming and often humorous story about a young woman's pursuit of happiness.

Taxicab to Wichita **by Aaron Asselstine** (Fiction) Quinn Jacob is a drug-addicted taxi driver with no options, no money, and no destination. Rocky is a thief with no getaway car, no driver, and no time. In the gathering darkness of a perfect storm, can they trust each other, risk it all, and recreate themselves on the high-wire roads to Wichita?

Discover more books and learn about our
new approach to publishing at **booktrope.com**.

CPSIA information can be obtained at www.ICGtesting.com
Printed in the USA
LVOW06s1803190215

427562LV00004B/347/P